In Loving Memory of
Mr. Roman W. Malynowsky

Other Books by Kala Trobe

Invoke the Goddess: Vizualizations of Hindu,
Greek & Egyptian Deities

Invoke the Gods: Exploring the Power of Male Archetypes

Magic of Qabalah: Visions of the Tree of Life

The Witch's Guide to Life

THE Magick Bookshop

Est. 1342

About the Author

Kala Trobe (London, England) believes that daily life may be lived in full magickal consciousness. An active esotericist for over fifteen years, she is always in search of living magick, and has found it in many locations and mystical systems during her travels. She is the author of numerous articles and books on metaphysics, including *Invoke the Goddess*, *Invoke the Gods*, *Magic of Qabalah*, and *The Witch's Guide to Life*.

To Write to the Author

If you wish to contact the author or would like more information about this book, please write to the author in care of Llewellyn Worldwide and we will forward your request. Both the author and publisher appreciate hearing from you and learning of your enjoyment of this book and how it has helped you. Llewellyn Worldwide cannot guarantee that every letter written to the author can be answered, but all will be forwarded. Please write to:

Kala Trobe
^c/o Llewellyn Worldwide
P.O. Box 64383, Dept. 0-7387-515-2
St. Paul, MN 55164-0383, U.S.A.

Please enclose a self-addressed stamped envelope for reply,
or $1.00 to cover costs. If outside U.S.A., enclose
international postal reply coupon.

Many of Llewellyn's authors have websites with additional information and resources. For more information, please visit our website at http://www.llewellyn.com.

THE Magick Bookshop

Kala Trobe

2004
Llewellyn Publications
Saint Paul, Minnesota, U.S.A. 55164-0383

FIRST EDITION
First Printing, 2004

Cover design by Kevin R. Brown
Cover image © 2003, PhotoDisc
Drawing on page viii by Llewellyn Art Department
Editing and interior design by Connie Hill

Library of Congress Cataloging-in-Publication Data
Trobe, Kala.
   The magick bookshop / Kala Trobe
      p.   cm.
         Contents: Prologue — Magwitch — Orpheus — Living light — Thus spake Ron — Witch in the city, or, The early adventures of an occult bookstore manageress — Karma-burner.
   ISBN 0-7387-0515-2
      1. Occult fiction, English. 2. Antiquarian booksellers—Fiction.
   3. London (England)—Fiction. 4. Bookstores—Fiction. I. Title.
   I. Title.
PR6120.R485M35   2004   2004044128

Llewellyn Publications
A Division of Llewellyn Worldwide, Ltd.
P.O. Box 64383, Dept. 0-7387-0515-2
St. Paul, MN 55164-0383, U.S.A.
www.llewellyn.com

Printed in the United States of America

Contents

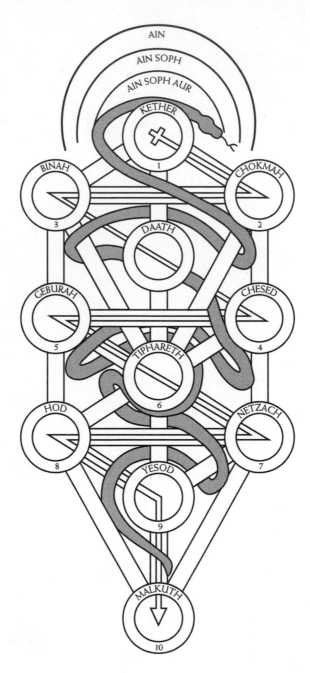

The Tree of Life

PROLOGUE

Let me tell you about our shop. It's the sort of place that makes people go "oooh" as soon as they step into it, and then maintain a respectful silence throughout their sojourn. It smells like a church, what with the combination of aged pages and the incense we burn for our various purposes. It is, however, smaller and more uniquely sacred than a conventional place of worship, and crammed to the rafters with ancient tomes.

The books both lure and intimidate—for who can resist the siren-call of a fat fifteenth-century vellum binding nestling on a slanting shelf, and then fail to feel slighted when the contents turn out to be indecipherable? Most of our texts are in Latin, some with Greek parallel texts; the rest are in Hebrew, German, French, and good old English. Luckily, ours is the sort of shop in which one is drawn, nine times out of ten, to the book of optimum personal relevance at the time.

The magickal skills of Mr. Malynowsky, the owner, cause it to be so.

We have some interesting early specimens written in the vernacular, as I always say to those whose intuition is failing them and whose linguistic skills are limited to modern tongues. To most of our clients, however, this is not an obstacle. We are situated in the heart of Oxford, and many of our customers are academics, or, as we call them, Denizens of Hod. Mr. Malynowsky, a Polish Jew who fled to England during the Second World War, is a practising Qabalist, and so am I. There are not many jobs which specify an active interest in esoterica as a desirable quality, so I was delighted to be made, five years ago, manager of Malynowsky's, Antiquarian Specialist in Ancient Cultures and their Religions. Mr. Malynowsky learned to be euphemistic during the War. He is brave, but not stupid. Oxford may harbour as many anthropologists as it does Christians, but an overtly magickal bookshop would meet the disapproval of the religious and the atheist alike. A danger of Hod is focus on fact, and not the mystery behind the fact. There is nowhere on earth as Hod-like as Oxford, except perhaps for Harvard.

The glass of our shop windows is thick and, from the outside, slightly convex, like the eye of a goldfish. Oxford flows around us, a river of modernity in which we swim immune to what Mr. Malynowsky calls "polluting mind-waves." He is usually in London, where he owns two more outlets, clad in an astral vestment of bright, protective violet. Just occasionally he pops in with a delivery and sits at the till, drinking tea so sweet and strong you could stand the spoon up in it, and tells us of his bibliophilic activities. He is a man possessed when it comes to antiquarian books. He has a knack for finding the manuscripts which are most secretly needed by his clientele. They come here to browse in the knowledge that their needs will be met and their privacy respected. Consequently, I have changed the names and locations of several of the customers mentioned, though others to whom I have talked about this project have agreed to go meta-phorically skyclad, believing that honesty is not such a bad thing. It is amazing, when you scratch the surface, to find just how many of us there are who would be prepared to come out of the occult broom closet, if only they could be guaranteed not to be labeled insane, or Satanic. The latter, of course, is an anathe-ma to us as to any practising Christian. We are not interested in back-to-front renditions of a new religion. We are spiritual seek-ers, referring to older, fresher sources for our inspiration. But you'll see this for yourself as you read the tales I've accrued dur-ing my time here.

One thing that's really become obvious to me since working in Malynowsky's is the way in which the Myths re-enact themselves daily, both for our enlightenment, and simply because they are well-established patterns. Many would argue for the latter alone, and many that the former was the whole point, but for me, both seem pertinent. I've seen the Old Ones walk into this very shop and buy a book. I've asked them if they'd like a carrier bag for that, and directed them to the nearest coffee shop or restroom. They are living archetypal energies, but functioning on the Earth plane, Malkuth, just like the rest of us—sometimes barely aware of their own divinity, sometimes with a foot so firmly planted in both worlds that they can be functional humans during the day, and psychopomps by night. As my boss likes to point out, it's a fascinating level we inhabit.

One of the first principles Mr. Malynowsky taught me was that Kether, the ultimate Divine, may be found in the heart of Malkuth, the material Kingdom in which we commonly abide.

He knows how to draw the magick out of life as a snake-tamer can take the venom from the serpent and use it to heal. Magickal awareness can be a venom, he taught me, if ignored or wrongly used. I certainly suffered from the former in my teens. I was scared by my differences, and tried to stash them away in my subconscious, the Yesodic Plane of the Qabalah. There they augmented, and manifested here as neuroses. Mr. Malynowsky is a great psychotherapist, and showed me how to retrieve my positive powers and put them to good use. Now, every day is a metaphor for Inner Reality, and not just in a heavy sense; we can laugh at it, at ourselves, and so can our favourite customers. Not all of them, however, view it that way, as you will witness.

MAGWITCH

The week I started at Malynowsky's, in June 1996, was the same that the newspapers carried the headings: "Majority of Britons no longer believe in God," and "God is dead: Nietzsche. Nietzsche is dead: God." The British Humanist Association had just conducted a MORI poll and discovered that, while 67 percent of the populace considered themselves religious, only 43 percent believed in a God. Not only this, but it rained and rained interminably. Mr. Malynowsky was undeterred.

"The rain is a wonderful sign, Kala," he told me as he handed me an antiquarian specimen with a binding like brie rind, "The rain is a symbol of knowledge, like this book. It comes from Chokmah, the sphere of Wisdom on the Tree of Life; it is God's thoughts descending on Malkuth, the Earth plane. Yes, the rain falls effortlessly from the unfathomable mind of God, fertilising all that it touches, even in these ancient city streets! The trick is to make ourselves a vessel for this Chokmah-rain, so that we can collect and hold God's wisdom."

"That's a lovely way of looking at it!" I said, putting this weather immunity down to his Polish origins as much as to the mystic bent. Britons, as well as not believing in God, complain endlessly about the rain, and then bitterly rebuke the sun for being too hot when he occasionally shows his face. Atmospheric intolerance and atheism seem to go hand in hand.

"Not just lovely—also true!" announced my new employer, his blue eyes dancing with merriment beneath salt-and-pepper eyebrows. "All of life is an analogy of the mind of God—magick teaches us this. There is no such thing as bad weather, only a bad attitude to God's many moods!"

I looked through the dusty, darkened windows at the silver streaks outside, and felt that pleasure which can only come when the rain is pummeling on the roof and flags, a cold wind weaving in and out of the liquid columns or blowing them sideways into wet explosions on passersby, and one is warm and snug inside. A shiver of contentment passed through me.

"Yes, we are like a capsule, floating on the river," remarked Mr. Malynowsky, a phrase which was soon to become familiar to my ears. "A bubble which many might like to burst. But we shan't let them, shall we, my dear?"

I looked at him, surprised. "What do you mean?" I ventured.

"Ah, my dear, so young, so much to learn. The first thing you must know is that every action has its equal and opposite reaction. For every good thing we believe and do, there will spring up an adverse reaction. You and I belong to the Pillar of Mercy, but there are just as many adherents to the Pillar of Severity. Not a bad thing; we need the balance. But then we have the flip-side . . . "

"Flip—?"

"Yes, I'm afraid we do. The Klippoth. The *husks* or *harlots*, as we call them. These are the spirits of evil, and there are just as many in Oxford as anywhere else, Kala, or possibly more. But I do not wish to alarm you, my dear, though forewarned is fore-armed, as they say. You will learn a lot working here; it is a focal-point for many energies, as you will see."

Had Mr. Malynowsky not been so gentlemanly, well-educated, and respected, I might have been deterred at this point. Actual-ly, that's a lie. I might have felt I *ought* to be deterred, but the lure of the shop, with its wondrous rows of tomes and spectral nooks and the fact that my boss was merely vocalising what I already thought—but was unaccustomed to hearing said out loud—far outweighed my desire to be sensible. I smiled at him with gen-uine confidence.

"I can't wait," I said.

I did not have to.

Two minutes later, a blur of brown Barbour coat crashed through the door, shedding silver beads of God's wisdom from its waxy surface, and generous streams of Chokmahic insight from the numerous bags clutched in the red hands of its breathless owner. The pigskin carpet* all around his feet was soon as sod-den as the gentleman's beard, over which he stared bespectacled. His eyes were large and rather frantic, and as they met Mr. Maly-nowsky's, the man, who was in his mid-forties I estimated, flushed like a teenager.

"I'll just put my bags down, if I may," he exhaled, depositing at the foot of the mahogany counter seven or eight extremely heavy-looking carriers from Blackwell's and the Oxford University Press Bookshops.

---

* Pigskin carpet: An ancient type of floor cladding or carpet made of pig hide. This needs to be lightly and regularly watered in order to keep it supple.

"Certainly, Sir," nodded Mr. Malynowsky mildly. "And how may we help you?"

The man looked at us both, and then swept the shop with his eyes. They nearly bulged, and he began to hyperventilate again. "I just want to look around and buy some books, if that's all right."

As he spoke, the man headed for the fine bindings shelf, his hands shaking—with the strain of his shed load, or with something else? He grabbed two or three beauties from the middle, then hurried to the next section, the incunabula, and pulled off the fattest specimens, piling them all up in his arms.

"You might like to put those on the counter, Sir, where you can study your selection," ventured Mr. Malynowsky, visibly concerned for the welfare of his books. Each was like a child to him; he knew its history, he had nurtured and tended it through the traumas of sympathetic renewal and meticulous cleaning; he had interacted with its inner essence. The customer, however, seemed reluctant to put his prizes down.

"I'm used to carrying heavy weights!" he announced, his eyes hungrily scanning the aisles and displays like a competitive child on a treasure hunt. He lunged for the next shelf, a row of historical tomes written in French.

This was too much for Mr. Malynowsky, who jumped to his well-polished feet and was at the gentleman's side in a flash, remarkably agile for a septuagenarian, I thought.

"Please, dear Sir, allow me," he cajoled, gently edging some of the pricier specimens from the man's damp and vice-like grip. Our customer did not know whither to look; at the articles rent from him, or at the others waiting to be seized. "Don't put them back!" he cried in my direction. "I want to take them all!"

Mr. Malynowsky caught my eye and raised an eloquent eyebrow. "Study him," it said.

Was this our first case of clinical bibliomania, I wondered?

The customer, however, was quick to complete his business, arriving at the till with two more armloads of eclectic texts and requiring that they be totted up, all within five minutes. Nervously, I put the books through the till. The words "That will be three thousand and fifty-four pounds, please," did not slip as easily off my tongue as I would have liked them to.

The man, still flushed and shaking and breathing like a fox just ahead of the hunt, put his hand inside the Barbour jacket and withdrew a pile of fifty-pound notes the size of a loaf. I looked at Mr. Malynowsky, unsure as to whether to accept them or not, and then remembered the pen we keep on the till to check whether notes are genuine or not. The man flicked sixty-one of his notes from the mass like a croupier, and placed them on the till with a flourish. I tested each with the pen, as swiftly as possible, trying not to blush. Mr. Malynowsky kept him talking all the while.

"So, you are a polymath, Sir?" he asked pleasantly. "What a rare quality that is nowadays!"

"Well, a polyglot, anyway!" gushed our customer. "I went to Oxford many years ago—studied Classics—ah, is that a Euripides folio there in the cabinet?"

"It is indeed, Mr.—?"

"Magwitch. Paul Magwitch," he smiled. Mr. Malynowsky held out his hand, and as they touched, I saw a flash of perception pass across the face of my new employer.

Magwitch tried to converse politely, but he was clearly agitated by the desire to extract the Euripides from behind its glass. Mr. Malynowsky nodded at me to pass the key, which I did, sending a fifty-pound note zig-zagging onto the pig-hide carpet. I retrieved it with a sense of money being rather like leaves on an autumn breeze. Magwitch's ideas must be catching.

"It's eighteenth-century diced Russia*," intoned Mr. Malynowsky, lovingly identifying the relevant faded backstrip. "Look
at this gilt back—beautiful, is it not?—and we find within, engraved portraits of Euripides, and Joshua Barnes, the publisher."

Mr. Magwitch could not wait to get his hands on the specimen. He clutched it to his chest, not even looking inside, as if
his very life depended on it. Within moments he had deposited a
further ten of his red notes on the counter.

I wrapped the books as carefully as possible, considering their
quantity and the speed of the transaction, while my boss tried to
extract conversation from our unusual customer. The latter was
soon so flustered that the ancient man of magick had to give up
his till-side stool to the hefty younger man.

"Thanks," breathed Magwitch, undoing his waterproof for the
first time. Beneath it I glimpsed a very fine tie of embroidered
silk, a crisp clean shirt, and an exceptionally well-tailored suit.
These did not seem in keeping with his demeanour, which remained on the frantic side of sane. His eyes still flitted hungrily
from shelf to shelf, and I could sense Mr. Malynowsky's reluc-
tance to lose further of his stock to the man.

"That's quite a selection you have there, Mr. Magwitch!" attempted the older gentleman once more.

"So many beautiful things," sighed Magwitch. "So little time."

"Would you like a box for these?" I asked, placing the last of
the brown paper over the medley of books. "It might help you
carry them."

"Carry them?" Magwitch looked confused. "Oh, carry them,
yes, well, if you wouldn't mind waiting for me, I'll fetch my car.
Oh, and bags are fine." He looked dazed. "Just fine." He arose almost immediately and bumbled out of the shop.

---

* Diced calf, or diced Russia: Treated leather or animal hide used in bookbinding.

"Do many of your customers spend that much money in one go?" I asked, at once impressed and disturbed. "And cash too! If it weren't for your intuition, Mr. Malynowsky, I would worry about that transaction."

"And you would be quite right to do so," replied the mage. "Indeed, there is much cause for concern for that gentleman."

"He didn't really want those books, did he?" I asked tentatively. "I mean, he desired them as objects, but he didn't even look inside most of them."

"Quite so, quite so."

I waited for an explanation, but Mr. Malynowsky sat like a sphinx and gazed out of the windows at the shiny slabs and slate-grey shadows slanting across the medieval college walls opposite. The shelves creaked, readjusting themselves after Magwitch's onslaught. The pharmaceutical breath of the thirteen genera-tions of midwives named Beth who once inhabited this premises caressed my cheek, though I did not know what it was at that point. I put it down to the herbs in the desk and a draft seeping through one of the shop's many fissures.

In a trice, a Mercedes had pulled up at the door of the shop, forties music emanating from it. Magwitch switched off the en-gine and bounded out, repenetrating our sphere with his book-craving bulk.

"Here, allow me to help you," I offered. I bore four carrier bags of the books to the boot in what was now a light drizzle, and waited for him to open it. He emerged, along with Mr. Maly-nowsky, each bearing six or seven more carriers containing pur-chases from our own or the other shops.

Magwitch pressed a button on his key-ring, and the boot opened gracefully. I tried not to gasp, for inside it were amassed the finest woven fabrics of India, and all the jewels of Arabia, it seemed, spilling from trunks and trousseaus, alongside delicately wrought troves of sparkling trinkets, elegant bottles of exotic perfumes, and everything that shimmered and shone with expensive lustre.

"Ah, we're running out of room in there," flushed Magwitch; "We'll have to put *these* little gems on the back seat."

Was he some kind of master thief, I wondered? The cash, the keenness to get rid of it, the boot of plunder from, apparently, a sultan's harem? I tried not to appear suspicious; after all, he had just spent a vast amount of money with us, and deserved our courtesy, at least; but I could not resist a glance at Mr. Malynowsky. He, meanwhile, maintained the perfect pose and profile of a hieroglyph.

We bundled the books into the back seat as requested, and waved him off. Noel Coward blasted from the car stereo as the engine started. We stepped back inside the shop.

No sooner had we returned to the till than Noel Coward became audible again. The car backed up the road, far too fast, and stopped outside. Magwitch leaped out, his Barbour flapping like the wings of a panic-stricken chicken, opened his boot, and dived in. Dashing through our door, he lunged at the till, managing somehow to catch both of us in the eye in the process—an earnest look, if ever there was one—and deposited a fistful of something on the till.

"For you!" he puffed, before bounding out again and pulling off at speed.

I gasped as I beheld the antique silver; a brooch studded with glittering star sapphires, and a beautifully engraved snuff box. No question which gift was for whom, then.

"Take it," said Mr. Malynowsky. "And don't worry. We're going to repay him amply for this. Now, time to cash up, I think."

I took the sapphire pin and attached it to my cardigan. I had never owned such a beautiful piece of jewelry before, nor one so valuable, and I sent Mr. Magwitch a *thank-you* on the ether.

To my intense frustration, Mr. Malynowsky locked up and retired to the basement to do some bookkeeping. I had so many questions to ask him, and would far rather have stayed and whiled away the evening chatting with him than return to my rented room. I shared an overpriced house with a very nice single mother, Sam, and her eight-year-old daughter Jasmine, but their conversation was not quite as intriguing as Mr. Malynowsky's. As I left, I tentatively invited him for a quick drink at the Turl Bar.

"No can do, my dear," he replied through a plume of aromatic pipe smoke. "At my age, you appreciate the faculties when they are in normal working order; you do not risk the vices. Tobacco is my one exception, a habit I picked up in the war and find conducive to the brain. You go now, and I'll see you tomorrow."

I smiled at him through the blue haze, walked up the stairs and across the pigskin carpet, and departed the shop.

Outside was like another world. I was almost shocked when I emerged to find taxis flashing by, queues of workers waiting for the bus, compounding the darkness with their umbrellas; girls in cocktail dresses giggling their way down the street, and boys in dinner jackets regaling one another with tales of getting "sooooo pissed that night." The usual army of beggars was out, hassling me at every corner for a spare 20P, some of them looking genuinely needy, others just trying it on. I thought of Magwitch and his four thousand casual pounds, and wondered what he was doing now. As I did so, stepping out onto the crowded High Street to cross it, the deathly white face of a heroin addict swooned into mine, her brown eyes dilated for her drug. They alighted on the sapphire brooch glinting beneath my unbuttoned jacket, and seemed to devour it with their gaze. I expected her to grab it. I took a step backward and my heel hit the gutter. I looked around, steadying myself; and when I looked back, she was gone.

The ghostly apparition left me shaken. The hunger in her stare was palpable and seemed very familiar. With a jolt, I remembered seeing the same need in the eyes of Magwitch.

I walked home with much on my mind, glad now to be returning to Sam and Jasmine and television and chat about trivia. A good dose of the ordinary felt like exactly what I needed.

The following morning I traversed the warm, wet streets with anticipation, unlocking the ancient door with a frisson of excitement, fully prepared for some sort of occult event. Even outside the shop the air seemed laden with portent, a whiff of incense on the breeze.

However, when my boss arrived, clad in his eternal grey raincoat and grey suit and purple tie, he declined to comment on our spendthrift friend. I reluctantly decided not to force the issue, intending to be an accomplice rather than a nuisance, especially in my first week. Instead, I made us tea, and sat studying books at the till while Mr. Malynowsky taught me about them.

The first printing presses, the way rags were used in paper, the first great scholars and collectors. I noticed him once or twice turning the snuffbox contemplatively in his hands, but the morning, though interesting, felt anticlimactic. Instead of the mystical atmosphere to which I was steadily becoming accustomed, it seemed almost like a normal shop. To make matters worse, at around eleven, when Mr. Malynowsky had just nipped downstairs, we were beleaguered by a chemistry don who had dropped by for a quarrel, it seemed.

"Ancient medicine?" he barked from the door.

"We have some Galen," I responded; and, lightheartedly, "Or there's Lavater's *Physiognomy*."

"Poppycock!" he shouted. "Galen I have, and I suppose the rest of your stock's all this spirituality nonsense." I gave him a look as blank as untouched parchment; it did not seem worth responding to the man.

Mr. Malynowsky emerged from the basement at just this point, and offered his assistance. The don strained at the leash of politeness. "I wondered whether you might have anything as scientific as a medicine book, but your girl tells me not."

Mr. Malynowsky smiled. "I take it from that, Sir, that you are one of the Godless 57 percent?"

The man smiled bitterly. "I should certainly hope so! Scientific explanation is the only way forward; but people are too lazy and impatient to wait for science to tell them the truth. It takes time, yes, and applied effort, and decades of learning to even begin to scratch the surface of the Universe."

Mr. Malynowsky raised a wry eyebrow. "And I suppose that most people are too unintelligent to understand it anyway?"

"Quite so. They want an instant answer. These peddlers of God, of so-called spirituality—whatever that may be—give it to them. Religion is nothing but instant gratification for the feeble-minded. We are heading for a repetition of the Dark Ages."

I detest this kind of person—I am not ashamed to admit it. They wring all the joy out of life, and cauterise all natural possibilities. As far as I can see, the study of creation does not disprove it, or identify the primal cause. I cannot be bothered arguing the toss with arrogant Denizens of Hod—or of Tipha-reth—for religious zealots are certainly just as bad. My boss, however, absolutely loved it. I suppose that his years of experience and learning had leant him a gravitas that I lack; so people like this don would happily indulge in a game of cerebral chess with him, whereas younger folk, particularly women, were not worth wasting their time on. I seemed like yet another student to him, no doubt, only less well educated. Disgusted by the whole scenario, I took a pointedly early lunch break.

When I returned, at a snail's pace, from the sandwich bar, Mr. Malynowsky was sitting behind the till puffing on his pipe with the air of one greatly entertained.

"Have a good debate?" I asked as I headed to the back room to make us both tea.

"Human arrogance never ceases to amaze me, Kala!" he said, raising his voice so that I could hear him from the tiny kitchen. "Scientists say 'there is nothing; it all just evolved'—but who set evolution into motion? With their stupid narrow minds, propped up by degrees and doctorates, they won't believe anything unless they can weigh it and measure it or analyse it chemically. Samuel Beckett's play *Waiting for Godot* sums it up beautifully. The two men waiting every night for Godot to appear and, like a commercial traveler, explain what it's all about so that they can then decide whether or not to accept it."

I brought the tea through, Mr. Malynowsky's as tan as can be imagined, and thick with sugar. Mine seemed like nothing but water and milk in comparison.

"We have to accept our own experiences, these being all we can truly rely on. Faith is not enough, in this the professor is correct; but personal encounters, particularly when these can be confirmed by independent witnesses; these are our guiding lights. I have believed and experienced the inexplicable more times than I have smoked this pipe!" He smiled and tapped the object.

"What kind of thing?" I asked, thrilled that the conversation was going in this direction again. I knew that after my initiatory week, Mr. Malynowsky would be leaving for London, and that this represented one of my few sustained chances to chat with him.

"Well, let us see. The most interesting thing that happened to me in early life was reading the thoughts of two men—I call this *brain-radio*—when I was a student in Vienna; thoughts so vile that they made me mentally sick for the day. The following day I was arrested by the Gestapo on a serious charge of affiliation to a political resistance movement, and kept in prison for two months. Later I learned that these two men had come to my house the day before to inquire about me—just when I had had those warnings. And that was just the beginning, believe me."

"Good heavens," I replied, rather inadequately. Mr. Malynowsky was just about to regale me with more details, when the door flew open, and in came—yes, you've guessed it—Magwitch.

He was clad in another fine suit, no overcoat this time, as the summer rain had let off for a moment, and today's purchases were not evident about his person, though I felt sure that he had made some. He was still short of breath.

"Hello again!" he gasped at me. "Ah, good, you're wearing your brooch. So nice when people know how to accept a gift in the manner in which it is intended! I shall have to bring you some more presents! Good day to you too, Sir!"

Mr. Malynowsky extended his hand, gave me a quick glance, and shook the generous paw of Magwitch. As he did so, I saw a change occur in our customer's aura. Something white and diaphanous exuded from it—visibly, like smoke or albumen—and in it I glimpsed, for the briefest of moments, the same brown eyes and hungry look I had encountered in the road the evening before. Shock jolted through me, and, had I not been sitting down, I might have raised a cloud of dust from the shelves behind the till. Mr. Malynowsky chatted to the man as if nothing at all had occurred. Age and experience certainly have a lot to be said for them, I reflected.

Today, Mr. Magwitch made only the most modest of buys—a set of Ovid at £300 in beautiful biscuit calf, and a couple of Theosophy first editions. I could sense Mr. Malynowsky restraining him, for though Magwitch was champing at the bit, my boss led him away from the items of desire on several occasions. "You don't really need that, Sir, do you?" he said, gently but firmly, and our customer acquiesced.

This was a peculiar type of salesmanship I was learning, I thought! Most shopkeepers would be delighted to have such an undiscriminating customer with a pile of cash on their premises. But Mr. Malynowsky, as we know, was one in a million. "Money and God do not mix," he used to say, and he was right. He fought Mammon every day, and won.

Very shortly, our customer had reached a pitch of agitation impossible to ignore. "To tell the truth," he panted, "I'm dying to get to Whistles and buy some clothes."

"Oh, do you have a daughter?" I asked. "It's a lovely boutique."

"No, I don't," said Magwitch, "I just love the fabrics—the designs—fabulous!"

I gazed at him, nonplussed. Mr. Malynowsky nodded to himself. Is he going to spill the beans soon, I wondered?

"Well, have fun!" I conjoined.

"Come and see what I've bought this morning!" cried Magwitch. "There may be something in there for you."

"You bring the car here, Sir," said Mr. Malynowsky. "I can't spare Kala right now."

He looked at my boss for a moment, surprised, even a little hurt perhaps. I saw the thought move across his wide face that maybe he was not trusted by us. His blue eyes, behind their shields of glass, looked even bigger. My heart went out to him suddenly.

"I'd love to see your finds," I assured him, "though I'm sure you've given me more than enough already! I adore my brooch; thank you so much! How about we keep your books here until you fetch your car? I'll lend you the barrier pass; it went up again this morning."

My ambush of thanks and special treatment seemed to do the trick.

"I'll be back in a moment! Don't go anywhere!" and off he rushed.

This time, Mr. Malynowsky did not keep me in suspense.

"You saw, I take it, what happened when I shook his hand? She's more tenacious than I had thought, that girl. Do you know what is happening, Kala?"

I had to guess, at least. After all, this was part of my job now. "Um, is he possessed?" I asked, feeling rather gauche.

"The story's a little more complex than that, my dear. You're not far off, though. See what you notice when he returns."

Magwitch's musical herald again reached us before he did; but today's was very different to yesterday's.

"I don't believe it!" I exclaimed. "He's listening to Moby."

The hypnotic beat and electronic tones of the superfast dance track blasted up the street, reaching rave proportions outside the shop. I suddenly regretted giving him the pass. Students on bikes stared and grinned, and upright gentlemen scowled at the Mercedes-cum-ghetto blaster. I dashed out to ask him to turn it down.

"What?" he said, blank and confused. "Am I listening to—oh, yes, of course I am. Right-ho."

Blissful silence descended on the street.

"Look! Come and look at this!" he cried, leaping from the driver's seat and heading for the boot once more. "Beautiful things!"

I followed him outside, while Mr. Malynowsky lingered in the shop porch.

The boot today was a child's treasure trove of dressing-up costumes. There were designer evening dresses, jackets trimmed with fake fur, long flowing gowns of silk, beautiful skirts in *à la mode* styles, and a plethora of trendy tops and jeans and garments of all colours and styles. There was even a sixties' afghan in there. I gasped.

"Aren't they gorgeous?" he sighed. Then, as if pulling himself together, "Is there anything in here that you would like? This, perhaps?" grabbing a paisley dress at random, "Or this?"—an embroidered Victorian mourning coat. I must admit to being seriously tempted by the latter, but I had already received enough from him.

"I don't think it's my size," I said, as an excuse. "But thank you anyway."

"They're all size eight to ten," said Magwitch. "They'd fit you perfectly." Then, suddenly, he slammed the boot down, and looked at me with panic. "I've just remembered, I've got to go and pick something up from the tailor's—a beautiful coat, just wait until you see it!"

I transferred his purchases into the back seat again, and as he started the engine and Moby blasted out, I saw him grimace at the music. Then his face became blank, and he drove off, the bass beat thudding from his car.

Mr. Malynowsky, who had been watching us closely throughout this exchange, escorted me back to our perches at the till.

"Any developments on your perceptions, Ms. Trobe?" he asked playfully. "You noticed that the lady's clothes were all one size; why do you think that could be?"

"Well, I suppose they're all for one person," I ventured. "Though who that could be . . . ?"

"Someone you've seen before, perhaps," said the master of magick cryptically. "Last night, possibly?"

The memory of the heroin addict loomed in my mind. "Surely he's not connected with *her?*" I asked. There seemed no point in inquiring as to how he knew of this brief encounter. Brain-radio, no doubt.

"Surely he is, young lady," he replied. "But think laterally."

My mind rummaged over a garbage-heap of possibilities, all equally insalubrious. Yet Mr. Magwitch, with his blunt kindness and sudden panic attacks, did not seem the sort to keep a girl, or be on drugs, or any of the other connections which leered at me with rotten smiles. Was he dying, perhaps, and spending as fast as he could? Maybe to prevent someone, this girl possibly, from getting his fortune? But then, why were the clothes her size? Besides which, I was unsure as to just how corporeal she was. Perhaps she was not "real" at all.

"The penny is beginning to drop," chimed in Mr. Malynowsky. "She is not alive, this girl; she died six months ago, run over by a car."

"By Mr. Magwitch's car?" I asked nervously.

"His old one, yes. He had it scrapped after that—a Jaguar XJS it was—and the Mercedes replaced it. I read about it all in the local rag—our friend was acquitted. She ran out in front of him, there was nothing he could do. She was undergoing what they call 'cold turkey' at the time, chasing after some drug dealer on the opposite side of the street."

"The High Street," I concluded, shuddering.

"Precisely."

"So now, she's—what, haunting him?"

"Hmm, not quite, though she's pretty close to it. While Magwitch was in shock, she entered his aura, and she's been moving in and out of it ever since, drawing sustenance from his vitality just as she used to draw it from her drug. His guilt—for he's a good, conscientious man—gives her access to him. At the moment, she's satisfying the unacted-upon desires of a lifetime. She never had money of her own; now she's making Magwitch buy all the things she would have had, if able."

"The books?" I asked, confused. "Surely she wasn't interested in Classics or Theosophy?"

Mr. Malynowsky's blue eyes smiled. "Unfortunately not. Those are the result of her compulsion to possess, acting on Magwitch's own inclinations. His discrimination was impaired on the first trip, but by the second, I had worked out how to make him separate one impulse from another. The jewelry and clothes and the like, however—and that dreadful music—they come from the girl. She is trying to solidify her own existence by externalising her cravings. Before too long, left to her own devices, this little madam will have Mr. Magwitch addicted to opiates, not to mention bankrupt."

I stared at him.

"So what are we going to do?" I asked.

"Ah, so you want to help him, do you?"

"Definitely!" I cried. "Of course."

"But there's no 'of course' about it, my dear. I require a shop manager who is *interested* in the occult, but nowhere in your job description does it say that esoteric first aid is also compulsory."

"True," I mused, "But I'd like to. He seems a good man, underneath—much nicer than that awful cynic you were chatting to this morning," I added.

"There we have the paradox—a man who denies his own soul will become immune to the perceptions of it. However, you are right about Mr. Magwitch. He is worth helping."

Visions of ceremonies in the basement ran through my mind. Would we work at night? Would Mr. Malynowsky be transformed by velvet cloak and ritual dagger into a living Thoth, candlelight flickering across the face lined by wisdom, strange chants emanating from some unseen portal into the Other World? What would I wear? My black velvet dress, normally reserved for my own rituals? Would I be the Priestess, my favourite persona?

"So you would like to, then?" he asked.

"Absolutely!" I enthused, envisaging the Grand Ceremony, the billowing incense, the Watchtowers seething with elementals, me in my dress, majestically calling on the gods. Mr. Malynowsky gave me a long look.

"I'm sorry to disappoint you, my dear, but I think you've been reading too many Dion Fortune novels. Silken robes and silver sandals are all very nice, but I'm a little bit old for all that palaver now, don't you think?"

I blushed. Damn this *brain-radio* lark!

"Nowadays, most of my work is done mentally," he explained. "Not that I object to the use of ritual to establish a pattern for future use. On the contrary. Had I not been involved in so many Lodges in the past, it would be far more difficult for me to envisage the correct scenario now."

"So, we're just going to use our minds?" I asked, disappointed. I am a Leo, and I love a bit of pomp and ceremony.

"We shall be using the same rays that we use in ritual, only on Magwitch directly, and in the shop. Imagine the scandal if we were accused of involving the mentally ill—for that is what most people would consider him to be—in rituals in our basement!

Oh, no, no, no. I've had enough interrogations and political-religious stone throwing to last me several lifetimes!"

"And what part would you like me to play?" I asked tentatively.

"You, my dear, will send me the rays I need when I ask you for them. Yellow to relax and heal him, and blue to freeze the spirit out if she won't come voluntarily. However, we mean to coax her from him; and that's where I really need your help. I need you to visualise, as vividly as possible, a scenario you think she would enjoy. Somewhere full of life, where she feels part of the hub. We need music, excitement, colour. Friends, drink, drugs—whatever you feel will appeal to her. Your job is to tempt her away, so that once she is out, I can seal Mr. Magwitch's aura against her coming back."

"So she can't discriminate between thoughtforms and reality?" I asked.

"She cannot discriminate between Malkuth, the Earth sphere, and Yesod, the Astral realm. She is living in both, yet in neither. The material and emotional-spiritual worlds seem equally real, and equally tenuous, to her. That is why I need you to perform a strong and detailed visualisation; the more solid it seems, the more it will attract her." Mr. Malynowsky retrieved his pipe from his pocket, and tapped it thoughtfully. "Had she died properly, her soul would have passed up the Thirty-Second Path, which links Malkuth to Yesod, and the break to the 'silver chord' would have been clean. Yesodic forms would then have seemed solid to her, and Malkuthic ones insubstantial, as is right for one who has left the earth. As it was, her spirit was already partially dislodged by her habit, and when her body stopped, so suddenly, she panicked and lunged for the nearest repository of life-force—that of our friend. She is sucking him dry now, etherically and physically; he hasn't the physique to keep up with a teenage girl's routine.

She's been making him go to bars and clubs at night, compelling him to dance for her and make a fool of himself. Half of the time, he cannot even remember how he got there."

"And when we've dislodged her?" I could all too easily imagine the girl's furious response when my vision faded, and she found herself tricked and locked out of her favourite link with life. I shivered.

"Then we will guide her to where she is really meant to be," he replied, "in the care of Gabriel and Raphael, until her next time comes around."

"Well, if I'm going to work with her personally, I'd better know her name," I said. "Do you remember it?"

Mr. Malynowsky opened one of the lower drawers of the whale-like mahogany desk, and rummaged around. It was brimful of yellowing newsprint. Eventually he emerged, flourishing a cutting. "In our line of work, it is always worth preserving these facts of local history, just in case," he commented.

I scanned the article. "*...The driver, Mr. Paul Magwitch, allegedly attempted to brake, but for the victim, Miss Juliet Spence, of Sutton Courtenay in Oxfordshire, it came too late.*"

Juliet? It didn't ring true, somehow. I continued down the page.

"*Miss Spence, who was known to her friends as 'Jude'. . .*"

That was more like it. Jude, the Patron Saint of Hopeless Cases, Jude, the outcast of Oxford, as in the Thomas Hardy novel.

"*The death of Juliet Spence is a tragedy, a teacher from her former high school, Saint Colette's in Sutton Courtenay, commented. 'She was a promising student who had done well in her A Levels.' However, the Police have since confirmed that Miss Spence had been sleeping rough in Oxford city centre since completing her exams in the summer of last year.*"

An intelligent girl who went off the rails, evidently. I recalled the hungry eyes, the vivacious music, the lust for life, the need to sate all desires immediately. Jude was not going to be easy to evict, now that she had found a home to call her own.

The afternoon was humdrum, for which I gave thanks. Several groups of tourists shuffled in and out, one of them on the Morse Trail (our shop was featured on one of the television episodes); I had my photograph taken with a variety of grinning Japanese companions. A couple from Aix-La-Chapelle came in and purchased most of our seventeenth-century Dutch bindings, for which they evidently had a passion. People popped in and asked me if we sold maps, or phone cards, or umbrellas. Mr. Malynowsky worked downstairs. It was all refreshingly mundane.

At a quarter to six, the inimitable Mr. Magwitch burst through the door, seeming at once hyperactive and exhausted. I leapt to my feet and offered him a chair; his breathing was so heavy, I feared that he might have a seizure at any moment.

Mr. Malynowsky emerged from the vaults, his grey suit surprisingly uncrumpled considering he had been bent over his books all day, shirt still white and tie still very purple—his only concession to personality in his dress. He looked rather stately, I thought, as he crossed his pig-clad premises and turned the sign in the door around to tell the world that we were closed. He locked up, but we all remained sitting near the window, clearly visible to anyone who might care to press their nose up against the undulating glass.

"Please," wheezed Mr. Magwitch. "Don't close on my account. I may not be spending much today—I mustn't—I mean, I'd like to—" His eyes scanned the shelves greedily. "Is that a Skelton I see there?" he said desperately.

Mr. Malynowsky walked up behind him, and held his hands over the man's skull, or rather, over his crown chakra, still unperceived by Magwitch.

Then, as he looked at me, there occurred one of the strangest things I have ever experienced.

"Visualise a brilliant ray of yellow light entering my hands," said Mr. Malynowsky's voice, but his lips did not move. Magwitch was clearly oblivious. Automatically, I obeyed, feeding into it all of my sympathy for this unfortunate man.

Magwitch's tense face began to relax a little. His breathing steadied as he stared into space.

"Now, give me that scene!" said the voice in my head.

Like an actress in her début with a new producer, I gave it all I was worth. Above my head I built the interior of a night club, complete with strobe lighting, thumping psychedelic trance music, pulsating bodies, and a group of friends for Jude. They were sitting round a table with bright drinks and dark eyes, painted lips and coloured hair, a crew from *Blade Runner* or *The Tribe*, only more intelligent. I even managed to weave threads of Hindi music into the drum beat, while making the imagined group emanate feelings of goodwill toward our heroine. I made one of them ask her if she would like a drink.

Then, a ghostly voice said, "You are the Lotus-Eaters. I cannot come."

My vision splintered like a stained glass window hit by a brick. Shards of it scattered across the desk.

"Build another! Quickly!" said Mr. Malynowsky, and I looked at him and saw that Magwitch was fading fast.

What could I do? With what could I lure her? A child-like Narnia, or a heaven for sophisticates? How could I plunder the inner dreams of one whose name and death alone were known to me?

"I'd like to order one Church, please," murmured Magwitch, his head lolling to one side.

As he spoke, an image arose in my mind of Notre Dame, of all places, at Easter. The altar was drenched in purple mourning. Nuns were singing of the tears of the Mater Dolorosa, their clear voices piercing the air like arrows of ice; Pergolesi's *Stabat Mater* sang itself inside my head with the clarity of perfect blood ringing in my ears. A group processed in black down the aisle, veiled, a mass of black, a mass of dissolution . . . I could feel the reality of the vision taking over the reality of my individuality; my cells were lending at least half of their energy to the ether. I was shocked by the swiftness with which the sounds and images registered in my mind and took them over.

"Good, keep up that Tiphareth projection," said a voice I thought was the priest's. "It is closer to God than Yesod."

Suddenly, something entered my vision: something frantic.

"Bacchanalia has entered the house of God!" cried the nuns. "We cannot allow this!"

Sounds, images, and implications fell in quick succession into my mind. It was as if I was dreaming lucidly, yet blessed with an innate understanding of the nature of the symbols. When I saw a thing, I knew exactly what energy it represented—*like*, I thought vaguely, *it must have been when we were first created*. Before dissimulation.

I saw a dark shape hurtle up the aisle and land itself at the foot of the altar, a shape about which black things clung, many-limbed, biting and clawing their host and causing her to thrash her arms about so that she looked half Hindu goddess, half Christian demon.

The priest, who wore a purple collar, placed his hand on the flailing creature, and as he did so, I noticed that his hands were glowing yellow, and that the little clawed and fanged things that clung to her ran like beasts from a flame when they saw it.

The girl struggled beneath the purifying grip, the final vestiges of her past gradually being seared away.

From the middle of the dissipated husk there emerged a slender flame, many-coloured, a face and body dimly visible in its outlines.

"My child," said the priest. "Leave Malkuth in Peace, and enter now another level in the Mansion of God. You will have a chance to return, when you have rested. Lessons learn; So Mote It Be."

He circumflexed.

"Ateh, Malkuth, Ve Geburah, Ve Gedulah, Leolahm, Amen," he intoned, with a gravity that would move mountains, a low vibration that I shall never forget.

I saw light streaking down to where the thinning flame was, in a terrific bolt. Then it transported her up and up, impossibly high, pulsating with the motion of ascent, and at the top, I thought I saw a golden hand reach down to welcome her.

Raphael, the voice said.

The next thing I knew, I was sitting behind the till at work. I felt exhausted, as one might after a trans-Atlantic voyage, lagging both physically and mentally. Mr. Magwitch was there, as was a pale, serious-looking Mr. Malynowsky, who placed a cup of scalding tea before me, dark and sweet.

"Drink this, my dear," he said.

I was freezing cold, and obeyed with gratitude. As I reached for the cup, I noticed that the clock said seven. Surely not; I had only been visualising for a few minutes, I was certain.

"You gave us quite a turn, there, Kala," said Mr. Magwitch, sounding much more measured than he usually did. "You fainted. How are you feeling now?"

I looked at Mr. Malynowsky, who winked at me. "You must be overwrought, my dear, what with the move to Oxford, and your first week in this stuffy old shop. It's no place for young girls, really."

I protested, and acted out my part, but of course I was dying to hear what Mr. Malynowsky had to say about it all. A glance at our former customer told me that our exorcism had worked, but the details eluded me, and I was concerned for Mr. Magwitch, returning to accounts ruined by a spectre. How long would his health last, once he was confronted by the toll of the last six wild months?

Luckily, our companion soon excused himself.

"Did it work? Why Notre Dame? What will happen when Mr. Magwitch realises the state of his affairs?" I demanded, overstimulated by the psychic experience and the sugar in the tea.

"Yes, it worked."

Mr. Malynowsky lit his pipe, and took a deep inhalation. The aromatic smoke billowed from his nose and mouth as he spoke. "Juliet was raised in the Roman Catholic Church, and she secretly wished to repent, not compound her sins, though it was reasonable of us to assume she would prefer a modern afterlife. Jude would have, but Juliet was the eternal side of her personality. Once we got her away from Magwitch's vitality, her spiritual tendencies showed through at last. At first she wanted, through him, to 'buy her way into heaven'; but then her true spirit shone through, and she wished only to commit herself to God, as she remembered being taught by the nuns at her school—the nuns who both taught her and terrified her; that girl was afraid of her own nature. That is why she chose to negate it."

"Will Mr. Magwitch be ruined?" I asked.

"Far from it!" replied the mage. "What Juliet spent was peanuts to him, though certainly, left unchecked, it would have ruined him eventually. No, most of his capital is bound up in stocks and shares, and he owns a beautiful house which, once he has painted over the fluorescent purple and peeled away the fake fur, will still be worth a fortune."

"Thank goodness for that," I said. "I'd hate to see him out on the streets like Jude."

"Ah yes, that was another point. She was never properly mourned; hence the veiled procession in your vision. She needed that, to compensate for the fact that her family refused to attend the funeral. They were hurt and angry—and embarrassed—by her lifestyle, and the way she died."

I paused for a moment, thinking of my bizarre experience.

"Is that how normal magick works?" I asked. "I didn't even feel as if I was doing anything except watching it all unravel—I could sense order within the melodrama . . ."

"Psychodrama," corrected Mr. Malynowsky. "The key to a very great deal!"

". . . yes, but I wasn't controlling it myself. How did you do it?"

More smoke issued forth. "It's taken years of practise, and of trial and error, but almost anyone can get to grips with the mechanics of the Universe if they really set their minds to it. Such skills do not develop overnight. But you helped, Kala, by sending me the energy I needed. You also acted as my eyes—my spiritual lucidity is not what it once was. But ritual itself, though an essential practise in earlier stages of magick, is no longer necessary to me. You entered the scene I had set mentally, and on that stage, Juliet played out the final psychodrama she needed to get her onto the next level."

Two pleasantly humdrum days later, the door burst open, and in flew Magwitch, at least ten bags clutched in his hands, his Barbour flapping. My heart sank.

"I'm off to Paris with my work," he gushed, "But I thought I'd drop these off for you first. They're of no use to me now. Must dash. Regards to Mr. M. Au revoir!"

He departed as he had arrived, in a flash.

I edged around to the front of the till to see what he had deposited there.

In bags marked "Kala," I found the clothes, all my own size, from his boot. At the top of one was the Victorian mourning coat I had craved.

I sent Jude and Juliet a *thank you* on the ether, put it on, and sat down again behind the till, wondering what would happen next.

ᴏRPHEUS

I

The first full-time member of staff I took on in my new role as manager of Malynowsky's bore the resplendent but ill-fated name of Eurydice. Her mother was an actress, partial to Greek tragedy. Witness now the power inherent in a name.

Eurydice was a nervous girl with a penchant for Rimbaud and Baudelaire, and henna in her long hair; qualities which made me take to her instantly. She had the most incredible blue eyes. If blue could boil, her irises were that colour. She was in her mid-twenties, a romantic soul always on the lookout for "the Love of Her Life," and I believe a major attraction of working in our shop was the opportunity to sit and stare out of the warped and ancient windows for "the One."

It was a beautiful spring day when Eurydice started at Malynowsky's. The bell-ringers were in the towers, showering us with chimes unchanged since the reign of Henry VIII. Many of the college bells were cast in the sixteenth century, and their mellow tolls frequently announce in complex synchronicity the season, day of the week, and any marital contract in the city. The trees were in blossom, though hail had wrecked them the week before. This day, however, was like a burgeoning of new potential in Oxford, with promises on the pollen-kissed breeze.

I was busy, busy, busy, and loving it. You know those days when everything seems vibrant, significant—it was one of those. I was zipping around on a high caused by caffeine and gainful employment, feeling very much a part of my environment and of society. Every so often I called over to my new employee—"Okay over there?"—and she nodded and smiled shyly over the ziggurat of books I had given her to price.

The medieval walled gardens and yellow sandstone edifices of the college opposite (leaned on by many bikes) were basking in the sun. It was a Saturday, and the town was bustling with humanity. Our own dark niche was proving particularly attractive to those specialising in incunabula and pre-Christian conceit, and Eurydice was doing her best to fend off feelings of ignorance in the face of so much knowledge, the common complaint of workers in bookshops around the world. Elegant bibliophiles from France and Spain, ruddy German scholars of Hebrew and Aramaic, hirsute wild intellectuals from America mellowing naturally from mescal into magick, were weaving all the faster through the ancient, crowded streets on this bright day, called to by Malynowsky's fine copies of Creech's *Lucretius* or exquisite *Magiae Naturalis* fermented between limp vellum.

The city's own shuffling dons positively drooled as they perused our recently replenished stock, muttering, accustomed to displaying their thought processes. They appreciate the age of the tomes, their weight suggestive of labyrinthine reasoning, even if they loudly declare "Piffle!" or "Modish drivel!" at the contents when these move from the reasoned clarity of history and philosophy to the conjectural or metaphysical. They rub shoulders with Thelemites and Wiccans and Pagans, who scan the shelves with an equally eagle eye.

Eurydice tried to hide politely behind the shimmering auburn hair which fell across her face like a veil whenever she inclined her head, while I bustled around chatting to the regulars and pointing out scripts of possible interest. I had half an eye on her in case she needed help, but also because she fascinated me. I employ only staff who can arrest my attention. Otherwise, life becomes too Malkuthic.

I thought it a good omen that she was starting on such an "up" day.

"You're going to love it here!" I enthused at her during a lull in the afternoon.

"I believe I am," she replied with a radiant smile. It was like the sudden lifting of a veil.

Eurydice said little at first, her thin hands fiddling with anything that might distract her from eye contact, and it became quite an obsession of mine to get her to open out.

"Penny for your thoughts?" I would try casually if her eyes alighted absently on my own; but usually, she simply smiled.

"I was just thinking . . . stuff," she might manage, if pressed.

"Sweet, but a little insular," was the immediate verdict of myself and the staff.

"Give her time," quoth Mr. Malynowsky when he flew by for our managerial meeting.

And true to form, the Malynowsky magick worked on Eurydice in a way which was governed by forces stronger than we. In many senses we were just the channel by which she lived out her subconscious pattern. We were her props. But isn't all of life like that, when you look at it closely? I'm beginning to think so.

Eurydice learned swiftly, and because she worked many more hours than the others, was soon indispensable to me. She was adept at display, and created fantastic designs in the windows, which attracted the tourists.

"I was at Camberwell Art School not so long ago," she reminded me when I admired her window-dressing skills, and we managed to have a little chat about that. She had left due to some indiscernible financial problem.

"It's okay, though," she said, her voice containing just a hint of a lilting Northern accent. "Things happen when they're meant to, don't they?"

I agreed. "That's what I think, anyway. Are you from Scotland, originally?"

She started.

"Why?" she asked defensively.

"Just the accent," I replied, a little startled by the sudden intervention of psychological barriers. I thought it an innocent enough question, even imposed on one so shy.

"Close to there," she responded, running a slightly sticky hand through her hair so that it came down over her eyes again. "Shall I go downstairs and tidy now? I noticed the Anthropology section's a bit of a mess . . ."

When it was quiet—which was most of the time during the week—Eurydice would sit and write pensively at the till. In most establishments this would be a no-no, of course, but the inimitable Mr. M. has specifically told me to allow the staff (and myself) some personal leeway. He's not the sort to think that looking busy means value for money. He actually wants his em-

ployees to be artistic and self-expressive. I looked for signs of the
latter in Eurydice as she scribbled away, red-tinted head occasionally raised and thrown back a little, eyes blind to the mundane, smiling, focused on some other land, like so many others
who have lived and written in this city.

It is important to set this typical scene so that we might see
what, in a few month's time, young Orpheus will encounter as
he strolls along our street from the Jacqueline Du Pré Music
School, where he is studying, or rather, being studied as the most
remarkable prodigy in the country. He will be deep in thought,
abstracted, unconsciously upsetting the busker* girl with her fiddle—she knows who he is and feels instantly inept. Inside the
shop, Eurydice will enjoy the sudden respite from the busker's efforts, for the screech of horsehair on catgut is setting her teeth on
edge. These teeth are typically English, uneven and off-white,
strong and certainly idiosyncratic, at this moment tarnished by
the strong coffee she continually drinks in the shop, and showing,
because she is smiling. Why this is she knows not, but a presentiment of happiness has wrapped her in a glow of ease, and the
customers enjoy extra rapport with her today, which will continue to surprise us all until eventually she talks with Orpheus, and
Charon's penny drops. After that, she will be entranced.

On the day in question, the premises seem particularly sensi-
tised by portent, the odour of sorcery saturating the air and
books like frankincense in a cathedral. Seen through the thick,
uneven glass of the windows it looks like a warped but ordinary antiquarian outlet, crammed with mysterious tomes, but this element
of mystique is tripled as one pushes the heavy door and breathes
the first lungful of arcane dust. The fusty air is much loved by

---

* Busker: someone who performs live music, poetry recitals, etc. on the street
  for money randomly given by passers-by.

bastions of the Old Path. Many of these paths are older than one might think.

"*A living cell of antiquity,*" says the *Oxford Bookseller's Guide.* "*Not for the health faddist.*" They had originally put, "*Not for the health-conscious,*" but I vetoed this at proof stage. We need our American customers.

Eurydice was well into the swing of the shop by the time Orpheus manifested himself. Every morning she watered the carpet, keeping it supple and its hairs erect. The stone flags are clad in pigskin, and many a century has passed since that particular stock grunted its last.

Then she would make us both a strong cup of coffee, and select two or three vellum-bound books, or one of speckled calf or engrained Morocco, to clean and polish at the till. As she rubbed the ancient bindings in soft, circular motions with wax and cloth, she felt, she told me, that she was both perceiving the book itself and imbuing it with her own being. Indeed, the books responded to her loving care, the soft vellum melting in her hands, the yapp edges* growing limp with pleasure, the deep red of true Morocco shining like a blush behind the dulling dust. What a sanguine specimen it would be when she was finished! The books she had treated in this way were nearly always the first to sell, for everybody covets a book that is loved.

Sometimes she thought of them, the books from the past which had passed from her hands into theirs, thought quite anxiously of their well-being like a mother, hoping they were comfortably shelved, not cramped or in damp conditions. Of course, the shop is damp, too, with entire colonies of algae dotting the walls, quite a visual feast for the biology students, but Malynowsky's damp seems somehow different. It is a medicinal vapour,

---

* Yapp (edges): In bookbinding, floppy edges which extend from the outer perimeter of the cover.

good for the books—and to the customers, a sort of penicillin-laden tonic, an antidote to the fast life, to time moving on apace. We abide, one might say, in a timeless sphere.

Eurydice watches the students out of the window. They do not notice her at first, engaged in being well-spoken in public and in-termingling in the street, but after a while her scrutiny begins to seep to the roots of their hair, and they turn, just as she does, catching nothing but a blur of black alternately magnified and made concave by the thick glass. Sometimes, if they slip out alone, they catch the gibbous moon of her head floating in dark-ness behind the counter before it turns inward, and then they are impressed by the intensity of azure eyes which can penetrate the glass with their colour. She knows all their names: Gabriel, Ali-cia, Camilla, Cosmos.

Through unintentionally eavesdropping, she has learned that Cosmos is so called because he is legendary at Oxford: "He knows everything in the world!"

Eurydice has witnessed him blithely answer queries on the chronology of the Aztec kings, the breeding habits of brackish water-fauna, the Jewish Diaspora and back again. His favourite area is Elizabethan economics. Eurydice quips to me about leap-ing out and asking him questions on Enochia.

One evening I managed to drag her to the pub after work, and she told me over a red wine that for her, magick is a progressive discipline, a striving for perfection, a healthy spiritual ecology. She too followed the natural rhythms of the year and worked with them, her most relevant being Beltane, the Rites of Spring epitomised on May 1, and Samhain, the Day of the Dead, on Oc-tober 31, the year's dying end. She told me that she employed as-tral archetypes for specific positive purposes, and was typically eclectic in her adoption of pantheons and philosophies.

Most of those she has encountered in her ten or so years of active occult work, she confided, were also of this school. They worshipped the Cosmic Intelligence in whatever form befitted them or the season; they evoked power to aid their own evolution and to help others. The use of magick had quantum-leaped their minds, creating a perpetual spiritual overview. Eurydice said, brushing the hair from her searing blue eyes, that the Craft has enabled her to leave behind a past which would have strangled her had magick not empowered her to cut the cords; it had literally resurrected her from the Underworld of her own psyche.

I wondered what she meant by this, of course, but knew she disliked being questioned.

It had given her lust and fascination for life, she added more confidently, and the tools to appreciate it to the full. It had also given her extra perceptions, for better or for worse.

Some of our customers we know to be lacking in integrity— and more are still totally inept. We discover this through the conversation they impose on us, and by conducting small astral experiments at the till. Once, Eurydice placed a vast ankh of violet flame in the middle of the shop, in order to observe people's reactions. A woman, who was on the premises for entirely nonmagickal purposes, looked from it to Eurydice, startled, but said nothing, fearing she was hallucinating. A bombastic warlock who frequents the shop at least twice a week, wooing the recalcitrant assistants with information on conspiracy theories (and who believes Homer to have been the first Freemason), failed entirely to notice the blazing hieroglyph. This came as no surprise, but was rather ironic, as he carries a much-brandished golden statue of Isis about his person, and often announces his particular rapport with this most feminine of deities and the symbolism of Egypt.

Eurydice methodically concealed her occult prowess from these more dubious personalities.

"Well, it's a job, isn't it?" she would smile when they waxed lyrical about her fortuitous placement. She had no intention of ending up as an altar for their conversational desecrations.

Of course, you would not think it to look at the place—Oxford, the very bastion of the decent classes, stiff with High Church formality, crowded with clergy—but look again! Beneath the robes of black, the *fusc** full or otherwise, there might be found, on some of the more exclusive University members, or beneath the voluminous cloaks of the priests, the brand of something much older and more sinister. Not the gentle paganism of the Wiccan this, nor anything that might be engendered by a New Ager intent on ascension, but the blood-steeped tradition of brute Bacchanalia.

It was my part-timer, Olivia, who alerted Eurydice to this hybrid tradition. Olivia is our guide in all university-related issues, a D.Phil. student of vague physical dimensions swamped in Indian silks and velvets, more often than not leaving a trail of tiny silver bells or mirror-fragments behind her in the shop. Eurydice used to enjoy retrieving these from between the bristles of the hog-hair carpet. She said they reminded her of two favourite great aunts, who used to hide silver things in flowers and say that the fairies had left them there. Olivia also reminded her, she admitted to me once, of these aunts because of her accent, an old BBC English rarely found now, immaculate pronunciation in league with a polite deference even rarer.

Though in the all-important Oxford pecking order Eurydice does not even figure, having studied elsewhere, and though she cut an unusual authority figure sitting there in her secondhand short dresses or cosmic designs, depending on her mood, the

---

* Fusc: At Oxford University, full fusc means fully robed in academic gowns. A play on the word "subfusc," meaning dark or almost hidden.

newer Olivia treated her with all the deference she probably showed to the head girl at school, and I am like the headmistress. Olivia's sense of hierarchy is inveterate and quite charming. She is naturally friendly, thus lifting the shop from the musing quietude by which it is lulled when she is absent. It was through Olivia's cheerful oratory that Eurydice learned of Aristo, and the Latter-Day Hellfire Club.

Eurydice was shocked by the tales, but not surprised. She had heard of Sir Francis Dashwood and his band of merry debauchees, and had witnessed that same autocratic hedonism latent in some of our stiffer-lipped customers. They buy books on the Infernal, which we would banish from the shop if able, but they sell too well for such niceties. Mr. Malynowsky being both eclectic and fiercely opposed to the censorship which drove him from Poland during the War, no tome is excommunicated for its content, only for its condition. Split joints and unsympathetic renewal offend this man as a child's rough handling offends its mother. His broad views and sense of finesse act from a distance to attract those with an equivalent sense of quality, and the purse to equal it. Aristo certainly falls into this category.

Olivia was her grapevine as far as these matters went, and they had got quite giddy on their conversation about Aristo.

"He's at Christ Church, studying French Literature, the seventh generation of his family to do precisely that. Those from seven to fourteen studied Classics. He's a renowned decadent, and believes his body to contain the soul of his own great-grandfather."

Eurydice could not help but smile. What a character!

Olivia extrapolated a little on some of his more public displays, such as invoking Black Isis in the middle of the Quad in Fresher's week.

"But since then," she said, "he's 'grown up' and retired behind a veneer of sophistication. Despite his provocative statements and behaviour, the vast legacy incoming from the family ensured his security at the college; it is rumoured that they pay as much each term as if the entire line of gentlemen were in attendance!"

However, it was not until after Eurydice met Orpheus that she became fully aware of Aristo and what he represented. We shall rejoin her, scribbling and sipping coffee at the till, still smiling for no apparent reason, happy to be there surrounded by fusty books; happy, in fact, to be alive.

To a bird its nest, to a spider its web, to Eurydice this shop. She loved it. She had even ventured to clean it. With the loss of the dust she enthusiastically expelled from the shop at the beginning, she felt an indefinable change come over the place; a demi-octave's difference in the tone, a slight discomfiture amongst the shelves bent by books almost glued together by time; it was the threat of the *New* coming.

She sensed loss; she had thrown history to the wind. Specks of medieval dirt, grains of Tudor crops, mud flaked from boots whose owners had trudged under the weight of Civil War camp fever, their baked minds searching the shelves for an elixir of life, the alchemist's respite. The shop had long been an apothecary, run by thirteen generations of midwives named Beth, and their various husbands. Yes, she threw bits of them out, too, fragments of their herbs and splinters of dried bark, flakes of the disintegrating scalps and skins of their plaintives, spells which had grown like webs in the corners of the tiny shop. She swept them into the dustpan with the evangelical haste of one formerly seeking employment, chucked them all in the council bin outside, and then felt uncomfortable. Thirteen generations of Beths seemed to berate her for so carelessly dismissing the mortal remains of their legacy. Their mushroom faces grew out of the darkness, opening hollow mouths in dark corners, uttering a silent "O" of horror. She never cleaned the place again.

The clients like it dusty anyway. A splutter of asthma is a small price to pay for the pleasure of perusing a truly unspoilt pocket of Old England, and for unearthing some literary treasure in its musty depths. Americans go into positive raptures as they set foot on the moist carpet and loudly proclaim their love of books, as if we might expel them were they not forthright enough about their literary proclivities. We keep a row of Bibles and nineteenth-century novels near the till especially. Their bubbling banter gives us light relief from some of the more pretentious diatribes to which we are frequently subjected. Many of Eurydice's regulars hoped that their intellectual monologues might dazzle the spider in her web, leading her to dazedly discount their purchases, and perhaps meet with them for a jar later? She never did.

And what of the private life of this secretive woman, what of the real loves she might harbour? Many wondered, but only Olivia and I knew something of the childhood with Professor Dolon and a suffering mother in the bleaks of Northumberland, and that only sketchily with a few water-colour details. Eurydice saved the defining gouache for her own designs. She was not proud of having a difficult background, and attempted to turn it into energy for her arts, or to forget it. It truly depressed her, pitying the child trapped in a glass coffin, observed but not interacting, immaculately dressed and entirely mute.

"Children should be seen and not heard, and preferably not seen either," was the first motto of her Victorian-style stepfather; then, *"Go to your room."* In her teens, she fought back, which made it worse. Her melodramatic mother, lack of control heightened by Valium and endless glasses of wine, she told us, sleepwalked like Lady MacBeth at all hours of the day, wringing her hands and bemoaning her lot as mother to such an ungrateful child, just like her father. It was a tale of extreme dysfunction, and Eurydice did her best to eliminate it from her consciousness. The alternative, a perpetual wallow in the unchangeable, revolted her sense of liberty, which was one of her most dominant features.

She fought her neuroses with magick, but it took years to take effect. Gradual improvements had been evident over the last decade, but she did not yet feel fully in control of her faculties, the fundamental aim of all witches and magickians. Next would come the control of external factors, a level at which she was far more adept. However, a faulty operator brings about a faulty operation. It was her aim to eradicate the final vestiges of her unfortunate past before subjecting herself and another to an intimate relationship.

Of course, we cannot always pick our moment.

Orpheus had the beginnings of a symphony in his head as he strolled down the street, enjoying the sunshine, taking deep, unselfconscious lung-fulls of vibrant spring air. Up and up his mood was lifting him, an ecstasy of harmonious, interlacing melodies in his soul. He gasped in raptures of music, making him feel he could levitate at any second, so strong was the prana and the music in his mind. He glowed with a Grecian golden aura of which he was almost entirely unaware. Many stared, but his head was in celestial spheres. Only the squeaky creetching of a novice violin-player tore his thoughts and brought him down to earth with a jar. The violinist stopped abruptly.

Where was he? Ah, opposite Lincoln College; must be between High and Broad Street, then. And what was he doing here?

His mind, devoid of music, was an absolute blank.

Orpheus looked around, and found his gaze caught on the azure hook of a dark woman's intense stare. Feeling foolish beneath her scrutiny, he redoubled his efforts to recall what he had come into town for, staring up and down the street like a tourist, though he had lived here for a good six months.

Slightly flushed, he returned his gaze to the window of the bookshop, or rather, to the particular square of it through which those eyes had pierced, but now in the pane only indefinable dark shapes were visible. Had she been swallowed by the shadows? Orpheus felt a sudden bolt of concern, then berated himself for his romantic notions. And why consider the matter further? Clearly the woman had taken pity on him and relieved him of her acute attentions.

Inside the shop, her back turned on the vision of loveliness, Eurydice was sitting in a welter of emotion, thoroughly willing him to go away. She had seen him before, once from the bus and another time as he cycled over Magdalen Bridge and she walked from the Inner Bookshop back into town, and had felt slain by his beauty. Nothing horrified her more than the thought that he might come into Malynowsky's, thereby trapping her in a confined space with him. She would be unable to breathe until he left, and thoroughly at the whim of his desire to browse, or, horror piled on horror, to buy a book. She felt sure that she would faint.

This was not the simple reaction of a hysterical teenager's libido repressed, though there was something of that in it. Eurydice, who had long studied the vicissitudes of her own psyche, knew that she was scared of him because their interaction augured intimacy.

With the wisdom of the crone she saw their chemistry written on the wall, sure algebra, certain as life and death and the grave itself. He was too beautiful, he would become too innocently hers. She knew that he would love her, could feel it every time their paths began to cross, and for this reason she avoided him.

His poetry, his soul would be a lyre in her fingers. Her dark mysteries he would long to illuminate with his love, her words he would hang on, her kisses he would crave. As sure as the grave.

She shook as this allusion coursed through her veins, a physical shudder which made the one customer present look at her and leave. Thoroughly alarmed, she sent out psychic defence barriers, effectively excluding her potential lover from the shop.

She need not have bothered.

Orpheus had decided to buy a giant fresh cookie from the Covered Market (nice, but not a patch on his mother's celestial delicacies), and return to the school. He ought to commit the symphony to paper before it blew away on the breezes of spring like so many dead blossoms.

After five minutes of extreme discomfort, Eurydice turned to look out through the window. A drunk was rummaging through the bin by the stationer's next door, and two students on bicycles were discussing Plato in the middle of the street. The golden boy was gone. Eurydice felt intense disappointment.

Dejectedly picking up the keys to the many cabinets which clutter the shop, she opened one of the cases and pulled out a book at random. She often did this, opening it at any page, using whatever she read as a form of divination. As many of the titles were faded or blind, her chances of random enlightenment were greater than they would have been in a newer bookstore, where her subconscious memory of the titles might have played a role in her selection. And Malynowsky's continually received new stock from the owner's supply of frail bibliophile buddies. As each collector passed through the Veil, a vast influx of literary gems would be released on the book-selling world, and most of them left their beloved stock to Malynowsky, knowing it would be in caring hands.

One such which had come in recently caught her eye. An indecipherable title was inked on the backstrip in an ancient hand; the jaundiced vellum was brittle. A flake of it came off at her touch, adding to the drifts of animal and book particles which softened the corners of the premises. She opened it carefully.

"Pluto me ad Inferos vocat."

"Hades calls me to the Underworld."

She clucked her tongue; this kind of melodrama revolted her. Fine if it was positive, but this was all too reminiscent of her mother issuing loud lamentations with bloodless lips and wild, dark eyes, their pupils massively dilated from opiates. *Great, just what I need.*

She felt like telling somebody off for guiding her to this depressing sentence, but a little quiver, the breath of a Beth perhaps, or one of the vault-like currents of air which rose up from the basement, warned her against such hubris. *You ask, and you receive.*

Thoroughly depressed now, Eurydice waited for Olivia to trundle in, her glasses steamy with the exertion of cycling too fast, as always late by one or two minutes, as always aware and apologetic of the fact.

What will she be wearing today? Eurydice wondered for distraction, being quite partial to many of Olivia's clothes. As a student, her own sartorial tastes had veered in the same direction; Pre-Raphaelite velvets, voluminous cloaks, long hair, and Pendants of Significance. The hair remained, but Eurydice's confidence in her figure had grown alongside her experimental streak and a desire not to wear her beliefs on her sleeve. The gothic urge was tempered, a sleeker look developed. She felt less of a cliché in more linear clothes. This in no way detracted from her certain knowledge that she was far from straight herself.

The clock struck one, and a few minutes later in came Olivia, puffed-out and smiling.

Eurydice chatted for a moment; *How's the thesis going? We sold that Salmasius. There's a pile of early Literary Theory for you there*, though really her mind was on the man with the golden aura. She set out on her usual walk to the bank.

The fresh air filled her with delight; she could smell sweetness on the breeze reminiscent of the Scottish glens in summer, as if the air had particles of honey in it. Despite, or perhaps because of, our dank working life, Eurydice loved the sun with a passion, thrusting the pale oval of her face into its cleansing rays, basking in minimal clothes when the rare opportunity presented itself. Sometimes she felt like an etiolated seedling shut up in the shop, pale and straining toward the light, yearning for the great, warm outdoors. Malynowsky's receives no direct light, that being absorbed by the walled garden of the college opposite. It must have been that way for centuries.

Because of the beautiful weather, Eurydice decided to prolong her walk by continuing to the end of the road and taking a right into Broad Street. She crossed over in order to walk in the sun, enjoying the bustle, the life-energy of the city centre. It was like another world out here; or rather, it was as if the shop existed in another dimension. Malynowsky's is a bubble of old air floating on the surface of the river. How long before it bursts?

She crossed over again, toward Waterstone's.

Orpheus, meanwhile, had eaten his cookie with a strong, sweet cappuccino, and felt revived. The sugar had reached his brain and stimulated the memory of what he had set out for; a new set of strings for his guitar. He left the covered market and headed down Cornmarket Street, suddenly intent on visiting Blackwell's Music Shop while he was here. He turned right at Waterstone's.

er hair smelled like frankincense, like an old church, with a hint of the vault to it, but he liked vaults. Despite his sunny appearance he enjoyed few things more than wandering around graveyards, the older the better, listening to requiem masses on his Walkman, or composing them in his head. He told her this by way of an apology after he had careered into her and nearly knocked her off her feet. She smiled up at him, and that was that.

Those eyes! Stunning. Flecks of green standing out against bright blue, sparks of yellow, each colour holding its own, yet enhancing the collective, like instruments in an orchestra. And were these not the eyes that had witnessed his confusion earlier? And now he was acting the buffoon again, charging into her like that. He went as red as prize Morocco.

Eurydice, somehow calmed by the violence of their encounter, perhaps with the wind still knocked out of her, recognised this as a prime opportunity to confront her fears by talking with this man.

"You look like you could use a drink," she said.

She sounded like a long lament, spirit lambent underneath, a mourning song, grief held in tight control, structured on a dirge not devoid of melody: notes like bruises, then purple as a priest's robe on Maundy Thursday, currents of the Styx, a river of tears . . .

"I'd love one," replied the celestial beau, who found such qualities irresistible. He hoped laterally to salvage his dignity. "Where would you like to go?"

II

espite Eurydice's resolve to avoid relationships until she had smoothed the kinks in her own psyche, she felt herself falling with irresistible inevitability into the open auric arms of Orpheus. So honeyed were her senses that she barely tried to resist, drinking instead the delightful new sensations which coursed through her body and soul like ambrosia. Sitting beside him in the pub, she had seen it all; she and he together forever, as the Fates intended. She perceived in a trice the demi-life she had been leading until now, an existence played out in the shadows, closer to the Other World than to this one. But now she wanted to experience the abundance of terra firma, to revel in the midst of Matter, scorch herself in the sun, burn out the spirits and dank corners of her latter-day psyche. Suddenly, she wanted it all.

As he talked to her in the Mitre pub, he produced a golden lyre, rather effete-looking she had thought, like no self-respecting instrument she had ever seen. Holding it as casually as another part of his body, he occasionally punctuated his sentences with waterfalls of notes. Usually, she would have found this intensely embarrassing, but as it was, it seemed at worst hilarious, and at best sublime. He was one of the country's première musicians, after all.

The strings, plucked and brushed, produced music so light and bright she visually saw dark spirits scatter, physically felt parts of her own psychic gloaming illuminated and made familiar. He was changing her constitution as he played, affecting the environment like some kind of Messiah.

The woman behind the bar, their only drinking companion in this industrious city, ceased her cleaning and leaned over the counter, looking pleasantly startled, a mask beneath which she was sucking in the music as if her life depended on it, Eurydice could see. Already, she felt proud of him. Already they had been eternally united in a Mysteries ceremony, bound together in a temple through all incarnations, blessed by the priests and priestesses whose edict may not be evaded, as well as by those more homely ones of Hera and Hestia, who smelled of the hearth, of baking bread, of burning pine torches announcing childbirth.

It was not love at first sight because they both knew, as yet tacitly, that this was their past as well as their future.

Clear, clean happiness flooded every cell of Eurydice's previously taut and dark bodies. Sitting beside Orpheus and listening to him talk and play, she felt pure bliss.

That "the whole course of my life could change in an hour!" provided a topic for breathless commentary when she returned to myself and Olivia, flushed and radiant. "Not that I let it show too much," gabbled Eurydice. "I don't want to put him off!"

She thought Olivia seemed a little reluctant to extract the details from her, but put it down to ineptitude in the world of love. Olivia was wholly dedicated to her academic work, and was rarely attracted to another person. With most of those who did manage to catch her eye, she established a rewarding cerebral rapport. Thus had Olivia managed to avoid the quagmires of emotion which so often destroy a good student.

"Don't you approve?" Eurydice asked playfully. "Don't worry, I won't let it interfere with my writing. In fact, it'll inspire me. He can be my Muse. He says his mother's his; isn't that lovely?"

Olivia, looking awkward, jerked her head toward the back of the shop. We turned around just in time to see the character known colloquially as Aristo, but officially as Mr. Aristaeus, emerging from behind the central cabinet, a look of absolute contempt aging his young face. I hadn't seen him either, having just returned from an errand. He sneered at Eurydice.

"How perfectly sweet is love's young dream," he sniped.

Our cupid-smitten friend looked at him, embarrassed.

As usual he was immaculately dressed as a gentleman of leisure at the turn of the century. His silk suit was cut to perfection, displaying both the strength and tactility of his limbs, or was she imagining that? No matter how hard she tried, Eurydice could never help but visualise the body beneath the suit, the spice-scented Adam's apple pulsating behind the Chinese collar, the bare feet within the shoes, the hairy toes.

Eurydice, abashed more by the style of her chatter than by the subject matter itself, put on the persona she used for these rich, confident types, of which we serve several. They are Mr. Maly-nowsky's rent.

"I do apologise. I hadn't seen you there."

"Me, specifically, or just anybody?"

Eurydice decided not to pursue this track. "We received some Huysmans first editions this week," she said instead. I was impressed by her swift subterfuge. "I seem to recall you requesting 'A Rebours' some time ago."

"Indeed," he rejoined with a wintery smile.

Eurydice, grateful for the brandy still in her veins, produced the book, a marker with "Mr. Aristaeus" written politely on it.

"Most kind of you to remember," he said, staring at her.

"It's my job," she replied defensively.

"Indeed."

He browsed for far too long, causing us considerable discomfi-ture. Eurydice, her nerves suffering somewhat from the strains of the day, albeit delightful ones, was desperate for the loo, but could not use it until Aristo had left the shop. Every little movement in the back room is audible in the front, and the idea of this man listening would paralyse her. She padded up and down the tiny aisles like a caged tiger.

"I'll take them all," he said at last. Then, turning to me, "I have some books which may be of interest to you. Classics, most-ly—Basil, Catullus, Aristophanes. I shall bring them in."

"Right," I replied, unable to think of any excuse to deter him, and simultaneously wondering why I wished to do so. He was a good customer, and the books were bound to be fine. "I shall look forward to that."

I wished I had omitted this final nicety. He stared at Eurydice again. His eyes, dark, powerful, filled her with sensations of excitement and fear. We felt the dead midwives shudder as his gaze penetrated the space which they had inhabited for so long. Eurydice felt she should use the Witch's goodbye, *Merry meet again*, which shocked her. She knew that if she gave but one clue as to her proclivities, however different to those of his own school, he would pounce. His dark stare was an attempt at drawing her out. She began to feel bits of herself separating from her inner core and floating outward. I could see it happening too. With a supreme effort of will, she mentally packed them in again. A flicker of faint surprise fluctuated within his left pupil.

"Your receipt," I broke in. "And would you like a bag with those?"

"I'm only going round the corner," he pronounced with utter disdain, causing Olivia to blush rosy-pink in my defence. She hated it when university people were surly; she thought it reflected badly on them all.

"Yes, but it might rain," she almost spat.

We all looked outside. A few drops were beginning to fall.

"Then I suppose I shall have to take one of your bags." His resentment at this tiny back-down was palpable.

He gave Eurydice one final burning look. His jet black hair seemed to grow before her eyes. His olive skin was pale with determination. A canine aura, so subtle it was almost a scent, betrayed the civilised veneer. She thought of "mad dogs and Englishmen" running down a Grecian mountainside together, lips red with—was it wine?

She felt the pentacle she wore scorching her solar plexus. She never wore the pendant on the outside, thankfully. Or did he see her naked, too?

As soon as he had gone, we broke into expostulations about his vile behaviour, and warned Eurydice not to become too fascinated by him. He reminded me of nothing so much as a prize Rottweiler secretly planning to sample the hand that fed it, complete with owner. His cold charm affected us all, but his interest in Eurydice was pronounced and, we thought, dangerous. She agreed that he was unwholesome, and that she should set up barriers against him, but admitted that she found him glamouring.

Still, she soon forgot all about Aristo and the creeps he gave her. She had beautiful Orpheus to occupy her thoughts, and besides, the wealthy customer was not to return to the shop for two seasons. She was still in the springtime of her incarnation.

Never before had she imagined that love, that life could be like this, blessed by a thousand harmonious currents of potential. Everything Orpheus wanted coincided with her secret dreams; they seemed compatible down to the tiniest details. They shared a love of Robert Graves, Dion Fortune, Tarot cards, music, candlelight, wine, fine cheeses, country walks, sacred sites—everything, in fact, that would have caused them to reply to one another had either advertised themselves in a Lonely Hearts column. "Too good to be true," they would have warned themselves, but the lure would have been irresistible. Eurydice soon became convinced that they would have met somehow, no matter where they were or with whom.

There were also enough contrasts to keep it interesting. Orpheus' knowledge of music left her dazzled, and his compositions entranced her. Eurydice's occult activities stimulated his imagination, she having taken things much further than his career had ever allowed. As well as music and his beloved parents, he now had a space in which to listen to a new symphony, one which carried the scent of herbs on its higher notes, incenses in its nuances, networks of spells in its structure. The magick and the musick wove together on the causal and etheric planes, and spirit became interlaced with matter as a finer fabric, the richly embroidered blanket of love. Or so wrote Eurydice in her diary, sitting at the till and smiling still.

A week after they met, she took him back to the house she shared in Abingdon with her friend Shade, another frustrated writer, better than she—but less equipped to take the rejection that Eurydice saw as part of the experience, but which to Shade was as a mortal insult. This young man envisioned himself as something of a rescued Chatterton, having attempted to do away with himself in his teens but being resuscitated by his adoring sister. The latter remained on hand, which relieved Eurydice of having to deal with her flatmate's suicidal impulses every time the postman delivered a letter from another agent or publisher claiming to have read, liked, but decided against his work.

"If anyone else tells me they're fully subscribed for the next year, I'll scream!" wailed Shade to Orpheus on their first meeting, secretly glad to have something to talk about in the face of such tongue-tying talent. Orpheus eyed the thin, sandy-haired writer with sympathy. He looked quite forlorn in his faded black t-shirt and bashed-about denims, a drooping roll-up hanging from the corner of his mouth. Despite being on the dole, Shade looked exhausted.

To Orpheus, he was a tune picked out on a discarded guitar; badly tuned, flat and immune even to skillful handling. He was wired, but rarely lucid. A distant hint of the Devil's own fiddle provided the soul's perpetual backdrop.

As soon as Orpheus escaped to use the facilities, Shade leaned toward her. "Bloody hell, Eurydice, you know how to pick them, don't you?" whispered the writer. "He's not exactly ugly, is he?"

"Hmmm, not quite," agreed the delighted woman. "What he's doing with me, I'll never know."

To her chagrin, her flatmate did not respond to this.

"Hey, you're meant to tell me I'm gorgeous at that point!" she laughed, trying to make light of it.

"Well, you're very nice and all that, but someone like Orpheus could get the pick of the crop."

Eurydice looked at him, hurt. His dry lips were taut with jealousy. Needless to say, it was Eurydice he was jealous of, not her lover.

I'm stupid, thought Eurydice. *Of course it must be nauseating for other people, seeing us together.* She knew that she and Orpheus already emanated solipsism, and did not blame Shade for his catty response. She heard his word processor tip-tapping all night.

Next door, in Eurydice's room, Orpheus was lying in his lover's arms, thinking about her house, her decor, her personality. The bitter drip-drop of Shade's catharsis in the orange-tinged suburban night made him think of the Underworld, and he attempted to eradicate this thought by burying his head further in his ancient love's ebony hair. It sounded like the cello.

The things he found in her abode confirmed his hopes: her books were either identical or parallel to his, comprising literary novels, though she veered toward French where his tastes were British; occult literature, of which she had more than he; poetry, though hers was a little sparse; and one or two extremely expensive-looking antiquarian specimens. The room was not her own, and had been left as found but for the green velvet curtains she had bought from Oxfam, someone's relics of Victoriana, and a few pictures on the walls. Most of these were of naked women involved in activities such as raising stigmatic palms to the moon, or standing on rocks looking moody. Circe raised her cup to Ulysses in the only framed picture, an image Eurydice had seen on the cover of Rider-Haggard's *She* and instantly loved.

In the eastern corner stood a round table of carved wood which Eurydice evidently used as an altar. Subtle tunes hung like diaphanous cobwebs in the sacred space; industry was indicated, steady constructive rhythms, thoughts, and energies intricately woven together. Above it hung a bold pentacle of yellow satin on black, a symbol which frequently cropped up about her person, stamped into a silver ring, or hanging about her neck. Most of the spell-vibrations were attached to the five-pointed star, either in the middle of it or at one of the points. Orpheus could hear the clamorous whisper of the sea as he studied one of these; the crackle of an open fire as his concentration alighted on another. On the table stood two tall red candles on either side of a squat green star candle, their intent concealed; beside these a censer for loose incense, a small bowl containing, he guessed, saline solution, as it sounded clean and carried a white glow with it; and a plethora of busy dried herbs to the back. A melodic chunk of rose quartz and an ethereal smoky crystal wand lay there also.

Eurydice had lit several scented candles and turned the lights down low. A carved clay lamp bought by a friend in Morocco covered the walls in shapes and shadows; Dead Can Dance ululated from the stereo speakers.

They slept in one another's arms that night, as content as unborn children.

Orpheus, for his part, was equally smitten. Walking along the river Isis with her the following morning, he watched the swans and thought how they, too, made white and transcendent by their love, floated above the murky depths of the mundane. His poetic soul soared on the psychic currents between himself and Eurydice, giving him a bird's eye overview of his life. It seemed to him that his entire existence had been honing him to this fine point, the moment at which he was to meet his one true love. The disappointments of the past, the girls he had set up as goddesses, only to be let down as they revealed to him their fatal flaws—the unkind words spoken by the last, Sally, as she made her passage through his life quite clear, turning the tunes he had written for her to cacophonies to his inner ear—all of these were eradicated by the all-encompassing presence of Eurydice. She was his justification, a Muse he could immortalise. She reminded him of his mother, the beautiful Calliope.

The young god was keen to introduce the three people he loved most in the world. Eurydice, conversely, was terrified. Her upbringing, remember, had trained her to believe herself inadequate; her stepfather's words and actions had to be continually exorcised in order for her to operate properly on this plane. Mr. Malynowsky had perceived her dilemma immediately, and given her meditations to perform which helped stabilise her persona. This encounter with Orpheus, however, had knocked her sideways. It was too soon. Her delicate soul was being scorched in the Apolline sun of Orpheus' concentrated love.

The family that had created him obsessed our psychologically orphaned friend. She conjectured, she asked for pictures and stories, she felt that she loved them before she had even met them. Eagrus, his ever-encouraging father, and Calliope, artistic and nurturing, had provided Orpheus with a solid foundation of unconditional love. They had tended without smothering him, allowing him to take the directions of his choice. Girl after girl had appeared on their settee since Orpheus had reached his teens, holding his hand, each introduced as "the Love of his Life." His trusting inclinations were something they secretly kicked themselves for; for having given him the best of themselves, he expected the best from others too. He had known little emotional pain until he began dating, and then the nature of the world had shifted in his eyes. His parents saw this continual stream of pretties as a necessary part of his education, and did their best to facilitate each as he would wish. However, some had pushed their patience to its limit; bossy little madams keen to get Orpheus under their thumb; or, worse, the ones who flirted with his older brother, Mal.

Malikin was Calliope's son from her previous marriage, his own father having died in Malikin's infancy. Sturdy Eagrus had raised him as his own, lavishing as much attention as was possible without pressuring the boy, but the amount received was greatly diminished by Mal's continual accusations of nagging. The latter, cavalier, charming, and undeniably handsome, attracted young Orpheus' girlfriends with his vices. He was rude to his parents in front of them all, surly with his brother, and self-consciously gorgeous as he lolled about the place in his leather jeans, white shirt, and long jacket, looking as if he'd just walked off stage. He wore make-up, which young girls always like. His vanity rubbed off on them, and they, too, saw him as the best brother. Beside him, Orpheus seemed to be clinging to the apron strings, and few traits are less attractive in a partner than this.

Sally had doubtless been the worst, Orpheus' first real love. For two years their relationship dragged on, Orpheus obsessive as his nature dictated, Sally prissy and critical, until Mal was in the room. Then she became giggly, a little flushed, as if tipsy. In these two years they had witnessed her transform from a girl of undeniably conventional tastes, right down to the court shoes which so revolted Calliope, into a bodice-wearing vamp, complete with

black lipstick and large doses of patchouli. In private they referred to her as Mademoiselle Whiplash, and truly wished that
she and Mal might have a fling and be done with it. But Malikin
had no intention of complying with her scheme. He did not
fancy her.

Eventually the love of Orpheus' life left him for a roadie she
met whilst trying to get backstage at a Fields of the Nephilim gig.
It was vaguely in her mind that if she could sleep with one of
them, Malikin might be impressed.

So much for Sally. They prayed that this Eurydice might prove
entirely different. They felt this to be so.

Knowing how important Orpheus' parents were to him provided a considerable psychological barrier to Eurydice. She
was terrified they would not like her; she could sense their love
for him from here, protective armour about his person, and suspected they would be up in arms if they knew her past. She
feared that they would look into her soul and find her wanting,
that they would see the damage done in childhood and declare
her an unsafe structure, a house built on shifting sands. Plus,
what was she but under-manager of Malynowsky's, and a would-
be writer, like practically everyone who works in the booktrade?
While Orpheus on the other hand was prodigiously talented,
steady, handsome, and young. Ah, that was the other thing. She
was six years older than their boy.

Still, love conquers all, she told herself. Over and over.

As they drove up the tree-lined road to the place of Orpheus'
nativity, they saw Eagrus and Calliope looking expectantly
out of the window. Eurydice's pulse raced.

"Don't be nervous, my love," soothed Orpheus, taking her
hand. "They'll adore you, just as I do."

To how many quivering women has that line been said over the centuries? wondered Eurydice. It vaguely comforted her to know that she was couched in an archetype.

As they approached the front door, Eurydice hallucinated festoons of laurel suspended on wooden staffs, quite an entertaining sight in this suburban cul-de-sac, and one which filled her with courage.

His parents delighted her. Their warmth was infectious, their conversation informal but stimulating. Both were well versed in Greek mythology, a discovery she made by commenting on a postcard of Delphi she spotted on the mantelpiece.

"We went there for our honeymoon," smiled Calliope from her armchair, twisting a long tress of black hair around her fingers as she spoke. The action was one of pleasurable languor rather than nervousness. "And Eagrus read the *I-Ching* in the cave."

"Wow," said Eurydice.

"We'll go there one day, my love," smiled Orpheus, stroking her hand. Eurydice felt intensely aware of this contact, little knowing that streams of girls had had the same gesture performed on them in this very spot. It embarrassed her.

"That would be nice." She removed her hand and used it to flick her hair back, as an excuse.

"I can envision you as a Pythia," mused Eagrus, stroking his short beard with a hand adept at many a stringed instrument, a fact confirmed by the pronounced calluses on various of the stout digits. This comment delighted Eurydice, who within her own circle was renowned for her oracular prowess. She wanted them to see this side of her too.

"Yes, I'm very interested in the art of prophecy," she said carefully. Orpheus retrieved the hand. "And I'd love to go to Greece," she added lamely.

"Do you know the myths of Apollo?" asked the expansive man. "Well—"

As he embarked upon the variations of Apolline mythology, Eurydice, though listening, used the opportunity to study the room. Up until this moment she had concentrated her attentions on his parents, not wishing to seem rude, but she was longing to get a proper look at the decor which had cocooned her lover in his youth. What a place it was, she thought, to produce such a specimen of human perfection!

Outside, the moon climbed into the sky, a sickle with which to scythe away the past. Inside, the room matched Calliope to a tee. The Indian paisleys of her clothes were reflected in details of the decor; the colours of her aura were redoubled by the orange and red paper light shades. Many leafy plants flourished in the house, and it felt healthy; a complete contrast, thought Eurydice, to Malynowsky's store or, indeed, her own parents' home.

If Oxford was Hod, then this house was Netzach. The energy here was effusive, creative; music and dance replaced ritual and dogma. Beauty triumphed over majesty; the natural replaced the contrived. *Or rather,* thought Eurydice, *it did not so much replace it, as counterbalance it.* Both were necessary. One excluded and discriminated, the other welcomed all. The God-name in Netzach is Jehovah Zaboath, Lord of Hosts; the atmosphere here befitted it.

The polished floorboards were warmed by generous Eastern rugs. A vast vase of fresh red roses filled the room with their delicate scent. The two generous armchairs and the settee on which the young lovers sat were Mexican, covered in dark suede of great softness, with chunky wooden frames. It was the sort of thing, thought the girl, you might find in Frida Kahlo's sitting room, and indeed, an illustrated section of one of the artist's diaries was displayed in an untreated wooden frame on the wall.

The mother's side indicated art and abundance, while Eagrus' portion of the room was slightly more Zen. A large brass Buddha sat near the hearth, and a teak cabinet inlaid with mother-of-pearl, which Eurydice suspected had been placed in accordance with the *chi* of the room. Wind-chimes in the window redoubled her suspicions of active Feng Shui.

Despite the differing origins of many of the objects gathered there, an overlying ambience knitted them together and gave the effect of expensive but comfortable hippie chic. There were also cases crammed with books, piles of musical scores and objects of interest; a Balinese carved wind instrument, several antique violins, a huge hollow rock crusted in amethyst, and a cluster of Jerusalem candles as well as tall monocoloured ones on arty towering candlesticks.

She peered over at the framed pictures, one of which, she deduced, depicted the entire family ten or so years ago.

"You can look at it if you like," said Calliope, reading her mind. Eagrus, not in the least offended, continued to regale them with Olympian myths, while Eurydice strolled around, occasionally nodding at him and smiling, happily absorbing all the available details of her lover's life to date.

Calliope watched the girl picking up the family portrait. She did so with the care of one who is used to being beaten for clumsiness; she barely dared touch, but she was too intrigued to resist. Calliope watched Eurydice's eyes rest on each image in turn; those of the parents, who had not changed, that of Orpheus, whose sensitivity had been written all over his face as a child, making Eurydice smile, and finally that of Malikin, then fourteen or so and already clad in black. Eagrus paused as Eurydice's lazer-blue eyes penetrated the picture. Through the mists of time, he thought he saw her lurk behind the friend who had taken the photo, and his monologue petered out.

The family portrait was replaced with infinite care. Eagrus and Calliope exchanged looks which Orpheus caught but did not understand. He felt upset. Didn't they like her?

While Eurydice continued to pry, in effect, with her hosts' permission, a small psychodrama played itself out behind her back. Orpheus, whose emotions had never been within his control, was pierced by anxiety about that look, for nothing would pain him more than his parents rejecting his beloved. That he loved Eurydice he had not the slightest doubt, and it had already entered his mind to marry her. Without his parent's consent, the situation would be unbearable.

Eagrus and Calliope, on the other hand, had just perceived the sound of Malikin on the approach, and the unmistakable bray of laughter, accompanied by the click-click of metal-tipped boots on concrete, filled them with misgiving. Not just Malikin's voice, but those of his hangers-on; Beltane's, Sanna's, Lenoir's, and that awful Meredith's sarcastic drawl.

"I think we have company," said Eagrus, attempting to put a cheerful face on it. He raised his voice. "Come on in, kids!"

"Kids, barely," muttered Meredith, walking in as if he owned the place.

The smell of teenage pheromones filled the room, though most of the crowd were in their early twenties. A solvent-like aroma flooded from one of them, a hint of patchouli riding its currents. A wreath of smoke exited Malikin's reddened mouth, adding a more stabilising aroma to the collective wreath of scents.

Eurydice was surprised by the sudden profusion of black in the doorway, and abashed by the animal presence of so many young men in one small space. Sanna smiled at her, pushing a lock of blue hair out of her proficiently kohled eyes. Clearly she had not done Meredith's, which were a mess. He glowered at her as if she had broken into his home. Eurydice thought, *Bad fairy*.

"Hi, Calliope," chimed Sanna, the only one to express any friendliness.

"How are the fiddle lessons going, Sanna?" asked Eagrus. "Have you got that chord sequence yet?"

"Not quite," replied the girl, "I—"

"Boring!" announced Malikin. "We're going upstairs now."

"Don't you want to meet Eurydice?" asked Orpheus, to Eurydice's chagrin. She just wanted them to go away. The room was becoming claustrophobic, and Mal's careless treatment of his parents offended her. What she wouldn't have given to have parents like that! Or even just one like that!

"Hello, Eurydice," snarled Malikin, tilting his head to one side so that it seemed at once insulting and winsome.

"Hi," she replied, a bolt of tension exiting her body in a manner she was sure was visible to all.

In her flowery dress, selected with parents in mind, she felt foolish. She wished she had worn some of her old regalia, the blacks and velvets, and then reprimanded herself for this impulse. Who was she trying to impress here? Her willingness to please this cult of egos pissed her off. She wished that Orpheus might exert himself a little, make his presence felt. It was as if she were alone in the room with them all.

"Allow me to introduce myself. I'm Beltane," said the one at the back, taller than Sanna but smaller than Meredith and Mal, who both exceeded six feet. He wore a black leather jacket like the rest, and torn denims patched in places where the denim had not torn. Numerous piercings studded his face and ears, which otherwise were nondescript. It was not until Eurydice took the extended hand that she realised Beltane was actually female.

"He's transgendered," carped Malikin, enjoying Eurydice's confusion. Beltane must have shaken her hand with this in mind. She wanted to say, *So what? I've met transgendered people before, you know,* but held her tongue.

"There's cake in the kitchen," said Calliope casually. The cool, lean guests strained toward the room of promise.

"What sort?" asked Mal.

"Coffee and chocolate."

"But I hate coffee and chocolate," whined Malikin.

At this point, Eurydice laughed. She could not help herself. She thought that any minute they would all turn around and tell her they were acting out a joke. But no. The *deathers* were heading for the kitchen, and Malikin's nose really was out of joint because his mother had failed to bake him precisely the right kind of cake.

"Leave some for Orpheus and Eurydice!" shouted Calliope into the finger-licking throng. She seemed not in the least perturbed by the scene which had left such an impression on Eurydice, who was hot with embarrassment at her untimely laugh and off balance with the presence of so many strangers. She began to feel quite ill. She wished she were at home.

Orpheus put his arm around her as she sat back on the settee, grateful for the support. All the same, the beloved arm weighed on her as the vampiric androgynes filed past on their way back out, and Meredith sneered at them, she was sure, through his flop of dyed black hair. His face was older than the others, sallow, pitted by abuse. He had lines, like her. She did not like him. There was something about him that reminded her of Aristo, something sharp-toothed and canine. She felt faint with relief when they left.

Despite this interruption, the rest of the evening passed off successfully. The warmth which flowed between Eagrus,

Calliope, and Orpheus gave their guest much cause for reflec-
tion. The fact that they exchanged genuine conversation amazed
her. They really were interested in one another's opinions, not
just trying to impose their personal Will on each other, as had
been her own experience. Their relationship was alive, organic,
growing. Incredible.

As she studied the family, she was hounded by the sensation of
being watched. When she blinked, a pair of yellow eyes seemed
to float before her; or were they just retinal impressions from the
lamps? Eurydice tried to ignore this, along with the subtle scent
of dog-pelt which had invaded her senses somehow, she was not
sure when. In an attempt to eradicate this perception, she lifted
her chalice to her lips with greater frequency than was perhaps
advisable, a fact which was politely ignored by her hosts.

She swayed into Orpheus' incensed room, spotted the double
mattress on the floor, strewn with Indian cushions, and lay
down with relief. An entire chandelier had been lit prior to her
entry, so that the den was blessed by the glow of nine flickering
candles, which she perceived as approximately eighteen. Unbe-
knownst to her, Orpheus had anointed each one of these with
magnetising oil as a sort of love charm. It had, of course, worked
before it had begun.

On the walls, she noticed through the red-wine haze, were
framed several images she mentally labeled *Yesodic*, belonging to
the spheres of imagination, subconscious, the etheric planes. A
Burne-Jones angel edged with thick gold-painted wood, a poster
of Magritte's floating rock-castle, the sea far beneath the gravity-
defying orb, and a cloth hanging depicting a Buddha-like figure
complete with chakras. Ivies tumbled from high corners, and here
and there faces carved in stone peeked from between the leaves.

Most of his books were in his lodgings in Oxford, but a few deemed unnecessary remained propped up against countless vinyl albums—at least three yards of the latter—comic books, *Brewer's Dictionary of Phrase and Fable*, shiny book-club editions on the photography he would like to get around to if he ever had time.

"Do you like it?" Orpheus asked unnecessarily.

That night she awoke at some unfamiliar sound, and lay blissfully inhaling the atoms of their household. As she breathed, she consciously absorbed the psychic materials that had created it. Caught in the web of spirit translated into matter, she felt organically linked to Calliope and Eagrus, part of the organism through which they had their being and which had brought forth bright Orpheus. For the first time in her life she felt cradled by a household rather than threatened by it. Here, the air was good.

*B*efore they left, Calliope led her into the room she shared with Eagrus, a veritable bower draped with warm silks and faintly scented with musk. On the dresser were a silver comb and brush and a crystal bowl full of water, rose petals floating on its surface, and, at the bottom, polished pebbles of rose quartz and moonstone. The bowl gave off a delightful scent of roses, geraniums, and something sweet and spicy. Behind this was a carved wooden box. Calliope gestured her to pass it over.

Eurydice sat beside Orpheus' mother, watching her brush her long hair back and open the box. She thought, *You are going to be my mother-in-law.* She and Orpheus had barely discussed it yet, but both knew that it was right. Eurydice felt a surge of joy as she watched her future matriarch pull strings of sparkling jewels from the box, rings and earrings hanging off the shining tangles, Indian silver and carved wooden bangles, a dream jewelry box of apparently interminable intrigue.

"Wow," said Eurydice continually.

At last Calliope fished something from the bottom of the box and handed it to Eurydice, who was perched eagerly on the edge of the bed. A silver ring, a moonstone glowing dimly at its centre.

"It's beautiful," said Eurydice, unsure as to whether to presume to try it on, or wait.

"See if it fits," said Calliope in a matter-of-fact voice which took the sting out of the potential symbolism if it did not. Eurydice twisted Calliope's jewel onto a slim finger. It did.

"It's yours, love," said Calliope.

Eurydice swore to herself that she would never take it off, not for as long as she lived.

III

The longer she spent with Orpheus, the more involved she became with his family and music, the more desperately she loved him. It came upon her like a kind of sickness, a fevered state of perpetual anticipation from which there was no respite except in his presence. Her childhood hang-ups churned as she poured more and more love into the cauldron of her psyche, chanting over it—*Be Still, Be Calmed my Soul*—willing herself to know happiness at last. A touch of her mother's histrionics no doubt, but nothing that she could help. It pained her dreadfully that she had no equivalent to Eagrus and Calliope with whom to hook him, no lovely family he could latch into. The profound effect his parents had wrought on her made this knowledge all the more acute. She felt as if she had no force behind her.

Orpheus, ever gentle and loving, did his best to assuage her fears. It was obvious to all who saw them together that he was just as in love as she was. During that long summer, a rainbow-hued bubble formed where their auras combined, and to psychic vision they floated like one of Bosch's couples in Paradise, protected by their love, made more beautiful by it. The "polluting mind-waves" of Malkuth flowed around them, as they did our shop. They were inviolate.

The young musician translated these states of being into the most celestial music he had yet written, reducing people to tears in the street when he busked. With the money from his street-playing, he took Eurydice out almost every night.

And so it remained until summer turned to autumn and Hecate swept her dark cloak across the country, causing the leaves to redden and start to fall. The nights grew longer and darker, the birds picked the last of the berries from the bushes, but the couple's joy continued to grow. Eurydice looked radiant with the "in-love" aura wrapped around her; she was becoming truly beautiful. Her conversation flowed freely and her confidence was increasing. She was finally becoming what she should always have been.

It was obvious that Aristo could see this bubble and wished to burst it. Eurydice perceived the needle in his eye the day he brought in the books, the same day that Orpheus popped in on his way past and saw Aristo for the first time. The boy's besotted endearments made the customer look positively ill, and it was with some embarrassment that Eurydice furtively returned them.

Similarly to when Malikin and his friends were present, it annoyed her that she was playing to the stranger's fiddle instead of her lover's, a habit she had picked up from her mother. The latter always placed the new above the familiar, and deemed everyone else's opinions of more importance than those of her own household. "Familiarity breeds contempt" was her mother's favourite catch-phrase.

In defiance of this training, as Orpheus left, Eurydice almost shouted "I'll see you later, *Darling!*"

Aristo kept his expensive back turned during the exchange.

"Now, Ms. Dolon," he growled as soon as they were alone, smirking at her surprised expression; "Yes, I took the liberty of researching you a little. You will find that I always make it my business to know who is handling our family books."

I was off that day, and Eurydice was in charge when I was away. She attempted a professional nod, though shaken, and took the box of books across the till. Aristo had used her stepfather's name rather than her father's, which she usually employed. She had not been called "Dolon" since school, and hearing it pronounced here disorientated her.

Aristeaus' animal presence flooded the shop, and she feared their fingers touching as he passed the box over. She all but snatched it from the top of the ancient counter.

"These look great," she said, peeking in and aiming for casual ease. "Our head office is in London, and it's actually Mr. Malynowsky who buys in the stock, so I'll send these to him with our next delivery, if that's all right. I'll just write you a receipt . . ."

"Aren't you going to inspect them now?" asked the man. "I must say, I find that rather surprising. I had taken you to be a lover of antiquarian books, but perhaps I have been mistaken."

"You're not," said Eurydice firmly. "Only I have rather a lot on at the moment . . ."

He treated her to his habitual smirk. "What, in this place?"

She held herself steady behind the till, a generous mahogany affair which she was grateful placed a barrier between them. "Yes."

He affected a sigh. "So be it. I shall trust you." He laughed: an unnatural sound, a pitch too low.

"Here's your receipt," she said, aware that this was the only voluntary phrase he ever extracted from anyone at Malynowsky's.

"Keep it," he replied, and left.

As soon as he had gone, she rushed to the back room, made herself a strong cup of coffee, and sat down to scrutinise the books. In truth he had been right, there were few things which delighted her more than antiquarian acquisitions, but she had demurred at the thought of him watching her, testing her knowledge, sensing her interests.

The vellum on the Catullus was so limp it felt like skin, and she was surprised to feel that it was actually quite warm, as if someone clutching it for a long time had just laid it to rest. There was no heater on in the shop and Aristo had certainly not imbued it with his own body warmth, if he had any—at least, not in her presence. With a wave of shock she suddenly imagined the book to be bound in the living hide of a human being; she dropped it in horror.

Angry at her overactive imagination and horrified at her treatment of someone else's property, particularly a valuable book, she forced herself to retrieve it from the dusty floor. This time it was perfectly cold.

Moving swiftly on to the Aristophanes, she made notes, hoping that the perpetuity of the normal would calm her increasingly abnormal reactions. *Re-backed in old diced calf*, she wrote. *Contemporary blind stamped vellum.* As she sipped her coffee, the phrase "diced calf" bobbed up and down on its brown surface. She replaced the mug with disgust.

Lunging for the *Opera D. Basilii*, a folio edition in yellowing vellum, she felt her hand stabbed by something cold and metallic. Swearing, she looked at her ringed finger. It was bleeding.

She retrieved the object from the box with a sense of menace, knowing that Aristo had planted it there. An ancient rusted caduceus in which the snakes had been replaced by basilisks came out in her hand, leaving her skin orange where it had touched. It glowed with dark energy, and had obviously been used in many a ritual, but Eurydice was accustomed to magickal objects.

She *humphed* as she studied it. Such relics were ten-a-penny in this shop, and her opinion of Aristaeus was low enough to give her ease of mind. He seemed more like a precocious child out trick-or-treating than a magickian to be taken seriously. Still, her finger hurt.

Great, she thought, *I'll probably get blood poisoning now*, but it never entered her head that she really might. She was careless of her own health, being young and, she thought, robust. Cuts in the past had never bothered her. She absently stuck her finger in her mouth.

With the other hand she undid the fastenings and turned the pages. The book was dated 1540. The leaves were almost pink with age, thick as paper rarely is today. A copper engraved frontispiece caught her eye. It showed a caduceus-bound basilisk just like the one that bit her. She removed her finger from her mouth, and to her surprise, found it instantly beaded with blood once more. A fat berry, beginning to burst. On the way back to her mouth, the bead spilled and dropped right into the middle of the page.

A flutter of concern from the thirteen generations of wise women, but what could they do? They could see her, dear girl, musing at the till, wondering how to get out of this one—she could not exactly liquid-paper over the damage—the infection beginning to spread through her veins.

Their hearts went out to the beautiful boy whose radiance lit even the darkest recesses of their shop, and they tried to warn her, tried to—but Eurydice was accustomed to the strange cell of the shop, its unaccounted drafts, its flickering wraiths, the shapes she saw out of the corner of her eye. The chilly fingers on her spine that warned of danger seemed to tell her what she already knew: Beware Aristaeus.

"I will, don't worry," she said out loud.

That night, as Orpheus escorted her through Oxford to Pizza Express, she thought she saw Aristo lurk in every corner, every shady doorway. Her finger throbbed, but she chose to ignore it, as was the will of the Gods. Orpheus, concerned, kissed it and wished it better, and his girlfriend smiled and told him to stop making such a fuss.

Flashes of translucence distracted her: suddenly the place would seem as it must have been in the eighteenth and nineteenth centuries. In the wind-gnawed walls of ancient brick, strange faces lurked; the lost, the dispossessed, the ghosts of scholars past. As in some lost realm of Hades clamorous with whispers, clues half-perceived tip-tapped at her perceptions, taunting with an etheric code impossible to comprehend. And all the time, this sense of a pack of shadows in hot pursuit, panting hungrily. Huddled beggars in doorways developed the clawed forepaws and sly faces of ghost-dogs, seeming to crave her blood as much as her money. The atmosphere slavered.

When Old Tom tolled ten, Orpheus cringed. "The oldest knell in the city," he said, "and the most commanding. Such a solemn sound, it sets my teeth on edge. It keeps its own time and tone, listen. Flat and monastic, like a slightly warped Gregorian chant. Greenwich Mean Time is supposed to set itself by it, I think."

Fraught with tension, Eurydice entreated her consort to take her home. He was as willing to please as ever, despite a pending early tutorial in the morning. She tried to keep him talking in order to ground herself. Between his words, she was startled by the subtle sound of well-manicured paws on the cobblestones.

They spent the long night palm-to-palm in her sanctuary, dimly aware of a sense of impending doom. In cat-ruled suburban Abingdon, they thought they heard wild dogs baying on the wind.

IV

And so an illness auguring health was gradually ousted by another which threatened death. The finger which the basilisk had damaged was ignored for several days, but Eurydice felt that something malevolent had entered her blood. Knowing the ploy to be deliberate on the part of Aristaeus, she put it down to spellcraft, and did her best to counter him on the astral planes. Here she found him waiting almost whenever she concentrated, and she attempted to seize the serpent in her blood and return to sender. He, however, would lift his aegis and triple his Will against her.

Every night, she lay awake, twisting Calliope's ring on her throbbing finger, trying to find the antidote to Aristo's venom, building walls of protection around herself and her beloved Orpheus. She was scared that he might try something similar on her lover, maim or brutalise this Baldur-like innocent with some mistletoe arrow of spite. She realised that one of his primary deities was Loki, and she felt that the allegiance came largely from the human's will to do away with Orpheus. Primarily, however, her rival worked with Dionysus.

Every night she engaged in battle with Aristaeus, lying in fitful projections for hours on end, getting up to cast Circles and throw salted water about the place, stamping on the floor to try and earth herself. She banished Orpheus from her house, knowing that Aristaeus had an inroad to this room, via the bite, and that Orpheus could be accessed through it. She would rather die alone, than live to drag her lover with her.

"I need to write!" became Eurydice's perpetual excuse when her consort called for her. Pushed for further explanation, she made wild accusations of him getting in the way of her career. "I don't want to be stuck in Malynowsky's forever, you know! At this rate, I'll be a shop girl for the rest of my life. Is that what you want?"

Her fatigue made her careless of the boy's highly strung sensitivities. She played his soul with cruel fingers, unintentionally.

Orpheus, of course, knew nothing of what was going on, and was miserably convinced that Eurydice was going off him. She was tired, withdrawn, and rejected him at night. One evening he begged her to let him stay, and she, sure that he would become involved in psychic carnage, refused. He cried. At that moment Eurydice actually wished that she were dead.

All of this, yet nothing solid to back it up; the perpetual dilemma of the magickally active.

Aristo had come nowhere near her or the shop for a couple of weeks now, and there were times when she feared that she was simply going mad. Was this a function of her childhood neuroses, actively driving off the one she loved before, perhaps, he abandoned her? She cross-examined herself as she sat slumped over the mahogany desk, breathing in the fusty air but finding no cure in its bacterial silence. Then she would shut her eyes, and there he was, as clearly as if he were standing in the shop, but a thousand times more powerful. At least in the physical realms of Malynowsky's she had a panic alarm button; what was one to do on the astral levels?

She called out to the Lords of the Inner Planes to help, but they seemed to reply that this was necessary, a part of her fate. She hated that answer; surely it cannot be that she was meant to fall for Orpheus, just to lose him, just to make him suffer? Already the extent of his discomfort shamed her; she could not help wondering with trepidation what Calliope and Eagrus would say of her inexplicable behaviour, for he was bound to tell them; he told them everything. She clung to the moonstone on her finger like a priestess following the reflected luminary across the endless desert. It was her only hope and her only light, a condensation of all the blessed time she had spent with Orpheus. *Orpheus.*

Distraught at his lover's sudden strangeness, young Orpheus resolved not to make an idiot of himself, but to calmly sit it out until Eurydice was ready to explain. He told himself he could forgive anything so long as she did not have another lover, and of this he was—almost—certain. The peculiarity of Shade on the phone sometimes gave him cause for wonder; was his unfriendliness due to possessiveness over Eurydice, or just the artistic temperament? Orpheus would go a long way to forgive the latter, having one himself, and he had seen the flatmates together and witnessed the lack of attraction between them; it was not possible.

So what, then? Did she have a lover at work he did not know of? Or was she simply bored to death with him and his quiet ways? Would she rather be with one like Malikin? Would she rather be alone? Tortured, Orpheus lay awake at night and created musical aberrations which made his sponsors wonder why they had bothered.

One night the pain in her red-streaked arm was so bad that Eurydice woke Shade up and told him to call an ambulance. "The serpent's got me," she raved, "I need tranquilizers, Beta-Blockers." Then she collapsed on Shade's warm, sweat-scented bed.

When she awoke, she had a drip attached to her arm and Orpheus hanging over her, tears in his sky-blue eyes.

"Hello, my love," he said. Everything except for the golden man was white and sterile. He seemed the personification of Life itself.

"Hi," she husked. He looked like heaven and she felt like coming out with some clichéd comment to that effect. Instead, she asked what had happened.

Orpheus told her all the details he knew of, clinging to her uninfected hand as if it were a life-raft. "You had blood-poisoning. You collapsed. My parents are coming down tonight."

Eurydice smiled. Nothing would please her more than to be subjected to the tender loving care of Calliope and Eagrus.

The parental visit did much to speed her recovery. Still Eurydice hallucinated at night, and still she was infected by the terrible conviction that Aristaeus awaited her behind the Veil, but having said that, he had not been present for the couple of nights around Orpheus' parent's visit. Eurydice intuitively sensed that their power in the collective was too much for the bloodthirsty gentleman.

She absorbed their every attention as if it were her life-blood, and heartily wished that she could live with them forever. Her fear of claustrophobia shrank in the face of the grimmer reality of solitary spiritual combat against a force she could not even name. It irritated her that "Dionysiac" was the nearest equivalent, as she had a Bacchante streak herself and was attracted to Dionysus on several levels. No, Aristaeus did not encapsulate this energy, he merely used it, sometimes. There was a streak of Christian Hell to him too . . . but here, Eurydice grew weak.

She began to consider trying to tell Orpheus the precise nature of her plight. Her fear was that he would consider her insane, and leave her. Her worst nightmare, absolutely above all others, was that of losing Orpheus.

"I want to tell you something," she attempted the night he took her home in a taxi and tucked her up in bed. The finger with the moonstone still attached was bandaged now, and sterile. Eurydice felt cared for. Her only fear was of returning to our shop, and the encounter which might ensue. Orpheus looked at her carefully.

"Well, first, I love you."

He smiled, tears of relief forming in his eyes.

"That will never change." She took a deep breath. "Secondly—and you're going to think I'm really weird now—I'm under psychic attack."

"Yeah? Who from?"

Orpheus' attempt at taking it all in his stride had resulted in an unintentionally flippant-sounding answer. Eurydice realised straight away that his reply had come out sounding wrong, but she was still weak and she allowed herself to become irritated.

"It's not a joke, you know!" she sniped. "It's serious." *Now I'm sounding like my mother*, she thought miserably. She heartily wished that Calliope and Eagrus were here to referee.

"I realise that," said the wretched lover. "Truly. Please help me to understand."

"Well, it's not that easy."

Then an idea struck her. It came straight out of an occult detective novel, and seemed absurd on an ordinary level, but it might work for all of that. If she could get Orpheus to hide in the shop at the same time as Aristaeus' next visit, the attacker would surely reveal himself, having put so much effort into immobilising her.

He must have some ultimate purpose for all of this.

His books were the obvious excuse. She would arrange an appointment to offer to buy them, ensuring that nobody but the concealed Orpheus was around, and see how he acted. With her lover there, she would not be so scared. Orpheus would witness firsthand the plot of Aristaeus, and perhaps he could help her extricate herself from his unwanted attentions.

Everything was going to be all right.

Stammering with excitement and sounding quite overwrought, she explained her idea to Orpheus.

V

He thought she had lost it, the truth be told. It was not that he disbelieved magick, far from it; he simply could not see why someone like Aristaeus would bother with Eurydice when he did not even know of what she was capable. Surely there were scores of young girls he could choose from at the University, and he could barely countenance the fact that she had not told him of this "attack" until now. The masculine side of his psyche was affronted, suspicious of a crush. She sounded positively obsessed.

Exhaustion and overfamiliarity with her own thoughts led Eurydice to omit several important details when she told Orpheus of her psychic predicament. Her lyrical monody failed to convince him; she lacked ease at attaining the high notes. Still, he had to persist, for the sake of their future. His dearest hopes were bound up in her well-being.

She looked the embodiment of misery as she sat in her room or that shop, her face another fungus growing out of the darkness, like those of the occasionally-glimpsed midwives and former clientele. The presence of Aristo seemed to permeate the air all around her, even when she made her daily trip to the bank. Her finger still hurt. A head-on confrontation, however disastrous, could not be worse than this slow osmosis of his Will into her life.

Boldly she rang the college and left a message for him to pick up the quote for two of his books, if possible, at three o'-clock on Friday. The Basil she had sent to London with a note of explanation to Mr. Malynowsky about the blood. She could not afford to buy the book herself, Oxford keeping her poor as well as mentally overstimulated, and she had no intention of handing him back a portion of her life-fluid with his property. She knew that the kindly old bookseller would do his best to remove the blood or, failing that, to make an uninsulting offer to Aristo and find an alternative home for the DNA-splattered antique.

She cast a Circle in the shop before opening on the allotted day, carefully fumigating the place with incense and sprinkling it with salted water. She should not have done this, disturbing as it was to the spirits to whom she was accustomed, but she was not thinking straight.

Then she asked for protection, and fired herself up a violet flaming aura. To the Beths she looked like a wall of flame. They were impressed.

By the time ten to three came around, she felt almost jovial, considering a climax inevitable. Her fears of insanity would be allayed when Aristo gave himself away, in one manner or another. Orpheus was due to arrive any moment, so that he could hide in the back of the shop and witness it all.

Aristo arrived early and Orpheus not at all. Eurydice stood immobile at the till, staring at him. She played right into the leisurely magickian's hands.

"Good afternoon, Eurydice; I trust you are in better health now?" he said. Then, swift as a snake, he made the hypnotist's passes over her. So fast was he that she barely registered the action, and began to wonder what she had been worried about. She was perfectly safe with the gentleman.

Smiling casually, not even bothering to burn her with his eyes, he leaned his silver-tipped cane against the till (the subject of much hilarity among his twenty-first-century peers), and asked to see one of the books in a cabinet at the back of the shop. Eurydice fished the keys from the desk drawer and walked to the cabinet in a trance.

For a while now she had undergone the sensation that her blood was somehow *singing*. At first she had enjoyed it; solids became translucent when her blood was up, the Veil thinned and she peered from this precipice of time down and across at many others. New forms of being entered her consciousness, and her perceptions increased dramatically. Now, however, the singing was reaching a pitch quite painful, and she felt faint and spiritually empty as she performed her master's bidding. She entirely forgot to maintain her auric protection, and was dimly aware of etheric hands draining off the remains of what she had placed there earlier. Her last conscious thought was one of crying out for Orpheus.

Then she became a marionette, moving only as Aristo tugged her strings. Discarding the book, he grabbed her and brutally pushed her against the back shelves. With all her magickal preparations, it had not occurred to her that he might simply use his physical strength against her. Unable to struggle, she felt her mouth encased by his own, his teeth pressing into her lips with feral ferocity, the serpent's kiss Crowley wrote about in *Moonchild*. She felt both physically violated and insulted that he had not tried something more original on her. He underrated her intelligence. Yet still she was held fast in the grip of his dominant Will.

"You wish to be my Pythia," he told her. "You would like nothing more than to be a channel to the gods. You will be Dionysus' mouthpiece, Eurydice!"

She sent out a palpitation of resistance. He looked at her, wolven. "The alternative, dear lady, is a fate you would not enjoy. You have heard of the sparagmos, have you not?"

Eurydice recalled reading in Euripides' *Bacchae* of the flesh-tearing frenzy that beset the worshippers of Dionysus.

"Occult science must not be compromised by the proclivities of the tool! Paltry though you are, you are the best that this era can come up with for my purposes. We must put evolution before your personal whims; and you, Eurydice, *will* comply."

He kissed her, properly this time.

It felt like being smothered by a vicious dog.

This was how Orpheus found them when he came in.

You invited me there just to torture me!" sobbed the golden boy. "Does our love mean nothing to you? Have you forgotten it already?"

Eurydice was bound to silence. Despite her oracular prowess, she could utter not one word which rang true to his ears, all of her explanations limp as old lettuce. "You're not even trying!" he cried. "Maybe Shade was right."

"What?"

"He said you weren't what you seemed to be. He tried to warn me, but I believed in you. I should have listened to him from the start."

With these words, he left the shop.

Exhausted and disillusioned, Eurydice's thought processes closely resembled those of her childhood. She simply wanted to curl up and die, preferably in the bed she had slept in as a child.

Familiarity, however harsh, must be better than balancing on edge of this psychic precipice, she reasoned. A return to Northumberland seemed inevitable, other more pleasant sanatoriums being beyond her means. Dolon and Mother would not help, but their blindness itself would act as a shield of sorts; incredulity might, perhaps, replace this psychic warfare.

She needed to regain her physical strength, gather her energies together in order to protect herself. Her weakness was her worst enemy; without the poison, Aristaeus would never have stood a chance. In her present state of compromise she knew that if she stayed in Oxford she would be forced into ritual with Aristo's cabal. She must safeguard her witch's integrity from consorting with these demi-Christian eclectics, consciously or otherwise.

Her real urge, to make her way to Eagrus and Calliope, had to be suppressed for the sake of their son. If she knew him as she thought she did, he would take refuge in his parents this weekend.

As the coach crossed the river Tyne, Eurydice felt relief washing over her. Simply to be out of the hothouse was a blessing, and there was anonymity to be found in this colder clime. Streets and warehouses all bathed in the same grey light, no time for messing around with airy-fairy nonsense; too busy trying to keep warm and earn a living. No psychic shenanigans here, at least not most of the time. Catch a man on New Year's eve bringing in the coal through the back door and he might have a spooky tale or two to tell you, or speak to a nurse at the Royal Victoria Infirmary about those pale moonlit nights . . . but generally the atmosphere was geared toward humanity's immediate needs.

Eurydice felt reasonably grounded, until she reached her childhood home. At the road end of the winding drive, she paid the taxi-man. She wished to approach *au pas du loup*, though why this was, she was unsure. Habit, she supposed.

The house in which the Dolons lived was flanked by pines which stood like giant antennae against the stony sky. The tree which was struck by lightning during the storms of '84 still pointed parched fingers at the repository roof above, not one crow or a solitary raven to be found in its unyielding carbonated branches. The ancient oak, once poked at by Professor Dolon, and officially established as 2,300 years old, stood nearly strangled by creepers, its buds shoved back in the photosynthesis queue by pushy young twiners. Fearing for the old dryad, Eurydice stopped to pull some of the more insolent vines from the lower branches. In the crepuscular light, she could swear she heard them curse her.

She arrived at the tall black door dishevelled from her battle with the vegetation, hands stained with green blood, the dark rings under her eyes telling of a long journey under considerable psychological strain. Despite this, when the bell, still on a pull-string, tolled her arrival, and the lofty figure of her stepfather blocked out what little light was coming from the inside, and a chained crack appeared down one side of the door, she was greeted by: "Eurydice, how dare you disturb us without prior warning! You cannot come in. And that is final."

Things had not changed here, then. She had hoped that the years would have worked their magic; her outgrown teens making her more compliant, time spreading a haze over the hatred that existed between professor and stepdaughter, her regular polite phone calls finally paying their dividends. But Dolon's eyes were still as cold as death, grey concentrations of hatred for the memory of his wife's lovers past, for the money spent on the cuckoo child's education, lasers of suspicion and disdain.

"Please, Sir," she said, a phrase reflected in a lifetime's double-mirror image, repeated and repeated until the little Eurydice diminished into a pin-point at the centre of a drab grey mandala. He had always insisted that she call him *Sir*, just as her mother had demanded *Mother dear*. "Please let me in."

"That is absolutely out of the question," he pronounced. "We don't want you bringing your tantrums and upsets in here. Your poor mother is desperately ill, but I don't suppose you care about that, do you?"

Eurydice's face was bloodless, her features stark and drawn. She heard a dog baying in the distance. It sounded hungry.

"I implore you to let me in! At least until morning. I need to see my mother."

"Go away, Eurydice. You are not welcome here."

He was just about to shut the door in her face, the girl mentally preparing for a dash to the long-obsolete stables, when a blur of drifting white announced her mother's arrival on the scene.

"My baby! My little girl is here!" she shrieked. "Let her in, Edmune, let my little girl come in!"

Fearing a display of hysterics, the man opened the front door, releasing a whiff of sick air onto the chilly night. The bony wraith of her mother flung itself over the threshold and at Eurydice, who, unprepared, failed to catch it. Her mother landed across the path in her nightdress, a sick blossom on a river of black. She made no sound.

Eurydice, horrified, stooped to help, noticing as she did the new thinness of her mother's hair where it had been flattened at the root by the pillow, the long grey roots which demonstrated a worrying neglect for her appearance. There had been a time when Madame Butterfly was always brightly painted, the belle of the ball, a blur of colour in a grey world. Now she was a death's head moth, the semiotics of her colours faded into in a dead tongue.

Dolon lunged forward with: "Now see what you have done! Once again you have compromised your mother's health with your selfishness. You will damn well help me put her back to bed."

And so it was that Eurydice was re-admitted to her childhood home.

The sprawling house had barely changed in the decade or so since she had last been allowed into it. The walls were still a noncommittal white, the household objects shabby relics of Dolon's previous marriage, seventies tack devoid even of kitsch. The air seemed not to have shifted since she left. It still carried the palpable frisson of fear, the mortal pain of her mother, the stark grief of a failed woman. It depressed Eurydice even more, the moment she entered it.

Just one missing detail, perhaps, to be investigated later. From the day she turned sixteen, her stepfather had marked all of his food supplies with an "E" in slanting black, telling her that she was permitted only to eat what her mother bought from her own earnings as a part-time editor. Cakes and biscuits, tins of baked beans, and pints of milk alike had been subjected to the prohibitive pen. Occasionally, following a long search, more often than not spied upon by Dolon, Eurydice might find some morsel left over by her mother, and turn that into her meal. More often than not she dined on Special K.

When her mother was too ill to work, Eurydice was reduced to six stone, then five and a half. Luckily a new antidepressant arrived just in time to raise her back up to six. Dolon had drawn the line again at eighteen, saying that she could have been married for two years by now, had anyone been stupid enough to take her. As an adult, she could jolly well find her own board and lodging. "Selfish parasite" had been his term of endearment for his stepdaughter.

Because of her total removal from the premises, only a very few objects of her own remained. A small crocheted owl hanging in one of the windows of her room, a revolting nylon nightdress hidden in a drawer, a large black statue of a three-headed dog bought by a school-friend in Greece squatted on the windowsill. The latter had been too heavy for her to carry.

Nothing had changed, not because of any sentiment on her guardians' part, but because they were simply too wrapped up in their own tortuous affairs to express interest in the room which had once encapsulated their growing daughter. A faded poster of David Sylvian hung near the oval mirror; a postcard of Colette in a man's suit was propped up on the desk. The single bed was still covered by the very sheets and blankets she had stepped out of ten years earlier. They bore the faint imprint of a heavy trunk tearfully packed. In her bathroom, the same old toothbrush she had left a decade ago, its bristles now moulded green. The same bar of soap with which she had washed her hands of the past. In her living room, the campus map she had sought when she reached Leeds University. A veritable time-warp.

How different, she thought, to Orpheus' childhood home! His family were Life, while here was decay and Death. It was what Mr. Malynowsky might have called the "flip-side" of the Thirty-Second Path. A painful demise into the inevitable, as opposed to a joyous exploration of the possible. She thanked the Goddess that Orpheus was not here to witness this shameful monument to spiritual decrepitude.

She lay exhausted on the austere single bed, watching the moon through the window. One thing she had loved about her room was its two windows, which caught the Huntress as she traversed the night sky, an early tutor of her psychism. In this room she had learned in silence, caught in a silver bubble of communion with the Goddess. Currents of fresh water had conjoined the

Styx at this point; tides which would eventually carry her to another shore—a shore on which she would live, laugh, grow, and
eventually meet Orpheus.

The distance between herself and her lover felt like be-
reavement.

The last thing she thought before she fled this Underworld for
the somnolent realms of Morpheus was about that pack of dogs
baying in the distance, and where it had come from.

VI

It was not until the following day that Eurydice was able to
appreciate precisely how ill her mother was. Histrionics were
normal; silence would have shocked her more; but what had
once been the conscious expression of specific emotions had de-
generated into a quagmire of disjointed subconscious sufferings.
In the pale face of her mother, furrowed and streaked by foundation years old, she saw no comprehension reflected; she was an
actress mindlessly repeating her script.

"He did abduct me, sweet Eurydice!" she wailed over breakfast, staring wild-eyed at the black-backed chair from which
Dolon reigned upright when present. "Fell down the chasm and
my flowers were lost." She began to cry. "No contact have I had
for twenty years."

Was she imagining it, or was her mother speaking in Iambic
pentameters? Surely not.

"Could you pass me the teapot, please?" she tested.

"The pot is there. Oh daughter, rescue me!"

"How? I asked you to leave a hundred times during my childhood, and you always said you couldn't," she said furtively, aware
of the prying ear of Dolon, whom in her teens she had nick-
named *The Lurker*. Already she felt that she was becoming part

of the play, acting her part with pain but not passion. Still, a change is as good as a rest, as they say.

Thinking laterally, as her magickal training had taught her to, Eurydice understood that her mother had slipped into Pythia-mode, but lacked the art of prophecy. She was becoming an oracular archetype, as did her daughter when the atmosphere was right, but her mother as mouthpiece merely transmitted echoes from the emotional depths of her personal Underworld. The entertaining thought occurred to Eurydice to present her mother to Aristaeus as a substitute.

Well, if you can't laugh at your own situations, what can you do?

Her mother jolted her from these reflections. Staring at Eurydice across the breakfast table, running a hand through her sparse grey hair, the woman began to recite. Her pronunciation was perfect, her stresses heavily melodramatic. Her head began to tilt toward the end, causing a strand of saliva to rock on her lower lip:

> *Grief is my lot; greatly perturbed I live*
> *A demi-life in Hades' midnight gloom,*
> *Sadly awakening each day alone,*
> *Abandoned by my daughter and my Love.*
> *Cares no-one for my wretched state? Is this*
> *The thanks I get for rearing you so well?*
> *Such moneys as were lavished on this child!*
> *Her education scrimped for, and her food*
> *Rendered from the very blood within my veins:*
> *My tears redouble as upon my eyes*
> *This sight is forced; my cruel Eury-dice!*

Eurydice heartily wished that Orpheus, or even Shade, were here to witness this. Nobody would ever believe it if she told them.

These poetical onslaughts did little to endear the mother to her only child. Of course, Eurydice was deeply worried, and she still carried a little love for the woman who bore her, as is natural, but all the same she would be one minute steeped in concern, tentatively hatching plans to rescue her mother, when the miserable woman would explode into psychodrama, screaming and beating her breast, tugging at her hair in a manner which would have delighted ancient theatre-goers.

> *O, shame upon thy head, Eurydice!*
> *In Subterranean gloom I pay the price*
> *Of marrying with a parent's fond intent;*
> *For thee I wedlocked Dolon; All too bad*
> *That as a Father he was curt and cruel.*
> *My fault this was not; only for my child*
> *Did I endure the trials of lovelessness.*
> *Ungrateful, proud, so like her Daddy lost,*
> *Lacking in backbone; Curse-d be her name!*

and so on. At such times, taking her back to Abingdon did not seem such a good idea.

Between attacks, holding her mother's papery hand in her own, Eurydice told her about Malynowsky's, about the young man she had met, Orpheus is his name, you should see him Mother dear, you'd love him. The frail moth nodded, her vapid hair swept back from her head for a moment, remembering. Those Halcyon days of love were a honeyed tonic. The best of her life, with Eurydice's real father, before he left. Left her for some slip of a nymph.

"Kor-e, Kor-e!" squawked her mother suddenly, flapping her thin arms about in mock-playfulness. "I am the raven of Doom, and I come to tell you that you will never escape your Fate, Eurydice!"

She flapped some more, pushing her suddenly malicious beak into her daughter's smooth face. The smell of death fanned up from her unclean nightdress.

"Kore, Kore, you can't escape your genes, and in them is the blueprint of your future, as sure as Hell!"

"Thanks, Mum," said Eurydice, feeling fifteen again, getting up to go to her room. "You've really helped."

Thanks, Mum," smiled Orpheus. "You've really helped."
"That's what we're here for, Love," chimed Calliope, smiling back at her son.

"And we really did think she might be the One," said Eagrus. "And faint heart never won fair maiden, remember."

"Apart from anything else, she's my best friend," confirmed Orpheus.

"Then go and speak to her!" said Calliope warmly. "You won't get anywhere sitting around here and moping."

"I shall!" cried the young knight. "I'll go and tell her I love her; I'll win her back if it's the last thing I do."

Looking up from his game of *Tomb Raider*, dark-eyed Malikin smirked.

I'm frightfully sorry, Orpheus," gushed Olivia, flushing, "But Eurydice was called suddenly back to Northumberland. Her mother is unwell, apparently. I say, what superb roses!"

"Here, you have them. They won't be much use to me now."

"Are you sure? How wonderful! Thank you! Shall I pass on a message?"

"I need to talk to her. It all went wrong," He blushed. Olivia seemed to resonate in sympathy, so he continued. "I caught her with that Aristaeus."

Olivia's face pinched. "What do you mean you 'caught her with him'?"

"Well, I walked into the shop, and there they were at the back of it—" he flicked his hand at the offending cabinet; "kissing. She was obviously having some kind of fling with him, but I think we can work through it, I mean, what's a crush compared to our eternal love?"

"I cannot believe it," cried Olivia earnestly. "Do you know how many times I have heard stories like that about that man? In the two years since he arrived there must be at least, oh, eight or nine instances I can think of in which girls have found themselves somehow obsessed and dominated by him. Charisma is barely an explanation. I rather think he uses mind-control techniques on people, you know. Eurydice would never willingly be unprofessional in the shop, and besides, I happen to know that she is utterly in love with you. She talks of nothing else; at least, she didn't until recently."

"And then?" Orpheus was nervous. The scales were beginning to fall from his eyes.

"And then, you're right, she did enquire rather a lot about Aristo, particularly after the blood-poisoning incident."

Orpheus' face fell. "So you think she might have . . . ?"

"No. She loathed the man. Whenever he left the shop after one of his visits, we made no bones about our mutual detestation of him. The man's a cad, and Eurydice knew that. She was more interested in his 'religious' practises; the Bacchanalia and all that. He worships Dionysus, you know."

"Yes, she said something to that effect, but I didn't take much notice at the time. But she's always loved Dionysus."

"In his more civilised aspect, perhaps. But Aristaeus is rumoured to combine the wildest rituals of Bacchanalia with a sort
of Satanism, something one of his decadent ancestors came up
with as empowering at the time. In the era of High Church it
probably *did* achieve something by way of liberation, but you
know as well as I do, well, probably better, that Eurydice's interests are not of that ilk. Aristo certainly does not intend to 'heal
the world.' I don't pretend to understand it all, it's not my field,
but Eurydice is a good person, and there is no way she would
willingly consort with that man." The legato changed suddenly
to staccato. "But I would have thought that you would be the
first to know that."

"Will you be speaking to her?" asked the young man, his lumi-
nescence flickering with misgiving. "I don't have her parent's details, you see, and . . ."

Olivia gave him the feminist eye, unsettling him further. "She's
on call in case we need her at the shop, but she did ask me to reserve the facility for real emergencies, so I'd rather not ring her unless it's utterly urgent . . ."

"Please, please tell her that I love her and need to speak to
her."

"Certainly, if I don't speak to her soon I'll leave a note on the
till, for when she gets back."

"Thanks."

She looked at the crestfallen musician, and her heart went out
to him.

"Here, have her address," she relented. "Only, tell her you discovered it for yourself. She is my colleague, remember!"

Olivia arranged the roses beautifully in an old vase and placed
them on the shop counter, where they died within the day.

VII

Even though she considered him lost to her, Eurydice spent every spare moment in Northumberland reconstituting Orpheus in her mind. Every inch of him was remembered by day and by night, each particular feature a gateway to some other aspect of her lover. A hand, for example, would lead to the lyre, and in the strings she would find her own soul lodged. Without him to play her, she was mute; the mere thought of him made her aeolian.

She remembered proud students with harps on Broad Street, and how Orpheus had referred to them as "*Carpers carping their harps.*" She recalled the impure sound of the trumpet, which had caused him physical pain when the Salvation Army played on the High. He had talked then of Mozart, a composer for whom he felt much sympathy, though Orpheus' celestial compositions went well beyond the vanities of Vienna and the need for love. Orpheus recounted the tale of Amadeus, also made ill by tones ill-conceived and accidental polyphonic paradoxes. Orpheus, though barely conservative, was fiercely pro-melody, pro-harmony, and most definitely an advocate of lyrical poetry. He favoured for his own use simple astrophic arias, monodic madrigals which made time revert to ancient Greece, where of course he had conducted many a musical feat at the games at Delphi.

Both Orpheus and Eurydice remembered large chunks of their former lives. They both recalled being hand-fasted in a cavern, an eternal bond blessed and sustained by the Mystery tradition, which no doubt was responsible for their present proximity. They both recalled children they had had together at various times; such thoughts comforted Eurydice as she bided her time in the little blip of circumstance which was her present physical condition. They went back a long way, that much was certain.

And for the future?

Other parts of his body elicited different responses; the thought of his heart chakra flooded her with helpless emotion, green love with which she could do nothing, all the power of the flourishing potential of what might have been, the sap of regeneration.

His wood-spice-scented throat brought thoughts of guides and gurus who might perhaps help them in their plight; she called out to them, the Lords of the Inner Planes, called out to all the good prophets that ever trod this earth, begged for help from each and every Messiah that Earth has known, but answer came there none. Instead, came the cruel conviction that the Fates had willed it to be so. The three sisters held her threads in their withered but steady hands, and their ears were deaf to her beseeching.

Ye Lords of Air, she cried, thinking of his mind and spirit; *Ye Lords of Fire, hear my prayer. Ye Lords of Water, Ye Lords of Earth, Let him be mine!* But only darkness held.

Orpheus, meanwhile, had plunged into the baritone night and was forging his way toward the trapped Eurydice. He realised now how she must be compromised by her magickal knowledge; the fear of sounding insane, and always the impossibility of explaining adequately, words being so one-dimensional, or two at best, but either way no fit means of translating astral experience into common sense.

He was composing hymns of guilt-catharsis as he sat inside the train and watched Southern autumn diminish into the early winter of the bleak North East. He wished to pick her up bodily and carry her to a place of total refuge.

When he reached the house, Orpheus was almost deafened by the aural phenomenon coming from within. It reminded him of music he had seen depicted on broken vases in the Ashmolean Museum, fragments of laments, shards of public performances, the mutilated splinters of ancient instruments. He could pick out, behind these painful, confused edges, a rigid backdrop of black which he knew to be the monody of Dolon. It had a particular traditional male resonance, typically Victorian. Who else could produce such a sound, other than the briefly described but clearly much-detested stepfather of his beloved?

He pulled on the bell several times. Inside, no response. Outside, no light. He was relying on the moon for help, but what with the clouds and the shadows of the pine trees, the torch of the Huntress was elusive. He could hear dogs quite close, howling and panting. He wanted very much to be behind a solid wall.

Tentatively, he began to walk around the side of the house. He dimly recalled Eurydice saying that her own room backed onto the orchard. A gate confronted him; he pushed it gently. It screeched open. His heart thumping, and half-expecting to be shot at any moment, he crept to the one window from which a light was glowing.

"*Eurydice,*" he hissed, tapping ever so lightly on the window.

He heard a scream within. Then, a pause. Suddenly, the light went off and the curtains trembled open. The white face of Eurydice peered into the gloom.

He climbed in through the window. They lay shaking in one another's arms for a good ten minutes before the explosion happened. Not that they were surprised, as both were expecting disaster at any minute.

The door was nearly thrown off its hinges by the force of Dolon in the doorway.

"Get out of my house," he boomed.

"Sir . . . ," started Eurydice, but she knew it was hopeless. He was standing like a basalt statue, one arm pointing in the direction of the front door. There would be no reasoning with this man, if indeed he was one behind the rictus mask.

Behind him, her mother floated up the corridor, phantasmagorial.

> *In deepest night in soulful plight*
> *I rise like Kore from Hades' bed,*
> *Oh! Ghostly sorrow . . . !*

"Mother dear! Come with us!" cried Eurydice, knowing that blows would rain down on the last of them to leave him. "Come now."

She was running with Orpheus' hand held tight in hers, Dolon looming behind, all the tortures of the past accumulated into one long, solid shadow, running as fast as she could stumble, clutching his dear hand, her nightdress plucked at by her mother's blind fingers, both of them following her toward the door, the door so distant at first and then within the minute, reached . . .

Out into the night spilled the desperate triad. The furious Dolon stood for a moment on the threshold, deciding on whether to lower himself by commenting or not, then opting against the effort. With infinite dignity and finality he closed the door of his ample abode.

No sooner had they established the rhythm of their own breathing than the three realised that the loudest pantings they could hear belonged to none of them. Clutching one another like characters in *Scooby-Doo*, they tried to penetrate the darkness with their fear-blurred vision. Canine eyes devoid of domesticity met their own. At least seven pairs were bent upon them; even one would have been enough.

"Cerberus and his death-inducing pack!" shrieked Eurydice's mother, no sooner released from Hades than hammering at its door once more. A pause in the portal; then the door briefly opened, admitting his wife. The lovers heard the chain pulled across the door inside.

They looked at one another.

"Walk slowly," whispered Orpheus, "Legato, now. Don't make any sudden movements, my love."

She felt acute relief simply that he was hatching a plan, taking control. Holding his hand very tightly, she walked slowly behind him.

"Don't look back," he said.

"Or you," she replied in a barely audible tremolo. She could feel canine breath on her heels. Could hear the pad of clawed paw on the familiar terrain. The worst thing was, the humans did not know where they were going.

As if reading her mind, Orpheus husked: "I'm following the Music. I can hear healthy life in the distance . . ."

They continued thus for a few minutes, growing almost confident at the rhythm they were establishing.

Then Orpheus stumbled on a pothole on the driveway, and their hands lost contact. His first impulse was to turn around to check that she was still there.

No sooner had he looked, than the excited dogs fell upon her. He could hear sharp tooth scraping on bone, sweet flesh being torn from still-flailing limb.

Strangely, she died in silence. Perhaps she did not wish to scar him with her screams.

Thinking of Eagrus and Calliope, he ran. He knew that no effort on his part could save his girl; escape was the only means of salvaging anything. He ran until he reached the safe place he had perceived, and though it was three AM, the kindly Northern couple admitted the terrorised stranger and called the police.

The police were nonplussed when they reached the scene. The witness had described a pack of dogs, but the girl they found, though wild-eyed, had not a tooth or claw mark on her body. She appeared to have died of shock. Two small grass snakes had wound themselves around her middle finger, on which a moonstone ring shone dimly. Her heart had failed, the coroner's report concluded.

At his wedding two years later, Orpheus played the lament he had written for Eurydice. His new bride, secure in the knowledge that her rival was safely dispatched to the Underworld, was too much in love to deny him this indulgence. She reckoned Orpheus would forget all the sooner if allowed this catharsis in public, and she was right. His optimistic nature and his need for love overrode his unique affection for Eurydice.

Malikin and Meredith sat watching the flower-festooned ceremony with glazed eyes, remembering more of his hand-fasted wife than Orpheus would ever allow himself to again. A single kohl-stained tear fell for the girl in the concealing dress whom they had secretly considered one of themselves—a darkling soul. Beneath the soil, Eurydice received the libation with thanks. Like a germinating seedling, she waited.

Even our magickal dog-in-the-manger, Aristo, was piqued at losing her. It had not been his intention to scare the girl to death; he had underestimated her sensitivity, having none himself. A heavy karmic debt now hung over his head, for these things never go unnoticed. Mr. Malynowsky could tell you more about this, if you made him a very strong cup of sugared tea, and asked him nicely.

Living Light

Here, for light relief, is the story of another girl, who found her salvation in a more positive manner. She used to come in and look around Malynowsky's quite frequently, apparently, though none of us recall her prior to the day she decided to share her secret with me. She was certainly what one might call nondescript, though the way she is now . . . well, you will see.

I was at work one afternoon, reviving a thirsty set of Livy with a beeswax cocktail from Maltby's Bookbinders, when in walked a student with an aura so bright that I was almost blinded. It did not so much emanate from her as envelop her; it was borrowed light. However, I could see that some of it was seeping inward and illuminating the soul within.

"Hello! May I help you?" I said, rather startled.

"You're Kala, aren't you?" She looked right into my eyes. "I recognise the green."

"Sorry?"

"Your eyes. He told me to look for the bright green irises."

"Thanks, but I'd barely call them that!"

What was she after, I wondered, attempting to disarm me with flattery?

"They are, from where I'm standing."

"Well . . ." I was quite embarrassed. "How may I help you?"

The girl, so ordinary on the physical level—plain face, slightly squashed features, short brown hair, jeans and sweatshirt—was moving inside an envelope of intelligent, refined, living light. I had rarely seen anything like it outside a Circle.

"Ah, so polite, so deferential!" she smiled wanly. "I used to be like that too."

Oh no, she's going to try to convert me to her religious path or some such, I thought. That Tiphareth-glow is such a give-away. She emanated a solar radiance reminiscent of the mystical sephirah at the centre of the Tree of Life, which often translates into the minds of its recipients as evangelism.

"Oh, really?" I said, more sharply. I lowered my head and began to get on with the book-polishing. "How interesting."

"Is it a convenient time? For a chat, I mean?"

There was nobody else in the shop (no one carnate, anyway), and I was certainly intrigued by her mysterious, burnished aura. I looked through the glowing gold light into her brown, run-of-the-mill eyes. "Well, I suppose I could spare a few minutes; but I'm not interested in having my soul saved, if that's OK. It's already doing all right, as far as I can tell."

"Oh, I'm not here for that."

"Well, you'd better sit down then," I agreed.

Even though Mr. Malynowsky's perch was right beside her, she drew up a kick-stool and sat on that instead, so that she was at a slightly lower level than me. I appreciated this touch, more like that of a supplicant than potential interloper on my privacy. She smiled up at me with her flat pale face. "There's someone who told me to speak to you, but if I tell you who it is now, you'll think I'm more than a little absurd. So, on a more ordinary level, one of my tutors, Olivia Bryant-Guily, also told me that you might be the person to talk to about it all. She works here part-time, doesn't she?"

I smiled. "Yes, she does. I assume, from what you've said, that it's something to do with the main subject area of Maly-nowsky's?"

"It is, yes. It's a long story, too, so are you sure you can spare the time?"

Few things please me more than polishing up an old book while chatting about subjects of significance; and I missed Eury-dice, with whom I had spent many a long afternoon thus em-ployed. I liked the idea of a good chin-wag while I worked, and so I nodded.

"Sure," I said; "I'll make us both a coffee first; but we'll have to stop talking as soon as anyone comes into the shop. I always think it so rude when the assistants are whispering at the till. How do you take yours?"

As I walked to the tiny back room, I passed straight through one of the Beths.

"Sorry," I muttered.

"No problem, dearie," she replied. "What a bright fire that is!"

The phantasmagorical apothecaries had gathered to warm their hands on our visitor's auric flames. Possibly, it was the first time she had ever been admired. I decided not to point it out to her.

I extracted water from the ancient lead pipes, and boiled the kettle on a system that predates the First World War. Health and safety regulations are not Mr. Malynowsky's strong-point. He has other ways of looking after us.

"What's your name, by the way?" I asked the girl inside the glowing aura, over my shoulder.

"Anna," she replied. She paused. Then, as I approached with the steaming mugs: "Are you Jewish, Kala? If you don't mind me asking?"

"I don't mind in the least. Yes, my mother's side of the family are Jewish, but my father was Roman Catholic—he converted from the Moravian Church, actually—and I was raised as such. I'm interested in aspects of Jewish lore; but orthodox religions aren't my cup of tea, really. Or should I say coffee?" I passed hers over. "Anyway, enough of me. Go on, tell me what you'd like to discuss."

For the first time since she had arrived on the premises, Anna's aura fluctuated. Clearly she was nervous. It must be very difficult, I thought, to approach a virtual stranger with one's most unique experiences.

"Here, hold this," I said, rummaging round on the desk for a moment, and handing her a smooth pebble of yellow topaz. The idea was to help her channel her Tiphareth. We keep many such gems and herbs in the ample drawers of the mahogany desk, for emergencies and general use.

"Thanks." She smiled, took a deep breath, and stabilised herself. "I'm just going to let it spill out, so please forgive any digressions or whatever. He's with me; and when He is, I speak better."

"I know what you mean. It's enhanced eloquence, isn't it?"

"Exactly. And perception. OK, here goes."

Anna's glowing body-sheath reached a pitch of intense light, and I watched it spiraling into her crown chakra, through her third-eye area and into her throat. She was visibly absorbing it. As she began, the pitch of her voice changed too. It was clearer, that's the only way I can describe it. Her pronunciation became refined and perfect. Her Higher Self and a Tiphareth-deity were clearly in operation here. She was virtually swallowed by the light; I wondered what on earth anyone with Sight would say if they came into the shop at this moment. I am accustomed to such things, and I was dazzled.

She began.

"It didn't start at Oxford specifically, I can see that now. What began here was utterly predictable, like the notes in the margins of my text books. No cosmic insights those, but the thoughts of thousands before me, and of thousands more to come.

"I was tired. Tired of analysis, tired of study, tired of myself. Exhausted by thinking the same thoughts day in, day out, until they were so engraved on my psyche that I also dreamed of them at night. Even the knowledge that it was almost over afforded me little comfort. I felt I was about to perform a much-dreaded bungee jump with no rope."

She looked at me, a blur of yellow surrounded by dark and ancient tomes. She needed some sort of confirmation.

"Yes, a lot of third-year students seem to feel that intimidation, don't they?" I attempted. "After all that academic work, it can be difficult to focus on 'real life'. . ."

She smiled, though her face had become taut. "Quite. The conclusion of these exams would lead to my graduation and then, in theory at least, I was free. Free for what, though? If decided to continue my education, to return to Oxford, to nail myself once more to a chair in the Bodleian Library, and to repeat the whole process at a higher level for five, maybe ten years! My soul grew dehydrated at the thought. This diet of intellectual creme-de-la-creme had given me spiritual scurvy. I needed something else. What, though?

"The alternative, a job in the 'real world,' made me shudder. No offence, Kala, but I had heard horror stories of those who had gone before me into underpaid menial jobs, or worse, into well-paid meaningless jobs in the city—and others, the sort I would probably become, catapulted back into public school, this time to be an Alpha instead of a Beta. Teaching others to follow my footsteps to the Dreaming Spires of Oxford or Cambridge, only to find themselves three years down the line in exactly the same position I am in now—at least, if they have any soul."

At this point, the door creaked open, and in strolled Professor Beaumont, tweed-clad, as ever, and featuring almost fluorescent orange tobacco-stains on the fringes of his ample white whiskers.

"Good day, Kala!" he said, raising his stick in salutation. "Anything new in my field?"

Anna looked crestfallen. She held her tongue.

"Are you still looking for a 1697 *Callimachi Fragmenta*, by any chance?" I asked him. He is one of my favourite customers, always cheery and informative, without being patronising.

His eyes lit up behind his thick-lensed glasses. "I most certainly am. Do you have one?"

I produced the vellum-bound specimen, aware of Anna quivering with frustration at my side. He began to examine it at the till.

Anna's phosphorescence increased, and the Beths gasped clairaudibly.

"I don't mean to be ungrateful," she hissed. "I know I've been lucky; advantaged, one might say. I can return only to the fact that there was undernourishment in certain other areas."

Professor Beaumont raised a hoary eyebrow at my companion's sibilant oratory. I tried to gesture her to be quiet, but the Power was in her.

"Of course, friends would have supplemented my psychic constitution, had I allowed myself to have any. I was nothing but a confused child when I arrived at Oxford . . . ."

"Ah, young lady," chimed in the don, "aren't we all confused at Oxford? Too many opinions, all of them perfectly justifiable; and so many options. It must be difficult for you youngsters to discriminate. Pick a path, and follow it, that's my advice. It's all this fence-sitting and course-switching that does the damage . . . yes . . ." He returned his attentions to the book, muttering.

I gave Anna a hard stare, which she misinterpreted. She continued to whisper.

"My parents were freshly divorced, and the final five years of particularly violent verbal combat were still clanging in my mind. Marriage—what a nightmare! I plan never to subject myself to it."

I looked at Professor Beaumont, hoping that Anna's expostulations of Artemis-like chastity were not encroaching on his appreciation of the Callimachus. His black-inked hands were stroking his beard absently, and the ancient mind was absorbing the details as merrily as a mug of malt, despite my companion's confidences. I returned my attentions to my plain yet captivating confidante.

"My one clear idea was to obliterate the noise with study. People, it seemed to me, were singularly untrustworthy, whereas a book might be opened time and time again, and it would always say the same thing. Lacking tribal ancients in my own circle, I loved to hear the wisdom of the ancients of mankind—Cicero, Plato, Sophocles; I saw them as my own grandfathers. I have always evinced a slightly personal approach to the subject in its many forms, which causes some amusement when noticed by others."

"Good for you, young lady!" interjected Professor Beaumont, suddenly alert at the litany of philosophers. "A personal attitude to the great thinkers is a positive attribute. Too much third and fourth hand opinionating going on these days; all this deconstruction nonsense, pretentious diatribes a hundred times removed from the actual text . . . unlike this wonderful work." He smiled at me. "I'd like to take it, please, my dear."

I wrapped the book in brown paper, while he wrote the cheque in his characteristic slanting black ink. I placed the package in one of our nifty half-size carriers, just the right capacity for a quarto.

"Thank you so much," he said graciously. "I shall leave you to your conversation now." He nodded politely at Anna, then at me. I gave him my broadest, most Leonine smile, partly because I think him sweet, unlike so many academics, and partly for putting up with the rather untoward discussion at the till with the discretion of a true gentleman. "Do send my kindest regards to Mr. Malynowsky when you see him," he added.

As soon the door had shut behind him, Anna resumed her story.

"So, as I was saying, Kala, instead of making friends, I went straight to the Bodleian Library and stayed there, more or less, for three whole years. By keeping my head down and speaking only when spoken to, as was my habit at home, I found that I could easily avoid the threat of intimacy, or, as I saw it, outside interference."

"So, you didn't want to make friends in case they let you down, like your parents?" I abridged, feeling more like a therapist than a bookshop manager.

"Pretty much. And after six months, I couldn't have made a hit socially even if I'd wanted to; I had acquired the reputation of being one of those academic hermits of which there are so many at Oxford. I was given a respectful berth by my more sociable peers. Great things were then expected of me, which I failed to deliver with monotonous regularity. I was subsequently perceived as one of those who must study continually in order to maintain their academic mediocrity. The berth became no less wide, but considerably less respectful. This troubled me not in the least. I was simply glad to be left alone."

I nodded at her empathetically. She was quite unusual, I reflected, despite her ordinary appearance when the aura was ignored. It takes courage to be alone in a group, to allow oneself to be judged an unsuitable companion by one's peers. I admired that.

Anna ran her hand through her short, mousy hair, sending shock-waves of golden light into the ether. She was a sun goddess, sitting here at my own till. People ambled past the warped windows, glancing sidelong at the books held open in displays by brass hand-clips. Anna was as invisible to them as she was to her peers at University.

"Once I had got over my pleasure at the Duke Humfrey Library, the part of the Bodleian crammed with vellum-bound books and arcane tomes, as you know, the thing I enjoyed most was the silence. This was something of which I had suffered another deficiency in my formative years. I would sit and absorb the quiet, especially late at night, with real gratitude. I consciously tried to superimpose it on my childhood cacophonies, to dilute them with its power in the present. Pure silence is not a common commodity in this day and age, is it?"

Surprised by the question, I spluttered out some sort of agreement involving traffic, economy housing, TV and radio . . .

Anna, not really listening, took a deep breath.

"It was under these circumstances that I gradually began to perceive the reality of the Gods."

Ah-ha, we were finally getting to the point!

I shuffled in my chair, and offered her another coffee. An un-
wise move at this juncture, you might think, but I needed one
after an early start coupled with this lengthy speech, and Anna
would be hoarse before long at this rate. She accepted. I was interested in the preamble, of course, and entertained by the
"well-written" style of the monologue, though I knew it was
spontaneous. How many texts had this girl swallowed whole during her hermit-like youth and adolescence? I underwent pangs of
mental indigestion at the thought.

I presented her with another caffeine dose, and she resumed
her tale. By this point, she was almost in a trance. Her concentrated thoughts were moving through her aura, close to manifest-
ing themselves as she described each. When she talked of the
Bodleian, I actually saw the long wooden rooms stretching above
the subterranean bookstacks, the oil portraits of various luminar-
ies and benefactors, the seats with their wooden partitions to
shield the reader from the eyes of the person directly opposite.

"One evening I was in the Lower Reading Room, contemplat-
ing my lot over a Paean of Pindar to Apollo. I had hit a real psychological slump; my life barely seemed worth living. It was an
effort just to get up in the mornings. It all seemed truly pointless.

"As I read the hymn, I found myself actually supplicating the
deity to heal and illuminate me. It is not that I was ill you understand, but I suffered an almost perpetual melancholy which
blighted my days, and disturbed, restless dreams which did little
to enhance my waking hours. The emotional aridity of my existence was starting to make itself felt, as was my self-imposed an-
drogyny. I'm a girl, but you'd never guess it, would you? My libido
was nonexistent. Sorry, I hope that's not more information than
you required?"

I liked the way threads of her personality would suddenly show
in the cloth of her intellect. It made her more human.

"Anyway, so there I was, silently pleading with Apollo Agyieus to cleanse my path of evil, and to purify and heal me. The nagging fear that it was I who was the root of my parent's woes was probably the subconscious prompt to this action, don't you think?"

I tried to look intelligently Jungian. It must have worked, as Anna was reassured enough to resume her flow.

"A luminous moment later, and I caught myself, looked defensively at the nearest readers in case they had read my mind, felt abashed, and blushed like a maiden hotly pursued by a callow but tempting youth. That's what he did, you know—Apollo—chased young girls; in his immature stage, at least."

"Yes, I *do* know," I replied, resisting the temptation to ask why the public always consider shop assistants to be unversed in literature, even when they are selling it. I have been told before that "Classics means Latin and Greek" by a helpful customer, but that's another issue.

"This was the first time I had ever felt anything resembling a personal rapport with a god," confessed Anna, taking full advantage of her free consultation with the Great Uneducated. "And it worried me. It is generally accepted amongst my peers that psychospiritual approaches to deities such as are popular in certain circles, including your own, I presume, are a laughable fancy."

"You mean 'Transform your Life through the Demeter-Persephone Relationship'; that type of thing?" I conjoined, wondering why I was being so helpful. And what *was* "my circle," in Anna's eyes, I wondered? Such thoughts would have to wait.

"Exactly. Working with gods and goddesses, indeed. We might just as well behold: 'Learn to Love Through Invoking Caligula,' or: 'Re-enact the Decline and Fall of the Roman Empire in Your Own Living Room.'"

I smiled. I could almost imagine those titles going into print.

"For we Classicists, the myths are evidence of an interesting but defunct religion, which help us to understand the workings of the ancient mind. They bring to light historical facts, not spiritual or personal truths."

I could see the dons dimming Anna's light now. Not sweet ones like Professor Beaumont, though no doubt even he had his limitations, but the ones with wintry smiles I know so well from working here; the cut-and-thrust academics who would sacrifice Kether for Hod, as Mr. Malynowsky would put it. "They'd rather see God dead on a slab than admit He exists—either at all, or in a form other than their own." Anna, educated in the heart of Hod for three long years, was showing signs of this already. Perhaps she caught her energy fading at this point; it visibly fluctuated when her mood became cynical and insular. She continued:

"Of course, that Persephone and Demeter were real to the initiates of their own Mystery Cults, we do not doubt—but what validity could they possibly have today? As you know, most of the Olympians were like tyrannical children, and an interactive relationship with even a human version is difficult to imagine, never mind a godform. They barely cared enough to permit one. Humans are 'wretched mortals' merely; the briefest glance at *The Iliad* is enough to put the aspiring devotee on her guard. If, that is, she is not so infused with romantic notions that she fails to recognise the signs."

She stopped, and took a huge slurp of coffee. I did not interject, not wishing to throw her off her stride. I was beginning to have a fairly accurate idea of what she might be about to tell me, and wanted to see whether I was right or not. Also, I was beginning to like her. It must have taken a great deal of courage to come into the shop and tell me all of this. I felt honoured. She replaced her mug.

"You understand my chagrin, then, at finding myself entreating such a being. I was also well aware of Apollo's own strict sense of separation between god and mortal, a celestial apartheid best left in the past. Not to mention the fact that the impulse seemed insane, the product no doubt of too much work and too little play. I had a sudden urge to go outside and be surrounded by crocuses and daffodils." She sighed. "But it was October, so I continued to sit in the library and muse. Were the gods, then, simply symbolic of parts of our spiritual and mental constitution? Traditionally not. Since the Greeks did not know of the subconscious, it seemed foolish to suggest that the Furies were Orestes' guilt personified, or that Persephone's descent into the Underworld represented a conscious deliverance into adult sexuality, or some such."

I nodded. Theories such as these, Jung and Campbell influenced, are rife in Aquarian belief. A lot to be said for them, in a modern context, too.

"And as for spirituality; on whose terms were we talking? The mind schooled by Christianity is very different to that produced by the Old Religions. It seems absurd to tack modern notions onto ancient practices when these practises could not possibly have been informed by the sensibilities we hold today. To us it was literature. History and literature. So, sitting there in the library, surrounded by sensible industry, the autumn night whistling about the towers of the ancient building, I resolved not to find myself saying silly prayers again."

She came to a stop, and looked at me.

"Right," I said, jolted out of the story, on which I had been concentrating with intensity. "Then what happened?"

"Are you sure you don't mind?" asked Anna, pointlessly. I was hardly going to chuck her off the premises now.

"No! Please—continue."

"Right. Well, despite my determination not to get sucked into all that New Age detritus—sorry, no offence meant, it's just the way I saw it at the time—I found that things were occurring which I couldn't consciously control. One night, for example, I had this incredible dream; though I hesitate to call it that, as it was so real. Can I tell you?"

"Please do," I said, wishing she might revert to her former storytelling flow. It was much easier to concentrate without these continual interruptions. If she didn't speak soon, I'd have another customer and she would have to wait indefinitely. "Just relax," I cajoled.

Anna fiddled with the thumb nail of her left hand. I noticed that it was heavily bitten.

"Don't let this bore you. There's a pot of gold at the end of it, I promise!"

"I really don't mind," I reiterated, hoping to convince her to spit it out, whatever it was. My intuition told me that this dream was more an astral experience than the simple byproduct of sleep. The Beths, gathered around us now like Girl Scouts around a fire, were keen to hear the refulgent woman's explanation. Together we attended Anna's oratory, with bated breath.

"I was in our homestead, and everything was normal, solid and familiar, except that each object and person was lined by light."

She looked at me, her plain face taut with anxiety. I nodded and smiled, like a mother encouraging her little angel at the school nativity play. Her tinsel grew bright again.

"This varied greatly in hues and lustre. The dogs sleeping by the back door looked fuzzy and red, while my parents were cocooned by pale rainbow-light. My sisters, slumbering in their curtained chambers, looked purest and clearest of all, and I wanted to wake them, make them see how beautiful it was at night. I touched Chloe, dipping my fingers into the long glow of her arm, but she didn't stir. It was then I realised that, though everything else was solid, I was not.

"Curious, I returned to my bed. Instead of the adult form I expected, I beheld a small child, thumb in mouth, eyes closed in deepest sleep. Strings of very subtle luminosity connected its body to mine.

"The light was increasing by the moment, though how long a moment was I could not detect. The tamarisk trees outside the house seemed to bud and blossom in the short time it took for the light to become almost blinding. Soon all I could see was fluid gold moving on a sea of white brilliance.

"Awe-stricken, I backed nearer to the bed. The next thing I knew I was sitting up in it, screaming '*Ieie Paian!*'—Hail Apollo—over and over.

"Clamouring and pale, eyes wild with import, my family (for I perceived that these people were my closest kin) asked me what had happened, and I tried to tell them, in my child's limited vocabulary, of the bright light I had seen, gold as the sun.

"'Apollo!' they cried. 'Apollo has come to claim you as his own!'

"'At last,' I heard my mother murmur.

"Was he tall, was he athletic? Was he as handsome as they say he is? How big were his muscles, asked my sisters; were they huge? I tried to tell them that the brightness had no shape, but they were carried away on a wave of their own imagery, and my limited interjections could do nothing to quieten them. Did he bless us with gold? A swift search of the house confirmed the negative. Exhausted, we returned to our beds, and I lost consciousness in more dreams within dreams.

"Perhaps my 'family's' suggestions had worked on me, for this time I saw the god as they had described him; a form quite human, though bigger and more powerful than any being I had ever seen, and glowing with a far gentler golden light than I had beheld previously. His hair was flaxen, curled and woven into plaits and patterns of almost impossible intricacy. He was naked but for a shoulder scarf, yet concealed between layers of what I thought of at the time as 'difference.' He looked naked from a human perspective, but he was by no means revealed. He held out his hand to me. The impression I got was that he wanted to make some sort of deal.

"I awoke believing myself to be choking on laurel smoke. In fact, pungent plumes of my neighbour's morning cigarette had drifted between our rooms and acted on my imagination. I lay in bed recalling the images of my mandala dream, the likes of which I had never before experienced, scared to move lest I disperse the magic which held them in my memory.

"Of course, most people protest that 'it seemed so real!' on awaking, but for me, queen of the banal dream, this experience was hyper-real; I did not know how to express it. Never before had I been so transported to another time, another consciousness; and then there was the deity himself, whose heat and light still scintillated my soul. Despite my resolution of the day before, I could have prostrated myself at his luminous feet there and then. I believe the only thing that stopped me enacting this physically was the fear of dispersing the dream by moving."

"I know what you mean," I enthused. "Levitation dreams are the same. Astral travel . . ."

"Well, I knew nothing of that type of thing then. But I was fascinated by what had happened. I really had been there, a child in ancient Greece. Lying in my narrow college bed I shone the remembered Apolline light on my mind over and over again, inducing the most delicious euphoria I have ever encountered. My entire body relaxed into it; I felt the tensions of nearly two decades dissipating and exiting my body. The smoke from next-door served as makeshift incense; entire wreaths of it seemed to be circling my bodies in cleansing motion. When I say bodies, I mean physical, etheric, and spiritual. Not a system I had previously considered, but one which sprung into my mind, and indeed my inner vision, with acuity at this instant. No perception of the human vehicle could have been more precise than this idea of layers. It made sense on every level. I was startled by the thought that those in the medical profession ignored it. What a mess they must be making of these subtle and essential energies! It was to the modern soul what medieval doctoring was to the body. It did not bear thinking about.

"My own layers, however, appeared to be reorganising themselves in a most efficient manner. The smoke had grown thicker and now did not even smell like tobacco, but rather bonfire-like, tinged with frankincense, the scent most guaranteed to bring to mind golden orbs swinging low and trailing the breath of God. Over my body I fancied that such an orb was swinging, sweeping away the debris of childhood, initiating me into an adult role. I knew consciously, of course, that, being female, I would have been under Artemis' jurisdiction rather than Apollo's, yet it seemed to me that here he was, undoubtedly he, and whether this be because I had specifically asked for his aid, or for some more occult reason I could not tell. Certainly the Ancient Ones must be less busy than they once were, and more inclined to be grateful for a line from a mortal. Perhaps we are not as dispensable to them now as we once were.

"A statement of my professor's suddenly rang in my ears—
'*Faced with a difficulty, a Greek will first pray to a god; but he must*

then reinforce the god's action on the divine plane by applying on the human plane whatever effort he is capable of making.'

"It was delightful and indescribably exciting for me to witness the first phenomena of my hitherto mundane existence, but I perceived in this timely echo that I had to act in order to pull the power through. This was the sign, not the event.

"To be elevated from the realms of the animal and intellectual impulses—for all I did normally was sleep, eat, read, think, write, and sleep again—to witness this etheric activity and feel it affecting me without the least impulse of fear! And all from the comfort of my own bed! What more could a supplicant ask?"

The telephone rang. We both jumped.

"Excuse me a moment." I picked up the waxy receiver. "Hello, Malynowsky's?"

Having dealt with the inquiry, I noticed that it was nearly six o'clock, time to shut the shop. I invited Anna to the nearest pub, and she accepted enthusiastically. Though intrigued by her story, I was fatigued now and grateful for the break. Her "inspirational mode" clearly emanated from an era much older than our own, and as you will have noticed, demands concentration. I thought it was worth reiterating it as she actually spoke it, though, as it tells us a lot about her and her spiritual sources.

We retired to the Turl Bar, ordered two glasses of red wine, which seemed somehow appropriate, and I urged Anna to continue. She looked around, somewhat unnerved by the setting which, unlike most students, still held some novelty for her. How different to mine or Eurydice's misspent youth! Still, with the lure of a willing audience, Anna soon ran a hand through her short hair, and recommenced her tale.

"So, there I was, lying in bed, just having had this incredible, life-like dream, and weird incenses poured over my bodies. I suppose nothing should surprise me after that, but when I awoke again, at three in the afternoon, I really was taken aback. I am an early riser, and always have been. Even during the most hormone-blighted and parentally harangued periods of my teens, I rarely slept beyond ten; I loathe the slovenly implications of lying in, for although never brilliant academically, I have always been a hard worker. My mother had invested a great deal of hope in me; essentially, I was to justify her unhappy existence by doing remarkably well in lieu. The least I could do then was to try. That a lifetime's economy of sleep should suddenly be replaced by a luminous dream, a waking vision, and a cataleptic stupor of which I recalled nothing, was enough to make me wonder whether I wasn't really ill. This would have been a perfect explanation, had I not felt better than ever before in my life.

"I jumped out of bed, and made an instant decision to forget my doubts over the process, and simply enjoy the results.

"My work that day was the most original and lively I had ever produced. I am sure that my tutor, when she eventually came to read it, thought I had been colluding with one of the Illuminati."

"Which, of course, you had," I slipped in.

"I suppose so, but it was all inexplicable to me at the time. I bought a bunch of daffodils and placed them in my room with a levity of spirit I had never experienced before. This tiny bit of nature, albeit out of season and thus unnatural, enhanced the few days of their duration to no small degree. Their colour reminded me of the Apollo of the second dream."

"So you were trying to bring a fragment of Apollo through into your conscious, working life?" I probed, aware of sounding like a psychotherapist, but what the heck. "To channel him, perhaps?"

"Definitely! It was the best experience of my life, and I didn't want it to leave me." Her aura became slightly dimmer. "But this state of rapture could not last. No doubt it was prolonged by my antisocial behaviour, for nothing destroys a mystical experience more effectively, it seems, than opening it up for discussion. Despite my silence, the golden light tarnished by the day; grim reality staked its claim on my attentions, and I no longer caught whiffs of frankincense from my hair when I brushed it."

She sighed heavily, and her brown eyes grew cloudy. "I was left like Tithonus, craving the love and light of the Divine, feeling myself deteriorating by the day, becoming less alluring to the god I craved, set aside from my fellow men but unable to fully assimilate the celestial state."

"How awful! It sounds like the sort of anticlimax that can occur after a Sabbat. Everything falls flat and one-dimensional, where before it was utterly vibrant."

Anna looked relieved.

"Oh, really, is it common? I suppose it must be. How can we sustain that kind of celestial rapport?"

"Is that rhetorical? Because it's almost impossible to maintain it permanently, but as to enhancing the frequency of contact, there are ways . . ."

Anna's pale face lit up naturally for the first time. "Are there? Because, you see, that's really what I came here to ask you. I can't bear the thought that it might go again. I don't want to return to that low level of existence."

"He's with you now, though, as you know, Anna."

"So you can feel it?"

"More than that—I can see it."

Anna's radiance increased.

"So I'm not just suffering some kind of psychotic episode, then?"

"I doubt it, unless I am too. I've never seen such a solar aura in my life—just walking around in the street, I mean. It's incredible."

"So, where can I go from here?"

"Well, what do you want, exactly?" I probed. "What is your precise aim?"

She paused. "Most of the time I didn't think about it. The more I observe those around me, normal people performing ordinary functions, the more likely it seems that my 'visionary experience' was the result of some kind of suppression I do not even wish to contemplate." With these words, her aura did its usual trick of fading.

"But you don't believe that now, do you?" I asked. She gazed at me through her golden veil.

"No, but I know you're sympathetic to the subject matter. This must be why Apollo suggested that I speak to you."

Her light increased again. It was incredible, I thought, how reliant it was on her mental energy; but then I remembered that Apollo is a god of intellect, among other things. She had accessed him through a mental channel in the very heart of Hod— so of course he was feeding off that quality.

I took a deep swig of my wine.

"Apollo suggested you talk to *me*?" I echoed.

The idea that a godform might think I had something to offer was immensely flattering, but also intimidating. There was no doubt in my mind that Anna was telling the truth exactly as she found it, but we still had not got to the hub of the matter.

"Well, could you teach me how to keep the contact?"

"You don't need to, Anna," I said. "The contact is already established. What you need is faith in your own convictions. In your heart of hearts, you know it's for real, don't you?"

She nodded. In a way, this questioning process was simply her mind going through the motions. She was so accustomed to subjecting everything to intellectual scrutiny, that even a miracle of mind, body, and soul must be probed and dissected. Still, nothing

wrong with a bit of discrimination, as long as she avoided the pit-
fall of complete disbelief.

"What are you planning to do with your newfound powers, by
the way?" I asked, hoping to compound their reality for her.

"Well, I've barely scratched the surface yet; I'm still growing
accustomed to the idea that this is a High Archetype, rather
than the proud, very human god found in Homer and the like.
Ideally, though, I suppose I would be able to use the energies for
healing. My depression lifts entirely when He is with me." She
grinned. "Actually, I feel amazing!"

"Healing would certainly be an appropriate use—as would
prophecy, though I wouldn't say that was necessarily an advantage. Perhaps we should concentrate on the healing."

"That's what I'd like. But where do you think this is coming
from? Why me?"

I contemplated the question for a moment. "Personally, I
would be inclined to believe that the subject of your studies—
Greek Religion—stimulated a memory of a past life. The dream
you mentioned sounds suspiciously like the preamble to being accepted as a priest—or Pythia—of Apollo. Your mother, or rather,
the mother of your past incarnation, exclaimed 'At last!' when
Apollo came to 'claim' you, didn't she?—as if she had experienced a presentiment that this would be your fate. And you
clearly perceived his energy—in two quite different forms.
Chances are, after an experience like that, you would be taken
into the care of the god's other servitors. I'm pretty sure that you
were a channel for Apollo in ancient Greece, and that your ability to perform that role remains. The energy of the god has
changed—refined over the ages—but his core functions are the
same. You, in approaching him in connection with one of these
aspects, both reestablished the link, and revived your own latent
memories."

Anna raised her eyebrows. "I've never believed in reincarnation until now, but that makes perfect sense. In the dream—I hesitate to call it that, it was so real—I had such a definite sense of self, even though I was outside my body—the child's body, I mean. I can only assume that the same thing happens on death; the separation of body and spirit is barely relevant. The consciousness remains intact. What I want to do now, though, is assure that my current perceptions remain, and aren't ousted by cynicism and the ensuing loss of power. Is that possible?"

Even Mr. Malynowsky confesses to experiencing times of doubt, I thought; we all do. It is proof of an active mind, of course, but also an annoyance. For Anna, who was much newer to these perceptions than we, the mundane vibrations of Malkuth were a positive menace. How could she preserve her mystic unity?

"Let's see," I said, thinking out loud. "You're working with a solar deity—so your link is with Tiphareth on the Tree of Life. That's the sephirah at the very centre of the psycho-spiritual structure, around which the other spheres rotate. If you want to preserve the qualities of Tiphareth—beauty, mystical insight, healing, willing sacrifice for the sake of others, perceptions of cosmic harmony—you will need to appeal to Tetragrammaton Eloah Va Daath."

"Sorry?" Anna looked alarmed. "You're beginning to sound like something out of *Star Wars* now."

"It's just the name of God in that particular context, referring to the fact that Tiphareth is the 'son' of higher sephiroth, including Daath, the hidden sphere of knowledge. In the Qabalah," I added.

"I don't know anything about Qabalah," sighed Anna, evidently thinking I had gone off on a tangent. "How can a Jewish system possibly be relevant to a Greek godform?"

"Ah, well, the Qabalah of the Western Mystery Tradition has been described very aptly as a celestial filing cabinet; each of the ten spheres encompasses a vast amount of correspondences to its particular properties. It's completely eclectic, and unites all religious precepts, from the inchoate urge to the complexities of theological philosophy, from cave magick to Hinduism to Egyptian religion to your Greeks. And everything else. It's relevant to all systems; it's religiously holistic."

Anna looked fractionally more convinced. "So this Tetragrammaton entity would allow me to access the 'body' of solar mythology, including Apollo's?"

"Exactly. The whole wavelength, with all of its correspondents. The name is like a password—to a mental state. Intone it later—you'll see what I mean. Then there's the Archangel Raphael, and the Choir of Angels, the Melekim, or 'Kings'—with all three behind you, you can't fail to perceive the level you're after. Or you could imagine an equilateral cross against a yellow background. Or you could visualise your way up the Tree of Life until you reach it . . ."

"OK, I get the drift," said Anna. Admittedly, I do not have Mr. Malynowsky's captivating charm when talking of such topics. I was once described, while discussing the Qabalah, as 'sounding like a heavy metal band thrashing out Mozart.' Oh well, I can but try.

"And if you're looking for a venue in which to perform your rites or meditations," I continued, undeterred, "there's nowhere more appropriate, in Europe, than a stone circle. Centres of solar energy, completely connected with the cycle of our stars and planets, the outer analogue of the inner constitution. The sun is Tiphareth from this plane, or 'in Assiah' as a Qabalist would put it. And the moon is Yesod . . . and so on. Yes, a stone circle—not

Stonehenge, it's too bleak—and you'll get no privacy at the Summer Solstice—"

"Rollright's nearby, isn't it?" chimed in Anna. "I overheard some archaeology students discussing it once. That would be nice."

"Or there's Wayland Smithy, next to the great White Horse carved into the hillside in Oxfordshire—it's a tomb, built in 5500 BCE; a good place to go for the resurrection-related purposes relevant to all solar godforms."

Anna looked at me. "Isn't it a little odd, attempting to invoke Apollo at a Neolithic burial site in Britain?"

"It seems it, yes, but the proof of the pudding . . ."

"I suppose it's this Qabalistic eclecticism again?"

"It doesn't make any difference where you are," I affirmed, "Except that certain places are more conducive to particular energies than others. You'll find that, if you go to a stone circle at the Summer Solstice, Apollo is just as accessible as Baldur—or Osiris—or any of the other relevant godforms."

A nd so it was that Anna learned to relax into her new abilities, for the fear of losing them was allayed by the knowledge that they could be restimulated when and if they faded.

We ended up going together to Rollright—only once, the following summer—through choice rather than necessity. By this time, Anna was completely attuned to her Apolline interaction, and she has been ever since. She chose to ignore Professor Beaumont's advice about switching tracks, and is applying her experience to a new course in medicine. She is trying to bring the perceptions of her vision—involving the various "layers" of the bodies, subtle and spiritual as well as physical—to bear on the world of orthodox science. A challenge indeed, but one which she is more than happy to take up.

The solar radiance she emanates has brought her a circle of similarly-minded friends, and the little brown mouse has transformed into a beautiful, fiery lion.

There are other godforms with whom she works now: Thoth, Asclepius, Isis, all those connected with healing; but Apollo is her "First and Last and Always." She uses his arrows to symbolise and direct precision healing, and has connected his energies with light-work and lazer use. She has taught me a great deal about the ways in which the Old Ones still operate on our plane—in Anna's case, rather literally. They have been refined by Time, just as evolution has refined us. No one wants a selfish, petulant God, and the deities have had to adapt themselves to this. Compassionate, helpful ones, however, are another matter. Whether Apollo himself might yet be termed compassionate I doubt, but he does make his energies available to persons such as Anna to do with as they will; and if they use these for positive purposes, he is effectively helping us all.

Such can be our interaction with the gods in the heart of the apparently mundane; or, as Mr. Malynowsky always puts it: "Kether is in Malkuth, and Malkuth in Kether. As Above, So Below!"

ᴛʜᴜꜱ Sᴘᴀᴋᴇ Rᴏɴ
Write with blood, and thou wilt find
that blood is spirit.

One day, the manager of the North London branch came over to the Oxford shop to pick up some stock. I had spoken to Lauren on the phone before, and always enjoyed a bit of friendly banter with her. Like all of Mr. Malynowsky's staff she was literary and esoteric, and we had much in common.

"The problem with the New Age," commented a customer as he stood at the till examining an Alice Bailey first edition, "is that it gives such scope to lunatics." He glanced at Lauren, who was rummaging among the *Oxford Sermons*, her raven hair hanging in lustrous lines against her thin body. She was entirely dressed in black, and though beautiful, was a little too overtly witchy for more conventional tastes.

"I mean, look at what the Theosophists believed," he continued to me.

I liked the way he divided his attention between us. I've always hated those people who are in a group but talk to just one person. Or who leave someone out! It's so rude. I warmed to him instantly.

"A group of well-educated, intelligent men and women, all of whom were convinced that they were being guided by Ascended Masters of the Great White Lodge. They even believed these occidental masters to materialise in their suburban British homes!"

I smiled at the beady-eyed man. He was a regular, always ready to chat about his latest purchases. His main interest was ancient religion; he was not, as far as I was aware, involved in any of the more practical applications that many of our customers grafted onto the subject.

Lauren appeared to be politely ignoring him.

"I know it sounds ridiculous," I agreed, trying to make up for her lack of response as much as anything, "But a Great White Lodge seems quite possible to me, to be honest. Doesn't it make perfect sense to have a group of entities watching over the planet, and humanity's progression, and so forth? Like Angels, but more flexible and communicative."

The man laughed, not rudely, but as if I had said exactly what he knew I would. "A great many theories make sense, but their convenience does not make them accurate."

Lauren yanked a wad of Victorian pamphlets from the shelves, sending a cloud of centurion particles into the air and over the desk, glanced through them, and lightly dusted herself down. Still she ignored our customer, which I found rather discourteous. It was obvious she was listening, but equally clear that she had no intention of joining in this debate.

"Alice Bailey herself admitted that her experiences were highly improbable," I rallied. "But that doesn't mean that they were impossible. When 'the Tibetan Master' first tried to use her as a channel, for example, she refused, telling him that she did not believe the experience to be real, or, if it was real, to be valid. As to proof—a woman who had no knowledge of Sanskrit, or science, could barely have authored the books he wrote through her—like that one you have there. And I'm sure she would have been bored rigid trying to figure some of those theories out."

"Was it Jung who said that 'the Tibetan' was her Higher Self?" asked my sparring partner.

"Yes, it was, but *she* was the one with the direct experience, and *she* stated otherwise." I grinned. "I know it sounds insane, but so does virtually everything when it's looked at in a certain light. Church, marriage, the way we live in the West—gurus are forever pointing out how absurd our lifestyles are."

"That's my argument entirely! Using this platform of all-encompassing possibilities, anything becomes viable. If we can accept that a person is receiving messages from a higher entity, or indeed a god, as is often deemed possible in New Age philosophies—what is to stop the most crackpot of people from issuing a theory and recruiting a following?"

"We need an Occult Police," I agreed. Lauren looked sharply up from her studies, but her darkly painted lips remained closed. What on earth was going on with her, I wondered? Was I annoying her by chatting in the shop? Perhaps I should try to tie the conversation up now.

"It's a question of discrimination, when it comes down to it," I concluded. The man nodded, and Lauren spoke for the first time.

"Coffee, Kala?" she asked.

Not quite the words of wisdom I had anticipated, but welcome nonetheless.

"Shall I go?" Lauren was my senior in the Malynowsky pecking order, after all.

"No, I'll do it," she insisted, and off she slid. With all that black and her bending over and around the till, she reminded me of an eel.

"If we're talking about the Theosophists," I continued hurriedly as she left the shop, "There were all sorts of confusions in there too. Poor Krishnamurti was picked out and hothoused to become a mentor from childhood, and then there were the petty jealousies, and the arguments over what Madame Blavatsky would or would not have wanted for the society—hence Alice splintering off and setting up the Arcane School. She did what she felt was right. At the end of the day, it was herself Alice Bailey had to answer to, as it is with all of us. Who wants to die, knowing that they've spread nothing but lies and delusion during their lifetime? We are each alone with our own conscience. An experience is valid if we know it to be so. I think that's the key," I concluded. "Sincerity."

"There are many sincere but misguided people," retorted the historian. "Mostly very intelligent ones, at that. Have you read about the Ordre du Temple Solaire recently?"

"Are they the ones who expect to reincarnate on Sirius, once they've committed ritual suicide?" I asked.

"They are. Doctors, scientists, businessmen, policemen, an architect—and an heir to a multimillion-pound sunglasses fortune—people with a lot to live for, you would think—have immolated themselves and their families in order to attain the goal of life on a distant star. It's a comic-strip fantasy—only taken to a tragic conclusion!"

I paused.

"What if they really *are* on Sirius now?" I asked. "Lots of philosophies state that the consciousness at the point of death determines the condition of the afterlife. If they died really believing and concentrating on that goal . . ."

The man looked at me, astonished. "A case in point," he said. "Don't let any strange French men talk to you for too long, young lady!" He shook his head a little, indicating his disbelief at my credulity.

"Is it not possible that individual truth is the real reality?" I banged on regardless. "Especially when it involves a group mind, like this Order? Perhaps all Muslims end up with Allah, all Christians go to Heaven, all Wiccans to the Summer Lands, and all Temple Solaire adherents to Sirius? Or an equivalent level on the Astral Plane, at least, initially?"

The man raised his eyebrows at me. "I'm not even sure that I believe in an afterlife," he confessed. "So its precise details are a little beyond me, I'm afraid. But there are plenty of people out there willing to sell you their theory—so be careful, won't you?"

I was surprised. This man was genuinely concerned for my welfare. I must sound incredibly naïve, I reflected.

"Thanks," I said, quite sincerely. "And you're right about the weirdoes. The world is full of them. So is this shop, for that matter. Present company excluded, of course!"

He decided against the Bailey, and departed with just a good old E. A. Wallis Budge. No one would argue with *him.*

I settled back to the *Hermes Trismegistus* I was cleaning. The solvent smell of the liquid pierced the air and, for a moment, my head. I hate the acerbic reek of this fluid; it gives me those one-eyed headaches that would become migraines were I emotionally disturbed; but I have to use it. Grime compounded over centuries of greasy-palmed handling and dusty storage is resistant to most other solvents.

As I moved the cloth over the vellum in gentle, circular movements, my mind played over the conversation I had just had. It is true that I am prepared to consider most theories; does that make me susceptible to the allure of the convenient? Do I "seize, abandon, but then commit again the errors that flatter," as that cynical chemist, Antoine Lavoisier, put it?

The motion of the cloth, cleaning away the past, creates windows of brightness; the motion of my thoughts, mandalas of memory and emotion, will give an insight into what lies beneath. As with negative experience to a metaphysicist, I suddenly reflected, the grime has become part of the structure now, a strength. We should not clean it away entirely.

Lauren arrived back with two tall lattés, and I asked her if she was okay.

"Fine," she said, a little defensively. "It's just too big a subject to go into in the shop—you know, the whole cultic thing."

"Okay, I won't ask you then," I smiled wryly.

"You can ask, Kala," she replied. "It's important, especially for people with our interests, to know what can happen when one idea or personality becomes religiously dominant." She looked at once paler and more flushed, but, since the shop was now empty and evening closing in, curtaining our cabal, she continued:

"The thing is, I am not exactly new to cultic thought processes, and most people, having undergone what I have, would hold their hands up in horror at anything vaguely resembling them. But I don't, not entirely. Have I therefore failed to learn, failed to evolve? I asked myself that for years, but in truth I do not think so. Life doesn't always have to be a theatre of extremes, does it?"

"I suppose not," I mused. "Though it has the tendency to be. Occult work brings it out, doesn't it?"

"You bet!" she replied grimly. "I can't possibly tell you what I mean here and now—but you can borrow this if you're interested."

She removed a fat, black, leather-bound journal from her bag. The book had a thick clasp and Celtic designs embossed into its surface.

I was unsure how to react. This was far greater a gesture of trust than I could possibly have expected, and I was not entirely comfortable with it.

"It's no big deal," she added. "I just happen to have this on me today—I felt the urge to pick it up as I left the flat this morning—and I'm guessing it was because you're meant to read it."

I held the journal in my hands, and could feel the energy in it—vivid and intense as a teenage dream. Only Lauren wasn't teen-aged, she was in her thirties.

"I wrote it years ago—most of it anyway," she said, "The relevant bit was written in my mid-twenties, to analyse it all and purge myself of the experience. It's ancient history."

"Well, thank you." I felt awkward. I actually did not want the responsibility of looking after such a personal item, nor really the intimacy of reading this woman's private journal. Still, I appreciated the implications. We would be friends after this—how could we not be?

When I got home that night, I eschewed Sam's offer of wine in front of the telly, and curled up on my bed with Lauren's journal.

A musky scent rose from the pages as I flicked through the many heavily inked paragraphs of spiky writing. Doodles abounded—spirals and strange creatures and astral images. But then I got to a page marked by a thin purple ribbon, and I knew this was the section ordained to me.

Imagine a girl whose mind is parchment awaiting pen; whose eagerness to learn exceeds her caution, a girl bred on suburban Christianity and whose idea of evil is being verbally cruel to a hamster (as was her friend Helen).

Spiritually inclined, and fascinated by Magick. A child who got her hands on a book on Qabalah at an early age, and spent time in her teens invoking Angels, scaring herself half to death. Someone inspired yet deferential, brave yet beleaguered by social graces, soul-searching and poetic, who knows the mundane run of things is not for her. A willing Persephone, if you like. But children never know what they are getting into until it is too late.

This girl, young Lauren, was as naive as Eve in Eden, even at seventeen, when she left home. An underlying belief that all people were essentially good, possibly misunderstood, misinformed her senses. She, me, whoever; the archetypal innocent.

Dress her in dark garb, with a good dose of the gothic. Let her hair be long and black, her body thin, her eyes heavily made up in the Egyptian style beloved of young occult types. A roll-up cigarette is constantly drawn at from between darkly painted lips; she wears far too much silver jewelry. Her student room is overpopulated with psycho-surreal imagery; a melodramatic crucifix, a black satin wall on which red roses hang upside down around a spherical Balinese war mask, eyes and teeth bulging. Another side of the small cube of habitation is devoted to overlapping photographs and peacock feathers—an Argos of eyes observing the visitor. "Intense," they would comment, before leaving the young neurotic to smoke and write in peace.

Litanies of pain flowed from the adolescent pen; poetic prose of a distinctly sombre nature. Life is a dolorous affair, don't you know. We only have a little bit of time to get to the bottom of it, and devote ourselves accordingly, before here comes the chopper, to chop off our heads. Books on Wicca, Magick, Buddhism, and lateral subjects were purchased and placed amongst the black and red candles, and read, sometimes.

You can imagine what a dream-come-true this kind of person is for an aspiring guru. A disciple waiting to worship. An ego-trip ripe for the plucking.

If I sound bitter, forgive me. Looking back, I feel protective—I was a different person then—the experience is part of my foundation now, my structure, and I do not refute it. I have never wanted to throw the baby out with the baptismal water.

With the utter inevitability of polar magnetism, this child attracts a wanna-be swami. Let's call him Ron. I can give him a regular name because, now that I know what to look for, I am amazed by how many of these "Occult Masters" there are out there. Usually, they are men in their forties; large of girth and sonorous of voice—when roused, anyway. In repose, they come across as "really nice—wouldn't hurt a fly." And, of course, they look "cool"—often sporting long hair or Eastern garb—and have plenty of psychological tricks up their sleeve. Let me give you an example.

Young Lauren is in town, shopping. Though she is usually in the company of friends, Ron is lucky today because she is alone, and dithering over, of all things, a teapot. A friend has requested one for her birthday; Lauren is stuck between a cat which pours tea from its paw, and a colourful Art Noveau brewer. Before she has had a moment to get her bearings, a tall, chubby John Lennon look-alike, reeking of dewberry oil, has walked right up to her, leaned over her and stared straight into the centre of her Egyptian-style eyes. His aura, which shimmers visibly, consumes her own. (She is trapped in front of the crockery display, and to step away from the stranger could prove noisy as well as expensive.)

"You're back again!" he exclaims joyfully. Then, "Oh, sorry, Lauren; it's just that we were so close—in countless other incarnations."

He withdraws, seeming to suck her soul out with his eyes in the process, and returns to where his younger friends are waiting, looking meaningfully over his shoulder all the while.

Yes, I know; a creep. But imagine how it would feel if you had never seen him before in your life, and yet he knew your name. Add to this a predisposal to reincarnation theories, the fact that the man seems somehow familiar, and the heavy influence of Eastern ideas regarding gurus and Ascended Masters. Then you might get some way to imagining how I felt when this great bulk of a man accosted me in the kitchenware department of Alder's Superstore in the first month of my nineteenth year.

He was wearing a vibrant pentacle, which I perceived instantly; I did not know any other Wiccans at the time, and was excited at the prospect of such an encounter. I was left hovering over the pots with a combination of outrage, intrigue, and a bit of an ego-tingle of my own. After all, Ron said I had been around in countless other incarnations. Who was I, then? My mind spun. It barely occurred to me that Ron might be lying. Lying is wrong, and nobody does it unless they absolutely have to, do they?

Then imagine the shock of receiving a letter at home, the very next day, from Ron. I had not given him any of my details, and according to the stamp, it had been posted before we met. Brightly illustrated with stickers, and written in felt pen like a child; a letter designed to be unthreatening. What could possibly be scary about a missive to which adhesive kittens clung? Even if it was from a stranger, celebrating an encounter not actual at the time of writing, and did ask for a date?

It was signed "Blessed Be." It resonated with witchiness, every well-chosen word. It was, to a potential priestess, irresistible. All it would take was for her friends to warn her off, which they duly did, to determine her to go.

"Incremental" was a favourite word of Ron's, and it describes perfectly the manner in which he insinuated himself into my life, so that, very gradually, I came to believe that this hulking forty-four-year-old sorcerer was an inevitable part of it. He tiptoed into my environment in these increments, alchemically designed to seem natural to me, meted out and measured so as not to upset the delicate balance of my psyche. I could flip fatally at any moment, incidentally. Ron was adept at demonstrating my neuroses, and how badly I needed him.

It did not take him long to confess, in a tearful moment, that he had only come back to Malkuth to rescue me from myself. Being spiritually and mentally perfect, his natural rapport was with Chesed, where the Masters abide, if not Kether itself. He had

reached Samadhi during the sixties, he confided, but was prevented
from Ascension by the inconvenient fact that I was not reincarnat-
ed until 1969. Poor Ron was forced to hang around twiddling his
thumbs, while I took my leisure on the Astral Planes. While he was
waiting, he ended up in prison. You can imagine how angry he was
with me, then.

Have I moved too fast, here? How can I describe the tactical
alacrity with which Ron progressed from stranger in the shopping
centre, to Wiccan in the pub with his (very nice) right-on friends, to
interloper on my spiritual integrity?

Miracles aside, at which Ron was highly proficient, young, deferential Lauren was impressed by the fact that he seemed to know
and be loved by everyone. Her stripling psychic responses to him
were intense enough to throw a seasoned priestess off her balance.

Though I can truly say that I loathed the man—and I did,
guiltily—I seemed to be at odds with everyone else who claimed occult ability. I would have sacrificed anything of my own, and undergone any personal inconvenience, in exchange for spiritual
insight. Ron convinced me that he could deliver this, if I would only
do as he asked. His self-belief was highly infectious.

This, alongside his thorough knowledge of many subjects, including sciences, religions, and languages (he would speak Urdu in
the corner shop, Russian to a regular at the local pub, or break into
fluent German, Spanish, Arabic . . .), and the ability to orate all
night on Qabalah and magick and Buddhism, complete with parables and personal illustrations, made Ron a force to be reckoned
with. He was also the head of Pagan Net in the Northwest.

If everybody else considered him "spot on," then who was I to
doubt him? Nobody but a neurotic teenager, just as he said.

So, take one neurotic teenager and mess with her head a bit. It is
not difficult. You can get her to discuss her childhood, her mother's
death when she was eight, her awful stepmother, how much she
hated school . . . then, when she has invested trust and information

in you, you can tell her, for example, that she betrayed you badly in another life, hence her feelings of discomfort and antipathy toward you—it's her secret guilt—and what can she do to disprove it? And how can she ever make it up to you?

It is impossible to brew up a real psychic storm, however, without a good sparkling dose of the inexplicable. This is essential to the belief factor—after all, most people who fall for bizarre beliefs are highly intelligent, and will need something of substance to encourage them. A little "proof" goes a long way, when combined with fervent hope.

Ron shone in this department. Imagine how amazed young Lauren was when he clapped his hands and produced a butterfly out of thin air, and in November! Such tricks have a timeless charm, and seem to signify positive things; the butterfly, a symbol of the psyche, of fleeting beauty—it is easy to impress a child as semiotically aroused as I was.

That, however, could be a stage magician's trick. Far more impressive was his ability to make large objects fly across the room; books especially. Seeing something levitate has a peculiar effect on the brain. If even gravity cannot be relied on to hold its own, what can?

He was also in the habit of reading my mind; everything from a subtle desire for a glass of wine, to people I was thinking of, to, unfortunately, what I was perceiving of him. He would sometimes burst into tears if the latter was particularly hurtful. If he was not genuinely telepathic, he was a freakishly adept psychologist.

The coup de grace, however, was the product of Ron's genius working on my psychic perceptions. I could visibly discern that his house was out of kilter; it operated on a different level to the outside world. Walking into it was an effort, like wading through water. The power on the other side was palpable. Inside his house, which he called "the Wiccarage," were sights and wonders such as I had never dreamed to behold so literally. Imagination became physical inside this psychic focal-point.

It was as if the entire world had been transformed into symbol-form. I saw quite clearly that a river ran through the middle of his home, flowing through the lounge, often with objects floating on it, or bearing aloft a boat complete with cowled passengers. It was perfectly superimposed on the contents of the room. Its reality was equal to that of the physical plane, only my physical referents belonged to the latter. I did not expect to get wet when I walked through it, but I watched it all the time, and was aware of it as being the Styx. A clue to get the hell out, you might reason, but I was so fascinated by the phenomena that I would rather risk the symbolic scythe than extricate myself from its vicinity. The follies of youth, or proof of my desire to transcend the mundane? That would depend on the judge.

This section of script lead to a page which was typed, folded, and carefully glued to the next page, on which had previously been some sort of ink drawing. The date at the top immediately told me that this was a recent addition to the journal.

I have just read Tahir Shah's Sorcerer's Apprentice *(Phoenix Paperbacks, London, 1999), and been relieved to discover somebody else as determined as I was to attain a coveted goal—his, to be a master of illusion—mine, to be mistress of Maya delusion, and find the truth and magick behind the screen. In this wonderfully rendered account, Shah describes his arrival in Calcutta and self-placement at the disposal of his mentor. The mentor then tests him, in the time-honoured style; for "success in any field always depends on forfeiture," as Shah says—a statement with which young Lauren would have vigorously agreed. They are tests of obedience and endurance, just as were Ron's. An example of Shah's: "Strip down to your underpants and crawl around the courtyard on your stomach, picking up fragments of seashell. Stop only when you have found two hundred fragments of shell." An example of Ron's: "Stare exclusively at an orange for a day. If you take your eyes off it or* daydream for one moment, you will start again." And when Ron said "you will," there was no getting out of it. This exercise took me four days, with no sleep. That orange nearly killed me. And the rotund fruit (about which I could tell you much) seemed innocuous compared to what was to come.

Tahir Shah progressed onto digging "a hole in the courtyard—two feet square, two feet deep—using a dessert spoon. The spoon may only be held in the left hand," while I was made to write a computer program which would greet me verbally when I switched it on; and this, for an unmathematical girl who could not even type at the time, was no fun at all. I was locked in a cupboard under the stairs, pending release on production of said program. It was very small and cold, and I am claustrophobic. Every so often, Ron would come in and give me a clue, though never the exact manoeuvre. Outside the cupboard, I could hear him and his friends, and sometimes my own, talking and cracking open cans of beer, packets of crisps, bottles of wine. I was allowed only two hours sleep a night until I had completed my task. Food of poverty proportions was brought to me at irregular intervals. By the time the computer finally greeted me by name, the mechanical appellation elicited a hysterical scream from Ron's obedient apprentice.

I like couching these details in comparisons, as it makes me feel better about having allowed Ron to do what he did to me. However, at this point, I must reluctantly part company with Tahir Shah. He has demonstrated a will to learn equal to my own, but had his teacher hit him, or made a pass at him, I wonder whether he would have stuck around. Perhaps, perhaps not.

In religious gurus, I find further parallels with Ron. Charisma-cult leaders such as Charles Manson exploit the group instinct, the need for belonging; Ron had this off to a tee. A "cool-factor" is always necessary in such endeavours; the members of the group must feel "chosen" and superior to the rest of humanity. Hence the danger of young Lauren's vanity; the willingness to believe that she was *as special as Ron continually told her she was. "Hand-picked by the Master," just like so many other cult members.*

Tal Brooke's Lord of the Air (Lion Publishing, Herts, 1976) describes his discipleship to Sai Baba, the agonies he underwent, so similar to mine, as piece by piece his personality was mortified on the altar of Higher Understanding. The abundant miracles and psychospiritual perceptions confused the issue further, as did the crunch, experienced by many of Baba's disciples, according to Brooke: "Baba got him alone, he did his usual number of material-ising things and telling him his inner secrets—the next thing that happened was Baba reached down and unzipped [his] fly . . ."

A key skill of gurus is to make the disciple see everything as a test. Of obedience, of endurance, of faith—whichever is the most convenient at the time. They are able to produce parables and lofty explanations at the drop of a hat. They have people with Egyptian-style eyes under their spell in no time at all.

In return for irrefutable Magickal Training and Spiritual Ascension, or, as Ron put it, "Crossing the Abyss," I was ordered to leave the student house I was in, and to move into Ron's spare room. I was promised privacy, liberty, and an on-hand magickal master. Everyone agreed that it was a wonderful idea. He was such a popular, intelligent, and compassionate man—"lovely" was his common epithet—and I was very lucky to have attracted his mag-ickal attentions. He was very well known in all the official Pagan and Wiccan circles, his kids (my own age, with whom I got on well) were always in and out of the house, as were his friends, and mine for that matter. My suspicions, my fears were unfounded, I was told. "Perfect Love and Perfect Trust" were obviously in order.

I looked about me. Spirits were everywhere; I could see and hear them clearly. The local dead flocked to Ron's place like light-seeking moths, jostling for the sustenance of our attention. Books flew off the shelves and opened at pages of relevance. Godforms shimmered behind the solid forms of strangers in the street. An old lady I had never seen before accosted me in town with "You are an old one! I can see it in your eyes! Hail Ra!"She vanished as quickly as she had come. Ron shape-shifted in front of me, and others; his favourite form was that of a wolf. Several of my friends were treated to this spectacle, and nobody could doubt its reality. Even if it were hyp-notism, which I do not believe it to have been, it was pretty darned impressive. It is not easy to argue logic with a yellow-eyed quadruped.

So, I decided to take Ron at his word. Perhaps he really was an expression of Godhead. He professed a particular affinity with Osiris and Jesus, and claimed to be a solar avatar. His aura was brilliant yellow, and he said his soul was pure. If it ever seemed not to be, he was simply trying to temper his brilliance, as Zeus wished to with Semele. "If you saw me in my full splendour," Ron assured me, "you would die."

And then there were the tests, which, reluctantly, Ron must force on his followers, particularly me, for compassion's sake. Without him, we were doomed to one-dimensionality and endless cycles of birth and death and rebirth. Ron could show us how to reach Samadhi. This was particularly relevant to me, he said, because I had already reached it in a previous incarnation, but then I fell from grace. What a klutz I must have been.

Many of my memories had been hidden from my conscious mind for the sake of my sanity, I was told. All I had to do now was to trust Ron, utterly, no matter what he did to me. There were tears in his eyes as he apologised to me, in advance. He did not want to do all of this, but it was his cosmic duty. I was to be melted down and remodeled into a vessel of divinity.

My heart rejoiced. Finding God was the only thing that I had ever really wanted.

Tal Brooke's response to the test, in this instance sexual, perfect-ly reflects my own. "My mind was reeling. Was the test not only that I comply, but that I see and acknowledge the holy in Baba's act? The Indian scriptures declared repeatedly, 'Anything done in total purity is without blemish.' Baba could ask, 'Do you trust me?' and I reply, 'Of course, for ever!' But until I was given cause to suspect him or question his integrity, the depth of my faith would remain uncertain."

I lavishly applied the rules of Eastern mysticism to Ron. With moral tales taken from the Upanishads and Rig-Veda, he trained me to see him as the Master.

My next feat of obedience came hot on the heels of the last. I was ordered to learn the correspondence table of Crowley's 777 overnight, to be examined in the morning. After a mind-scrabbling vigil, I was made to stand before a Ron, on whom Arabic and Hebrew words were delicately superimposed by my weary retinas, while he fired words at me, demanding my immediate response. He said "Saturn," I said "Binah." He said "Hindu correspondences?" I responded "Shakti, Yoni, Prana." The price for answering incorrectly was a punch in the face.

Several times I was knocked to the ground, and yanked up again by the hair. The logic was that, in a magickal working, the repercussions of a mistake are far worse than a physical blow could ever be. This was, said Ron, an example of "being cruel to be kind."

"You are going to be a major priestess in the new millennium," he told me continually. "You cannot afford to mess it up."

The rest of my training followed suit. I scrubbed the house, and was treated to a spirited blow if I missed a spot. I was forced to visualise psychic rays of different intensities, colours, and textures, and rewarded with a day's rest, or a phone call to a friend, if I met with Ron's clairvoyant satisfaction, and a night locked in the cupboard if I did not. He began to hit me frequently, even outside a training context. If I looked defiant, or contradicted him in any way, however subtle, I was kicked, punched, or slapped. This was nearly always on my body rather than my face, so that the bruises remained hidden beneath my flowing gothic garb.

The tiredness, the solitude, the fear I was beginning to feel toward Ron, conspired to put me further into his power. He talked continually, allowing me very little other input. I was not allowed out of his sight in case I "did something stupid," having reached the worst stage, apparently, of my initial training. I was kept hungry, scared, and short of sleep. My friends, and his own, were told that I was on the verge of suicide; only Ron could help. The slightest wrong move on my part could precipitate a violent physical attack.

Once, I gave him a cup of tea in a mug he said was the wrong colour for his psychology that day. The scalding contents were tipped over my head, the vessel smashed against the wall, and I made to clear it up shard by shard, by hand, still dripping with tea. My dignity had up and left, it seemed. There is little room for such luxuries when you are categorically told that, if you rebel, or worse still, try to escape, your mother and brother will be skinned alive. Ron made it clear that his threats were by no means hollow.

This violence was taken into the Circle, where my desire to become accomplished at Practical Magick was exploited to the full by Ron as priest. I had become the classic victim of cultic thought-processes.

The ridiculous thing, the fact that wrecked my head for a couple of years afterward, is that Ron's tactics worked. When I eventually escaped, after six months of sheer anguish, I wanted to disbelieve him totally, because I hated him and loathed what he had done to me—the beatings and sexual assaults above all; but I found that my power was flowing, just as he had said it would. What I still had to learn was that the power would have come to me regardless; and I could have chosen far better ways to induce it. Ron's brutality epitomises everything that is wrong with religion and the occult. Thus it was that I eventually reported him to the police, and had him struck off the Pagan and Wiccan contact lists, on which he had featured prominently. Even if I had escaped with my body and spirit still intact, others might not be so resilient.

The Styx flowed fast and thick through the centre of my soul, thanks to Ron. I escaped, like Persephone, in the summer, and *hitched my way to London. I had to abandon every single thing that I possessed, except for my Tarot cards. It was literally a case of running out of the back door, as fast I could. I promised myself that I would never go back, and I never have.*

Crazed warlocks are not, as far I am concerned, recommended.

I am thus capable of taking all occultists, however lofty their academic or magickal status, with a pinch of cleansing salt. I have never, however, allowed my mind to slam shut. That would negate all the genuine experiences I have had.

Mr. Malynowsky listened to my tale over a number of till-side counseling sessions. Violence indicates a serious imbalance of the Ego, he emphasised; the one thing that enlightened beings are supposed to be without. Genuine teachers are characterised by another feature: they never claim to be perfect. No good spirit would do that. No true Master ever forces his pupil. Ron's Karmic debt is vast.

My success was a happy side effect, rather than a direct result of his parlous methods, according to Mr. Malynowsky. He also pointed out that such techniques, though effective, "are not for this era." They belong to a dark age in which pain was offered up in return for enlightenment—but the whole point of the Aquarian era is that it has now become possible, indeed more expedient, to follow a joyous path to the Light.

The time for martyred saints and demonic, dualistic gurus is long gone.

I put the book down for a moment, allowing the train of images to move again before my eyes. No wonder Lauren had not wished to talk of such things—possibly, it would be beyond her verbal powers to dictate such a story. Better by far to have it committed to paper, a medium in which she could be measured in her task. And good old Mr. Malynowsky, helping her analyse it afterward. I smiled. That man truly is one in a million.

The next page of Lauren's dramatic script had caught my eye, and I was itching to read it. *Witch in the City*, it said, *Or, The Early Adventures of an Occult Bookstore Manager*.

I wondered whether Lauren would mind, and concluded that no, she would not. She had loaned me the journal, after all. I began to read again.

He that writeth in blood and proverbs doth not want
to be read, but learned by heart.

WITCH IN THE CITY
or, The Early Adventures of an Occult Bookstore Manager

I don't want to tell you a story about a girl locked in a cupboard, though that would be easy. Karmic guilt-trips and projectile fisting belong to another aeon; one in which the veil was as thick as a curtain in Madam Sosostris' séance room, dusty with the discharge of false hopes, false promises. Of course, in an era comprised of atheism, religious segregation, mutual suspicion, and scientific deconstruction, the "supernatural" seems a sham. As to the truth behind the illusion—well, that's another matter.

But now it's the twenty-first century. Time for a change. Time to experience Isis, and Osiris, unveiled. So now I will fast-forward you to the day, six months later, that I escaped Ron and his psychopathic version of Magickal Training.

It is summer when I arrive in London. I am surprised to remember, through the holes in my shoes, how hot concrete paving can become.

The citizens shock me. They are all so busy, so caught up in their particular networks of belonging. People are smiling, talking, rushing about. I see a particular man, in a suit and tie, musing as a shaft of sunlight illuminates his face. His eyes are lucid cerulean blue. I never would have dreamed that a man in a suit could look so beautiful.

I head straight to Kensington, because I've been there before. A friend and I absconded to London when we were fourteen. She told her parents she was staying with me; I told mine I was spending the night with her, and we caught an overnight coach to the distant metropolis. In Kensington Market we bought Eye of Horus earrings, and reveled in our conspiracy. Back at home we wore our earrings as talismans until they fell apart. These little memories thrill me; I have not had the luxury to think small thoughts for what feels like aeons.

I sit beneath a gnarled-bark tree in Kensington Gardens, hungry for shade and stasis, the blood in my head swelling and pumping too fast to support further movement. The sky is Siva-blue, with ashen dreadlock clouds. I swallow two of the paracetamol I have bought at rip-off rate out of my only five-pound note, and cradle my Tarot cards pensively.

They glow through their black silk covering. The old friends inside the pack jostle for position in my consciousness. The Fool, my current rootless persona, telling me to follow my dreams; the Hierophant chanting orthodox advice like a psalm; the pearlescent High Priestess with her comforting intuitive wisdom. They speak to me as I sit with my back up against the wily city dryad.

Don't become insular.

Send out beacons for a friendly hand.

Without aid, there can be no salvation.

And stop thinking like a religious maniac.

Who said that? My mind follows the thread of thought back to its source, and meets with Justice, Lady of Reason—Athena to the Greeks, to the Egyptians, Maat; the embodiment of balanced living. Not a goddess I have had much rapport with recently.

The silk burns in my hands. The Tower sends out fountains of flame, assailing my attention. Thoughts fall from the windows of my mind like fire-fleeing bodies, jolting me into remembrance of horrors lived through, threats inflicted.

For a moment I consider the rest of the paracetamol. But I don't have the energy, or the money, to get the analgesic mixers I'd need, and besides, I deserve a chance, do I not?

The Tower subsides, replaced by the lampen light of the Star. It has taken me months to extricate myself from Hades, and not even giving it a go would make a complete mockery of past efforts. The majority of voices in the pack concur. I have no underwear on and no toothbrush, but at least I am free.

I sigh heavily and lie down on the bumpy earth, the Tarot resting on my chest, between the heart and solar plexus chakras, to be precise. The memory of the word *chakra* makes me feel sick, and in a wave the other sneakling phrases hit me—sephiroth, auras, astral entities—the whole wear-worn thesaurus of my most recent experience. It has been snatched from me and returned inexorably annotated, its references warped. I need a new one, with lovely new words in it, words which have not been yelled at me or abused. I still want to keep the definitions, though. They are as much mine as his, after all: if not more so.

Words such as *prana, karma,* and *chalice* are probably not yelled very often, so my sensitivities are fairly unique. Then again, not many students replace university lectures with the magickal tuition of a middle-aged warlock, or are forced into fire-dancing when they should be sitting their finals. Not many at all. A word of warning to aspiring undergraduates: if you are ever approached by a strange man bearing cakes and ale, just say "No."

Perhaps my stepmother was right. Perhaps I really do go out of my way to be different.

I need a drink.

I rise from Gaia's lumpen lap, my head still thumping. In the nearest pub, I splash out wildly on a brandy and coke. The Fool within rejoices. It cheers me that they serve me, messily shorn hair, bruises and all. It must be my voice. Sometimes people refuse to see the obvious when presented with a more palatable alternative. My accent and intonations were bred in upper-middle-class suburbia, so nobody says to me, "Sorry, love, you look like a coven escapee whose only underwear is two hundred miles away, we can't have your sort here." They say, "Certainly, Madam, and would you like ice and a slice with that? That will be three pounds fifty, please."

I thank the barman with a special flourish of that fortuitous elocution—*every word a je-wel,* as my stepmother used to say, and do some swift mental calculations. I dislike math, but this sum is easy. Three pounds and fifty-seven pence, minus three pounds fifty, equals: London on a budget even George Orwell couldn't rival. The barman hands me a glass of my craved beverage, condensation running down its sides and chilling my fingertips. I drink to the challenge.

I emerge in the warm, polluted dusk and begin to wander down the crowded high street.

Almost immediately, my eyes meet with those of a profoundly grubby young man of the tie-dye variety, bearing an armful of tattered newspapers. In my hand, the black silk becomes hot with urgent signals.

I smile at him. His yeasty consciousness extends a bacterial tendril toward me, carrying a whiff of Bacchic frenzy on its undercurrents, a bouquet of mystic and chemically induced *fleurs du mal* in its overtones. I perceive him as characterising "clean dirt," having experienced an excess of subcutaneous filth for the past six months. He seems to think that I'm all right too. Soon, the pungent young vagrant and I are sitting beneath my tree again, carelessly divining cosmic truth from strewn-about sticks.

He has the squeakiest voice, a real rusted-gate number, and a paranoia complex which is probably not entirely misplaced.

"People are always trying to kill me, Lauren," he enthuses. The atoms of his aura fly about chaotically as he speaks, reflecting the manic mandalas of a fragmented consciousness. Most of his life-energy is encrusted, but glowing at the centre, like the earth herself.

"A few days ago I was sitting on a bench by a big block of flats, and suddenly a brick landed beside me and shattered into pieces. I looked up and saw someone leaning out of the top window, staring at me. I scuttled away like a rat, in case they tried it again."

Jess has an empathy with vermin. His mind is not feral, but his gestures are all tooth and claw, forage and store. He is a creature of snickets and nooks, a nimble den-finder. His papers and empty bags are nesting material. Hopping and skipping and scuttling between subjects, he tells me enough to reveal a man in a fox-hole, recycling his own breath, studying the psychedelic stratum of the soil in preference to the grassy, airy realms above, where danger lingers.

He makes twists and twirls in his erratic beard as he speaks, his fingers dark and thin as long-buried spindles. There is something deeply archaeological about him; he might have been buried in peat for a thousand years or more. His bones jut through clothing almost carbonated by dirt.

He sniffs out an abandoned bottle of wine—most of one—which we drink as the light fades. I am beginning to feel euphoric.

"They'll be locking up the park soon," he hints, and bang go my plans for the night. I had already spotted the leafy enclave of my choice. "Where did you say you were staying?"

I look at him enigmatically.

"You lied, didn't you? You little sphinx! When did you really arrive in London? A week ago?" He pauses, eyeing me with dilated pupils. "No—it was today, wasn't it?"

"Jess—do you live anywhere?"

He grins at me semitoothlessly. Clearly I am not the only person in London lacking in the apparatus of dental hygiene.

"Come with me, and I'll show you."

The Tarot still agree. It seems the least hazardous option.

It takes me a quarter of an hour to cross the threshold. The door is twelve feet high with no footholds, and it is the broken window above it through which we mean to gain access. The fear of cutting my hands on the jutting shards is diminished by modesty; Jess is holding my feet and would be able to see straight up my skirt, if he ever stopped looking over his own shoulder for long enough.

Clenching the shabby material between my knees, I nose-dive through the aperture and land in a heap on the broken wood and splinters of glass within. I do not stop to consider whether it has hurt or cut me; I am protected by four walls, utterly concealed in an obscure nook of Holland Park; I am safe. Safe and very grateful. This place is paradise.

Jess wheedles through the window above me. He almost floats to the ground, so light and divorced from reality is he.

We fumble our way upstairs in the thick, damp darkness, tripping every so often on a dilapidated floorboard, until we finally reach a rotten-slatted, amber-lit room. Several enormous mushrooms grow in the corners, from which city-curious spores vacillate. A Fly Agaric of impressive proportions points its white-dappled red nose at the ceiling, from a bizarre tangent, of course.

"I grew them myself," explains my host. "I brought the cultures here from the woods of Somerset and Oxfordshire."

They certainly add an unusual touch to the lofty Victorian mansion, I reflect.

A filthy, concave mattress lies on the floor, and a single poster is stuck to the wall.

"Glastonbury Festival, '89," announces Jess, on noticing me noticing the poster.

"Really? I was there that year too." A good time. The connection is comforting.

"I go every year," he continues. "But '89 was the only year I could afford anything other than acid."

I glance at his emaciated body. I suspect he trips pretty hard.

"Do you sign on?" How could he survive, other than on Government Benefit, I wonder?

Jess shakes his dreadlocked head. "I can't. No fixed abode. Anyway, they're dangerous, the DSS*. They take your details and capture your soul. One of them tried to knock me down in her car recently. They hate free spirits. I've got friends who help me out. I still get acid once a fortnight."

"But you're so thin! Shouldn't you—"

"My body will survive for as long as my mind wants it to. I get by. Today I had a solid and two liquids. I'm not hungry."

He looks at me edgily, a small smile appearing every so often. It is half Pan, half perverse. In Tarot terms he is the Hermit under the influence of the Moon; of male polarity but beholden to the feminine, mentally isolated, living in liminal realities. I think of the one-eyed Phoenician Sailor, and though I am no T. S. Eliot, I

* In Britain, the Department of Social Security; the branch of government providing benefits to the unemployed or those unable to work—"on the dole."

cannot help but make literary cross-references. I was studying English Literature before I went mad and signed up with Ron.

I yawn, and let my eyelids droop a little. Jess, his body racked by malnutrition, is already asleep in a hirsute ball in the corner of the room. He clings to sheets of newspaper in the same way that his body's cells cling together; against the odds.

I have made it into exile.

I am woken by the sound of traffic and the bright sunlight which streams through the vacant window. For five minutes I am jubilant, wondering whether Ron slept last night, hoping that he is suffering, knowing that I will never go back now. Twice before I have escaped and he tracked me down; third time lucky, then. I recall the words which came to me in the dream, the one that conveyed to me like an electrical charge the sure knowledge that, if I stayed, I would die: "Leave the Leo Solar Furnace while you can. Follow the Sun."

I look to my left and see the muck-encrusted Jess asleep, still huddled in the corner like some creeping creature prised from beneath its stone. What an improvement! If Ron looked the way he acted, he'd make Jess seem a freshly bathed babe. My new companion's mental health was ropy, to be sure, but he was spiritually hygienic. He had none of the urges normal to man; the drugs and starvation had taken him beyond such shenanigans. I determine to reward my paranoid friend for giving me a safe haven on my first night in the city. When I've earned my fortune, perhaps I should hire him a couple of bodyguards? Then again, they would probably turn on him, by all accounts. Breakfast might be safer.

Another reaction invades my blood . . . fear, self-doubt, the usual crew of ghouls and screeching madwomen. Yet I cannot ignore the fact that the only way is up, that nothing is at stake, everything to gain. I will ascend this mountain despite the pack of slavering memories nipping at my heels, the pale ferocious visages of demons crossed; I will leave the past beneath me, as Persephone left the dead in Hades every year.

I wash in Holland Park Ladies', and we breakfast on tea and a bread roll in the park café. My vagrant friend pays the bill, in coppers. My resolve thickens. It has occurred to me that I can attempt to read Tarot for money; in fact, it has occurred to me that I have no choice in the matter. When I fled, I had no idea what I would do when I got to London, beyond a brandy and coke, that is. I thank the Goddess for making me pick up the cards.

The park is brimming with other squatters, hoboes, and free-range patients from the local psychiatric hospital, and sprinkled with yuppies and tourists thinking how glad they are not to be us.

We are joined by friends of Jess—Roberto, an Italian boy-waiter with mocha skin and a cornet quiff, who shares our hovel, apparently; Dave, a middle-aged Australian male; a young woman with big brown eyes called Veronica; and a well-spoken chap in pink flares, who introduces himself as "Jesus—yes, *that* one." An intense conversation ensues, ranging from Dave's perception of Thai housing to Veronica's relationship with her mother (once a literary hostess of some standing), to the problems of Coming Again and not being recognised. I am thrilled to remember that other people exist, and are challenged by issues as complex and obscure as my own umbral themes.

Jess introduces me as "my girlfriend, Lauren," and I note with amusement how swiftly my ownership had been transferred. This time yesterday . . .

I am tempted to stay and enjoy the first real conversation I have had in what feels like aeons, but as you might have guessed, I am in no position to doss.

yde Park is quiet today, but its flat urban turf feels like the Promised Land to me, vibrant and full of opportunity. I look above people's heads, and when I see an orange light hovering there, I approach and offer them a Tarot reading. The cynic might say that I am acting in a manner indicative of certain mental strain, but the technique does not let me down, and as far as I am concerned, it saves much unnecessary legwork.

The first woman I approach pays me £5, which is encouraging. She gets the Tower and Death reversed, which is not. Luckily, they are in her immediate past and present; I do not wish to be a herald of doom. She looks at me expectantly while her friend scrutinises the small crystal I carry in the pack.

"Well, you look very happy at the moment," I begin. "But if I'm not vastly mistaken, you've recently suffered a violent shock."

The woman's face crumples. Her friend looks up sharply. The querent begins to cry.

"My mother died two days ago," she says. "Here, have a grape."

Soon I am sharing their picnic and memories, and explaining about the Eight of Cups in the immediate future being a positive sign. I begin to realise that my new job is not so much Tarot reader, as nomadic counselor.

Some of my clients can only afford to pay me 50P, or buy me a coffee in return, but very soon I am not in it simply for the money. The human contact is a therapy to me, and the accuracy of the readings astonishes the querents. If I can help a few people en route from Hades, all the better.

I earn a large hunk of stilton, most of a spliff, and £18.50 from my first day's endeavours. It is beautifully sunny, and I am beginning to glow with optimism. Fantasies of bedsits and Tarot stalls drift though my mind. I have nothing, just my cards and what's in my head, but I have all the tools that I need. Anything else would be an encumbrance, although a pair of cotton panties would be nice. But it seems too soon to be throwing money away on frivolities, so I set them as a treat to be bought if, and only if, I equal or exceed today's takings every day for the next week. In my present mood, anything is possible.

Jess dines on double egg and chips that night, and I eat cheese-cake and clean my teeth afterward. I feel like the luckiest woman in the world.

The next day I linger longer over breakfast, and read Veronica's Tarot at the table. She likes my green eyes and I like her doe-brown eyes. I am grateful to be alive, and sometimes this makes me sentimental. She is slightly doleful but very friendly to me. She pays me with a kiss.

I make £36 this hazy summer's day, and several loose-knit friends. In my state of regained liberty, it seems that everybody is opening out like flowers, and they are mine to gather. I wonder why it takes such extreme circumstances to underline the good in life? The simple things like human contact, and cups of tea, and not being beaten up by six-foot-four hippies yelling at you about Qabalah. At the moment, it feels as if my joy will last forever.

I am dreaming of his face, staring, cold eyes penetrating, fists pummeling, bang, bang, grind of teeth, when I awake, alone, to the continued sounds of destruction. Heavy feet on the stair-case, door opening. One, two, three, four—skinheads burst into the room.

Others are downstairs; I can hear them shouting and breaking up the walls and stairs. They have hammers and small axes.

I am trapped. I feel real fear for the first time since I arrived. They are staring at me.

"What're you doing here?" asks the gang leader. Several more of his mates pile in, presumably in case I turn nasty.

"I was sleeping."

"It's a tart!" says another.

"Shut up! What's your name, darlin'?"

"Look, excuse me," I say, my voice schoolmarmish with suppressed hysteria. "Would you please leave the room while I get dressed?"

Well, it's worth a go. I wonder what the hell they've done with Jess. I notice that they are very young, and clean, which is strange. They look shocked when I speak. They do not seem to know what to do with themselves now, and are all glancing nervously at their leader.

"We were looking for a squat."

"Yes, well, this one's already taken," I manage. Just. They might be clean, but their pheromones are filling up the room, and only a thin sheet lies between them and my nakedness. "Try down the road. Number 19. There's loads of people there—they might be able to help you."

"Sorry to have disturbed you, love," says the main man. They look at me disconcertedly, almost questioningly I think, and they leave. Very loudly, but they leave.

I leap up, shaking uncontrollably, retrieve my skirt from the old nail on which it hangs at night to keep it from creasing beyond all redemption, and, when the house becomes silent, creep into the corridor to look for Jess. I find him next door, cowering in a fixed wardrobe.

"You can handle people better than I can," he squeaks, smiling that paranoid smile again. His breath reeks of fox-fear, the vile scent of the cornered animal.

"There's no way I'm sleeping here again, now," I snap. It is not his duty to protect me, but I am angry that he did not even alert me to the danger. "I'll have to find somewhere else."

"I know somewhere. Acton. Trust me Lauren, I'll find us a roof for tonight."

"Do what you want. I'm out of here."

Yesterday's bliss has become today's bullshit again, I reflect miserably. The feeling of not being safe in my bed had cut a little too close to the bone. I also have an additional concern now— the harbouring of about £75 in dodgy environs. I feel even more determined to save up the deposit for a bedsit, preferably somewhere free from other people's testosterone overdrives.

The entrance to the Acton squat is so small that, though Jess can squirm through it, I do not even try. I am thin in human terms, but a worm would call Jess slim. He throws out some musty duvets and we sleep in the back yard. It is good to wake up with the sun on my skin, but the dirt rankles and there is no water with which to wash it off.

At Acton tube station I peck Jess goodbye, and the adolescent girl behind me shrieks, "How can you kiss *that?*"

I flush with unspoken retorts, but I know what she means. He is no Adonis; not even by Glastonbury standards.

I am beginning to smell of him. Unlike Jess, I wash daily, but there is only so much you can do over a sink in a public lavatory. Whatever would my stepmother have said?

I wonder what my friends think I am doing. There is no possibility of me finding out, of course. Ron has my address book, and I may as well butcher and feed myself to the poor depressed wolves in Regents Park, as try to stay at one of them. He'll be doing the rounds by now, no doubt.

I long for a bath.

My muscles cry out for one.

Instead, I content myself with the Holland Park Ladies'.

On the way past the old squat, I notice an eviction bill stuck to the door.

"It looks as if we got out just in time!" I comment to Australian Dave.

Blue amusement beams from his eyes. They are shockingly bright against his tan.

"You reckon that's a coincidence, do ya? Get real, Laurie—that gang you mentioned—did you notice anything strange about them?"

I nod, and reiterate their cleanliness and the newness of their tools.

"They were hired by the Council to scare ya, mate. They've been trying to evict the squatters from those rows for years now. Jeez, Laurie, you wouldn't have stood a chance with a real gang in there. They'd have broken you and Jess up, not just the flaming walls, mate. And a lot more besides. Nah, it's the Council. They'd rather have you sleeping in the streets than in someone's unused property." He smiles bitterly.

"Well, Goddess only knows where we'll go tonight. The cemetery, perhaps." I know I can get away with such phrases in Holland Park. Everyone's barking and anything goes. There is an unspoken code of mutual tolerance, and only those who break it are ousted.

"I'd just worked out how to get in the top window on my own, as well," I grumble. "The Acton place is a waste of money on the Tube. How the hell do you lot survive in winter?"

Dave smiles and shrugs.

"I couldn't take it," I exclaim, surprised at how angst-ridden I am becoming again. It has only been a week since my destitution began, and the seasons are already becoming a threat. I know I will not be able to survive on Tarot alone, once Britain reverts to its usual chilly drizzle. Not without a stall.

"I watch the leaves all the time. I'm telling you, Dave, if I'm not under a proper roof by September, I'll be a hypothermic tragedy."

He eyes me casually, bright blue eyes glittering in the sunlight.

"What happened to your hair?" he asks.

The question lures me into another muse. I had managed to forget, a little, about Ron.

"Not that it looks bad or anything. It's just so uneven—over your ear on one side, and under it on the other. Did you get it caught in something?"

"Someone cut it off, if you must know. It used to be down to my waist." I thought of Ron swinging the severed plait in the air, and throwing it into his draw of magickal equipment with a smug smile. "But it's just as well that it's gone. Totally impractical for squatting. I feel kind of liberated without it; a lot of my psyche was caught up in my hair, if you know what I mean."

He nods like a man who's suffered the long-haired blues.

"I used to keep my spells in it. Old ones. I'm glad it's gone."

Dave looks amused, cynical. "I guess you're the kind of girl that believes in spaceships and the Age of Aquarius."

I prickle slightly.

"And if I do?"

He looks askance at me, and I regret my auric spikes. This guy's okay.

"I've thought a lot about such matters, yes." Schoolmarm again. "It seems perfectly logical to me that there are beings of extraterrestrial origin alive on this planet today. An alien would hardly materialise in its natural form, which would probably be too physically strenuous anyway. No, what it would do is be incarnated in human flesh, indecipherable from the rest of us. Probably indecipherable to itself."

Dave laughs. "And its masters would beam up special progress reports from earth hey, nano nano?"

I smile. At least he doesn't try to convince me I am in need of immediate correctional therapy, or that I *am* an alien. "Something like that. Or maybe they'd go round over and over, gathering knowledge, and finally return to the source on shedding the physical shell—maybe they'd be special, have particular gifts, be perceived as prophets or gods, even. It would explain a lot. I think the Egyptian Myths are particularly influenced by beings from other dimensions—but it's a long story."

My heart is pounding quite heavily, I notice. I begin to feel very uncomfortable. By talking about this, I am allowing Ron back in. I can almost smell him now, his sickly dewberry and bergamot scents, so close am I to his native wavelength. "Have you seen Veronica today?" I ask, to change the subject.

Dave looks amiably about him. "Nope, sorry love. Buy me another cup of coffee will ya, Laurie? Jess is lucky having you. He hasn't eaten so well in years. Any chance of a croissant?"

Jess and I have an unspoken agreement: I provide the food, and he provides the shelter.

Only, tonight, he doesn't. He tells me he has had to spend the day hiding from the woman from the DSS, the one who tried to mow him down in her car, the one who's stalking him. He is indeed particularly tense tonight. He would be a sitting duck if he stayed still, he tells me, so it is imperative that we keep moving.

I have no desire to be alone on the streets of London, so I go with him. I am beginning to realise the impracticalities of hanging around with Jess, however, and fear that I will have to start making ulterior arrangements more quickly than I had previously intended. It is very important that I am well rested; I cannot read the cards properly otherwise. Also, the last thing I need customer-wise is to look as if I've been on the hoof all night.

London is funny like that. If you appear to have a little money, people will happily give you more. But if you start to look penniless, you've had it.

I perform elaborate ablutions in Marble Arch Ladies' in the morning, then decide to go completely mad and invest in a beautiful black silk G-string. Well, if I'm going to walk the streets all night, I can at least do so with the dignity bestowed by a pair of decent pantaloons.

Besides, it will help me hold my head up high in the public toilets of London, where I spend so much of my time.

I read the cards for a group of Cantonese tourists who shower me with money, smiling and giggling, but who clearly understand nothing that I tell them. I find this an unfulfilling experience, despite its lucrative nature. One young lady, who is about to be married, has mortal tragedy marked out in her future, within the next two years. I try to emphasise the need for her to be strong when this event occurs, and she screams with laughter at my mumbo-jumbo, and points and nods repeatedly at her friend in a bid to get me to read hers as well.

Their guide, a lanky English chap, returns from the ice-cream van brandishing cornets, and giving me a warning stare over their swirling creamy peaks.

"Have you taken money from these people?" he demands.

"Well, I offered to read their Tarot and they all threw money at me, yes."

He glares at me.

"I'm a genuine Tarot-reader," I say. "I didn't *steal* from them, you know."

"Well, that's a matter of opinion," he snipes.

"You can have their money back if you want. But first, you ask them if they enjoyed their readings. I think they'll tell you that they got value for what they paid. At the very least, as *entertainment*."

He slips into Cantonese, and the innocents shriek, clap their hands and nod. The guide shakes his head.

"Just leave us now," he says.

As I depart, I hear the sounds of disappointment in an oriental tongue. Perhaps they understood more than I think: or maybe it's just something to tell people when they get home. Either way, I do not think they will miss the thirty-odd pounds I have just earned in as many minutes. And I am pretty confident that they do not need it as much as I do.

I wander down by the river, and am struck by the similarity of the view beneath the bridge to the image of the Four of Swords in the Morgan Greer Tarot pack, with its weeping willows and gothic arch. The message of the allusion: recuperation, time to meditate, a mental and physical sanatorium. This is what Hyde Park is to me; I am delirious with liberty, yet rightfully attuned. Were I mad, damaged, the readings would be inaccurate. They are not. I know I am on the right path.

Three well-dressed, well-fed Indian boys approach me and remark in Etonian accents on my latter-day profession.

"I hope you don't mind us asking, but could you possibly read our cards?" asks Jiten, having introduced himself and his friends, Prameet and Nealam. "We shall pay you, of course."

We sit cross-legged on the turf near the Serpentine river, they in their fashionable smart-but-casuals, me in my grotty tie-dye vest, torn Indian skirt, and invisible but confidence-inspiring new knickers, and I tell them of their futures in science and medicine. All three have just taken their A Levels and are off to medical college, they hope. They are friendly yet cynical. At the end, Jiten asks me if I really believe in all this nonsense. I tell him that I could not read the cards convincingly otherwise, and besides, hadn't theirs just come out accurate?

"All this superstition has been the downfall of many peoples," he announces, tacitly implying Indians among others. "I don't want to seem rude, Lauren, but such beliefs are for peasants, not for well-educated Westerners like us. Still, it is very enterprising of you," he continues, evidently immune to the point I am making. "Gentlemen, we could make a real fortune with this one!"

"He's been trying to think up money-making schemes," laughs Nealam, whose teeth are Kether-white. All three have the crystal eyes, perfect skins, and abundant glossy hair indicative of quality nurture and unshakeable focus. They are a good advertisement for first-generation atheism, unfortunately.

"He's always trying to work out how to make a fast buck," grins Nealam, with a hint of apology. "Don't mind him, Lauren."

I smile genuinely at the polite youth.

"No, but seriously!" enthuses Jiten. "Just think about it!" He turns to me, excited by his flash of genius. "We've just paid you nine pounds for about twenty minute's work, right, and you said yourself that's cheap for a professional Tarot reading. So, if we had three or four girls all working from nine to five, we could make over a grand a day. Even split six ways, it's over a hundred pounds a day, without us actually having to *do* anything. Pay them an hourly wage—say five pounds an hour—that's good for just wandering round in the park—we'd be laughing! We can start with Jessica and Shireen."

"Yeah, Jessica'd be *perfect*," cries Prameet. Nealam giggles.

Jiten gets his second wind. "A small investment of a pack of Tarot cards each—that's it! Maybe a crystal ball if things go well."

"Tea leaves!" cries Prameet. "Tea leaves cost nothing!"

"Um, excuse me," I butt in. "I hope you're not planning on using Hyde Park as your fortune-making plot: I need this money to actually *live* on."

"Wow, it's such a bloody good idea, man," grins the Jessica-wallah, tears in his eyes at the beauty and simplicity of the plan. "Don't worry, Lauren, we won't tread on your toes. You don't want to work for us, do you?"

I smile sarcastically. "How are you going to avoid treading on my toes, if you have two or three of '*your*' girls working here? And can they actually *read* Tarot?"

"They can learn."

"Yes? Well, one dodgy reading on their part could ruin my clientele base. Most people think it's a con anyway—look at your own attitude—or they're scared by it. An inaccurate or badly delivered reading could confirm people's worst suspicions."

Jiten grins and shrugs. "But you actually believe in it, don't you?"

I nod.

"Well, Jessica might, but Shireen doesn't, so it wouldn't matter what their readings were like, would it? They'd just be written off as not very good, so more people would come to you, innit?"

"That logic is *so* warped!" say I, smiling despite myself at the incongruity of hearing an "innit" grafted onto the end of a cut-glass English sentence.

"So is metaphysics!" argues the entrepreneur. "You cannot prove anything about your beliefs; you have no basis for your argument. You are simply pursuing the follies which coincide with your personal hopes!"

There's some truth in that all right, I think to myself. My folly on the Ron-front was phenomenal—I allowed my suspicions and intuitions to be swept away on a tidal-wave of flattery, or fear, time and time again. A reason for being here—something very specific which justifies all past pain—is a Grail in itself. To drink from it, and in company; that feels sublime. But in addition to symbols of truth, the experience brings on hallucinations, and one's delusions of grandeur lead easily to external ego-manipulation.

Of course, I say nothing of this. It would complicate matters, and confirm Jiten's point. And there is so much more, besides the delusions. Another reality untainted by the ego. The spiritual realms which are beyond emotional pollution. It is on these that I hope to focus now—and always.

"I have no intention of trying to convert you, but I *will* say that my personal experiences of the so-called 'supernatural'—which I think of more as the cosmic ultranatural—have led me beyond all reasonable doubt as to their veracity. That's all the proof I need; otherwise I'd just be taking *your* word for it, wouldn't I?"

Prameet claps his hands. "Well said, Lauren! This guy gets far too carried away with his materialistic theories. There must always be room for hypothesis." He glances at his friends. "What is science without hypotheses? A bunch of sterile statistics. Innovation is the root of progression—and that requires imagination. At the very least, Tarot and so forth represents the faculty of imagination."

And so it continues. I am enjoying myself too much to move on, though I have spotted several potential customers, or rather the orange lights above their heads, scattered about the park. It is getting quite busy this balmy summer's afternoon. After a couple of hours, I decide to make my reluctant excuses.

Suddenly, I notice a rustling in the bushes behind my companions, and, to my horror, a grubby, feral face peeking out of the foliage. Jess, on perceiving his cover blown, emerges like a creature flushed out by wild fire. He positively hurtles himself at me, squeaking my name as if we have not seen one another for decades, audibly panicking.

Jiten, Nealam, and Prameet look round in alarm, and begin to rise to their feet. When Jess reaches me, he throws an emaciated, rag-haunted arm about my waist and displays the rotting stubs of his teeth.

"Ah, have you met my girlfriend?" he asks the horrified trio. "This is my Lauren. I'm Lauren's boyfriend, Jess. Are you ready to go now, Lauren? I told Dave and Veronica we'd meet them down at the café in half an hour."

"And you said *I* might threaten your clientele base?" quips Jiten, as I inadvertently turn crimson.

"He's not really my boyfriend," I desperately want to say, but how can I? Alienating Jess would mean being alone in the metropolis, and ceasing to hang out in the places I have managed to establish as familiar. My vanity cringes.

I tell Jess sharply that I will meet him in Holland Park when I have finished my day's work. I turn my back on him, and just about manage to meet the others' eyes, though I have clearly plummeted in their estimation.

Jess stays put, right behind me. I can tell from the boys' faces that they can smell him too; his rotten-sweet scent is, to say the least, distinctive. Other people begin to beat a path around, rather than via, us.

Evidently, I will not be able to shake off my antisocial companion until I have extricated myself from these three young men, who are causing Jess to puff up like a demented cockerel trying to compete for his hen against three lusty peacocks.

Before I leave them, I extract a swift promise from Jiten—for what a materialist's promise is worth—that he will not create false Tarot readers. He waxes lyrical about the free market, and how it improves standards in the long run, which is irritating, but, I reflect, chances are he'll be off to medical school before he can set his money-making posse on the innocent citizens and tourists of London.

I do not need the cards to tell me that all three of my new friends will lead steady and rewarding lives.

I am perturbed by the venal inklings which informed Jess' actions, the territorial adult suddenly evident in his suckling psyche.

Now, though, he grapples for my favour with runtish squeals, his animus once again consigned to some distant maze of his crop-circle mind.

"Are you okay? Sorry, Lauren, but you have no idea what those three were up to. I've seen them around before, and I'm sure they work for the DSS. That woman I told you about knows them, and . . ."

"Jess—shut up."

I walk away from him, furious at the blowing of my cool before an audience, and even more so at the idea of having been spied upon. He is beginning to remind me of Ron, with all this possessiveness.

I head for the bridge and he catches me up, bringing a waft of squat-stink with him, and reminding me of why I am beholden to him. He giggles maniacally. He is scared.

"Look, Jess, go and buy some batteries for your Walkman," I tell him. His Walkman is his one possession, along with the Pink Floyd tape that lives in it. Listening to it calms him down. I plunge a ten-pound note into a hand on which any palmist could read the lines; those of deeply ingrained neurosis.

"Veronica will go in for you," I add. None of the shopkeepers on Kensington High Street will let Jess past their door, even when he's brandishing the readies. "I'll join you all later."

Appeased, and keen to re-explore aural ecstasy as he defines it, Jess scuttles off and leaves me, thankfully, alone.

Now I can be Anyone again.

I go back under the Morgan Greer bridge, and saunter along the paved river bank, looking for astral lights. As the day begins to wane, more and more people are filling up the deck chairs and sitting facing the water, and, although the buildings will obliterate the sunset, they can at least look towards it.

Fragments of conversation arrest my attention.

"It is just like Chowpatty," a woman clad in a bright pink sari comments to her wealthy-looking white friend. "The popular sunset beach of Mumbai. But here there are women allowed, and at Chowpatty it is just the men wondering. It is nice to be having peace and quiet at sunset."

"What? Don't they let women onto the beach there?" Her friend sounds suitably indignant.

"Oh yes, but there the women are too busy preparing food at that time. Also, it is not a very nice beach, very dirty. Still, we are grateful for small mercies in the city, isn't it?"

Most of the occupants of the expensive deck chairs are young Arabians, children of visiting sheikhs, the girls with their eyes heavily kohled, their faces at once sultry and sharp, never missing a trick. Self-consciously exquisite in traditional, yet stylish, attire, and dripping with gold, they hurl words from rubied mouths with graceful gesticulations, then become suddenly languorous, opiate almost, imitating some ancient harem aesthetic. They are gathered in single-gender groups, but indulge in much eye contact with those of the opposite sex. They notice nobody who is not of their culture; but when the deck chair attendant forces them to register his presence, they each present him with a one-hundred pound note.

"'Ow the bleedin' 'eck am I supposed to change *this*?" he cries perfunctorily, his hands sticky with greed.

"Keep the change." They brush him away like a fly. He stuffs the fistful of notes in his apron pocket, and ambles off. Something tells me this is not an unusual occurrence.

There are also many Indians, Pakistanis, and a few London office girls using his facilities, the latter looking red and gossiping about that total bitch in reception, or lying with their heads clamped between Walkman headphones, toes wriggling in time to some tinny rhythm, a pair of shades balanced on a peeling nose.

I weave between them, catching a whiff of suncream here, Chanel there, until I come to a brightly haloed trio of what could well be princesses. Certainly, the look of disdain on their faces suggests some lofty status. I offer them a reading. They consent.

I sit on the grass at their gold-sandaled feet, and attempt not to feel servile. However, it is blatantly obvious that they feel this is where I belong.

"Tell me who I will marry," says the first. "Will he be powerful? Will he be rich?"

This, I soon discover, is all that any of them wishes to know. They are not interested in any other angle of their own lives; they define themselves entirely according to a future husband's status. I begin to feel sorry for them.

"You will be wealthy but unhappy," I tell the first, rather brutally, but I figure it serves her right. However, she looks ecstatic.

"How wealthy? Richer than her?" She points to her friend.

I gather the cards up in as dignified a manner as I can manage, though I feel that I am quite literally groveling, reshuffle them, and hand them to the second friend. She looks rather perturbed at having to touch them, but her curiosity prevails.

All three stare at me as I spread the cards on the black silk cloth.

"We need to know who will be richer," the first one reminds me, presumably in case I had lost track of this amidst all the other issues being raised. "Of the three of us, who will make the best marriage?"

"I would have to do you each a reading to tell you that. So far," I nod toward the first one, "You're the best off materially, but your friend here will be happier in her life."

The friend looks furious.

"And mine now," urges the third.

We repeat the process, and the same result ensues.

"But who of the two of *us* then will be richer?"

The first one has opted out now, smugly withdrawing her attention to superior matters, but the other two need to establish the pecking order of their own relationship. I realise I have the power to really mess them up with this one.

However, I do not wish to accumulate bad karma in my life over such an irrelevant matter. I tell them that they will be equally rich, and equally happy.

So absorbed have I been by the ins and outs of their financial lives, that I have barely noticed the large crowd gathering behind me. When I turn in response to a request for a reading, I find that several deck chairs have been moved to allow thirty or forty people to stand over me.

I am, in fact, entirely surrounded.

A very attractive, smart, black couple are at the head of the throng. The man, in his mid-thirties, takes a step toward me.

"See how she wears the sign of Shaitan!" he begins, pointing at the pentacle I wear about my neck. "She is in league with the Djinns!"

He nods at the Arabian girls I have just read for, and, ignoring me, addresses them.

"You should not have allowed this fortune-teller to work for you. It is against the Holy Law," he tells them.

"I know that," replies the older. "But we did not allow ourselves to be contaminated by her. It was amusement only."

"This girl is under evil influences," he continues, and, turning to me, "You must repent."

Infuriated, I tell him that I have nothing to repent of. Needless to say, this does not placate him. His wife looks adoringly on.

"You must go the mosque and pray four times daily for your soul! If you will not, I will do it for you."

"Fine. You do it for me then. No disrespect to your religion, but I have my own beliefs, and—"

"There is only one true religion. What you are doing defiles the Holy Law. You are nothing and you will go back to nothing, while the believers will be honoured and Allah will be revered across the earth."

The crowd stirs with emotion. Spirals of powerful dark energy become visible above their heads. They are beginning to lose their humanity.

"Well, anyway, I must be getting on now . . ."

I attempt to depart. The throng packs closer. I feel like a medieval witch, caught mid-sabbat.

"Tell me that you will pray for redemption!" he demands.

"I always do," I say frankly, "but to my own gods, not yours."

Bad move. A murmur of disapproval ripples through the audience.

"And who do you pray to?" he probes.

Then I really mess it up. This is England in the 1990s, I am thinking to myself, conveniently forgetting Salman Rushdie and his fatwa. Still, before I have finished saying it, I know that I am making a dire diplomatic mistake. "If you must know, I pray to the Goddess."

Most of the air in the vicinity is sharply inhaled.

"You hear that? She prays to the triple-horned goddess: this woman truly is in league with the Djinns!"

I have the fear. They are so intent on me that I can see nothing but a hundred eyes glaring at me, attached to faces righteously murderous. As with gurus, a religious belief can justify anything. I know that, were I in Pakistan at this moment, I would be stoned to death.

"And now I am going to leave, if you'll excuse me." I wait for them to move. They stay put.

I look around for a policeman, or even another infidel, but none is to hand. Growing desperate, I begin to push past them.

They let me through, reluctantly, though I am strongly aware that, in another time or another place, they would not have been so lenient.

Their spokesman yells after me. "I will pray for your soul! Four times daily!"

I decide my best policy is probably to keep my mouth shut.

My primeval terror transmutes into a strong desire for brandy and coke. It is not until I arrive at the refuge of the Ship Inn, that I realise I forgot to charge the three outwardly beautiful, inwardly ugly princesses.

I decide I would rather not be defiled by their ill-gained wealth. So much for their haloes. How much injustice is there in their bank accounts? Quite a bit, I shouldn't wonder.

Dear Goddess, I know this is a superficial request, but please can I have a bath tonight? A creature comfort would help me on my way. There are so many baths in London—surely I can be effortlessly connected with one of them? A bit of hot water in

which my tired and grubby body can relax: I Will to have a bath.
So mote it Be.

M eanwhile, in Holland Park, it is business as usual.
"Jess, my friend—haven't seen you in ages," says Jesus in
pink flares. "How are you keeping?"

"Jesus!" squeaks Jess. "Well, you know. Been having girlfriend troubles."

As he speaks, he shies away from the aura of cleanliness sur-
rounding his companion, fearing it might interfere with the gravitational pull of his own atoms. His dirt structures are essential to
him, familiar.

Jesus' face is an icon of selfless concern. "Not more problems
with Kathryn, I hope?"

Jess looks sheepish. "She's still in hospital. I visit her all I can,
and she knows she's the only one. But there's this new girl, Lauren. I haven't told her about Kathryn yet, and I know that I
should."

"You must, Jess. If she is good, she will understand."

"She showers me with presents, Jesu. She loves me. How can I?"

Jesus cups Jess' pencil-thin hand in his own. Inside, Jess shud-
ders at the soapiness of his friend's skin, but he does not wish to
offend him. He hopes that it will not dislodge any of his little
friends; the ticks and mites and millipedes he communes with
when the acid is in him. He waits for the wise response. Jesus just
sits and nods.

"So, how are *you* doing?" asks Jess after a very long pause.
"Any converts yet?"

Jesus looks sad. "I'm still waiting. I don't suppose . . ."

"Sorry, mate. I'm an atheist."

Jesus nods; sagely, this time. "Sure. I understand. And I don't
want the Chosen Ones to be forced. You take your time, Jess.

Your mind is full of other things at the moment. Do you like my new trousers, by the way?"

Jess glances. "Aren't they the same ones you always wear?"

"No, no. They are quite different. I took them to St Paul's last week, and they haven't been the same since."

"Of course. Sorry mate. I'm just wrapped up in these women-troubles at the moment, does my head in, if you know what I mean."

Jesus gives him a long look.

"Not really. I'm of the other persuasion, I'm . . ." He checks himself and gulps his confession down, ". . . celibate."

Jess is too caught up in his own tangents to even notice.

Veronica approaches, smiles at them both with her eyes—she rarely uses her lips for such things—and settles herself on the grass beside them. The long light of evening comforts them all.

"My mother's driving me mad!" she announces. "It's taken me forty-eight hours to get out of the house. The woman never sleeps. It's all 'Veronica bring me this' and 'Veronica fetch me that.' She thinks it's the 1920s, and I'm her maid servant. She knew them all of course. Virginia, Ottoline, Edith. Never stops quoting Bertie Russell, either."

"Oh," says Jesus.

"If we'd moved, it might be different, but here she's surround-ed by memorabilia. All we ever get is third-generation Sitwell hangers-on visiting the house, and Oxford D.Phils rummaging amongst the family archives."

"Oh," says Jesus.

"I like your trousers, by the way."

Jesus beams. "See! Veronica noticed."

Jess is too busy trying to breathe himself in to reply. His scent-atoms are dissipating in the open air, and he feels that he might decompose altogether if he does not concentrate.

"Where's Lauren, Jess? I haven't seen her for a few days now. How's her Tarot reading going?"

Jess looks despondent. "The other day I caught her trying to sell herself to three Indian pimps. She didn't appreciate it when I stopped her either. I'm going to have to let her down, I think."

"The forces of evil are strong in the city," chirps Jesus. "That's why I escape to Glastonbury when I can. It's the heart-chakra of the world."

"Aren't chakras Buddhist?" Veronica asks, smoothing her long black silk skirt, a relic of her grandmother's, over her thin legs.

"Buddhist, Hindu, and New Age."

Jesus is perturbed by this mantra. "How long must I wait? The spirit is in me . . ."

Jesus leaps to his sandal-shod feet and adopts his usual pose atop an upturned crate; arms extended, face radiant.

"Children of Earth!" he cries. "I am here to bring you great news!"

A couple of American tourists stop to listen, amused by his quaint eccentricity, along with the ubiquitous Japanese man at the end of a camcorder. At this rate he'll achieve cult status in New York and Tokyo.

Jess and Veronica sit in companionable silence, letting the melodies of their friend's voice drift them into euphoria.

The Tube, which in my younger days used to scare me with claustrophobia and fear of fire, is becoming one of my favourite places to sit and relax. In its comfy seats I can daydream with impunity, knowing that I am traveling and therefore doing something useful, and enjoy the safe obscurity of being in a tunnel in the earth, a chthonic hideaway so unlike the Hades I knew above ground.

I enjoy studying people. Like a Gypsy admiring her crystal and silver, I hoard the details of their variety in this transitory subterranean treasure-trove of human idiosyncrasy. Three weeks of endless Tarot readings have trained me to talk deeply with all sorts of strangers, and I have developed an instantly communicative quality that is unusual in the underground environment. The other passengers seem to sense it, and I have had some wonderful conversations between Marble Arch and the backyard in which we are still staying because Jess is too busy hiding from imaginary assailants to find us somewhere else.

One day I meet an actor from my favourite soap opera, *Brookside*. I am thrilled about this because, prior to Ron, I was a regular viewer, and, even better, the actor himself is a very nice man. He asks me about the septogram and pentagram I still wear around my neck, and I explain a little about Wicca, Qabalah, and the like. He is very courteous and interested. For five more stops we talk about Robert Graves' *White Goddess*, and whether the author's motives were primarily spiritual or academic. Then he alights, glowing with recognition, and I resolve to buy all the old *Brookside* videos I can, when I have made my fortune.

Another man boards the train and sits down opposite me. He is drunk; not unusual on the late service; probably a waiter going home . . . tall and thin with a big nose and a slippery smile. About my own age. Spanish?

"*Parlez-vous Francais?*" he calls over to me.

"Not very well," I reply, thinking longingly of hot water.

"Are you liking some wine? Do you like to go for a little conversation? You like to come 'ome with me, yes?"

"What for?"

"We are going to ze gardens and we are drinking ze wine, yes? It is so 'ot, first we are having ze bath, oui?"

"*D'accord!*" That's settled it. "But I'd like to take the bath on my own, yes?"

He looks at me as if I am crazy.

"Of course," he hisses.

He is a French Algerian with a name I cannot get my head, never mind my tongue, around. He lives in a shockingly small rented room in a family house, with pink and white candy-stripe wallpaper and three black and white postcards stuck to the wardrobe. He is indeed a waiter, and he explains that this box is the best he can afford, as he sends most of his wage to his family each week. A copy of Milan Kundera's *The Unbearable Lightness of Being* is lying splayed out on his bedside table. I am surprised.

"I like to read," he explains. "All sorts of sings. It is important to 'ave knowledge. To me, life is an adventure, and I believe in 'to live and let live.' I 'ate ze racists and ze bigotts. You agree, yes?"

I am beginning to warm to him now, inspired by the wine and the conversation. Soon I suggest that *je me lave*.

The bath is glorious. The water, the heat, the bubbles are sensual and soporific. A profusion of brown scum bears testament to its effectiveness. Smiling, I sluice it away. The last traces of Ron disappear down the plug hole.

Afterwards, I curl up on the French Algerian humanist's bed, and doze off pleasantly.

Suddenly I am a Druidic virgin cast into a pit of snakes for divination. They are trying to get at my intestines. They are writhing all over me, hissing and licking and squirming. Every time I push them away, they return, efforts redoubled.

Then one of them is in my mouth, forcing its way down my throat.

I awake bug-eyed, to find him kissing me ferociously. The softness of sleep keeps on calling me back, and I spit him out, push him away, push him away, feeling cruel. "Please, please," he begs.

"No, no," I retaliate, moving with alacrity onto the floor.

I am left in peace until 7 AM, when a little girl comes in and wakes us up. He shoos her out again, and sharply tells me to leave. He refuses to meet my eye, and hardly speaks another word.

"Thanks for the bath," I say at the door, smiling genuinely. "It was lovely. And the chat. Au revoir."

As I head back to my patch in Hyde Park, I hear the door slam behind me. The bath has left me buoyant; I feel wonderful. Good enough, in fact, to ring my stepmother at last.

"Lauren! Where on *earth* have you been?" she screams down the receiver. "That horrible Ron rang us about a week ago, and told us that you'd gone missing. We were on the verge of calling the police."

I feel sick and faint. His name, and hearing about his actions, has reopened the fissure in my mind which leads to Hades. The dewberry-thick fumes are almost visible.

"He rings us twice a day," she continues. Her voice is a rap on the psychological knuckles. "You had better have a jolly good excuse for all of this, young lady."

My confidence abandons me completely. It is as much as I can manage to tell her that I'm all right, and not to worry. She yells. By some miracle, I have passed my Degree, but it is not with the First predicted by my tutors, and her wrath is intense. She tells me my father does not wish to speak with me.

I allow her to vent their spleen, leaning against the red phone box wall for support. Terror invades me. I apologise, say goodbye, and burst into uncontrollable tears.

I am incapacitated.

I sit at Marble Arch and talk with the buskers, but my mind is far away, and I feel full of dread. Even their super frisky dogs, Zero and Bypass, cannot cheer me up today. My situation seems bleak and perverse. Ron, the Emperor crossed, is insurmountable again.

"Are you on smack, Angel?" asks David, one of the buskers, who looks like Johnny Thunders and is holding my hand. He always calls me Angel or Angie, for some reason. He strokes my cheek in a chaste, paternal manner, and for a moment, concern settles on his normally debauched visage. "It's just that I've noticed you sniffing, Angie," he says.

"Just a cold," I say truthfully, though it must indeed seem strange in this sweltering heat. The chink in my psychic armour caused by the telephonic "reality-check" is letting in bacteria, I reflect. I need some psychological antibodies, and am glad to be here, chatting with people who do not know me. There is strength in anonymity, I have found. A whole wardrobe of personae at my disposal, and nobody to accuse me of putting on a show. "*You* are though, aren't you?"

"My girlfriend died in my arms, Angel. I really loved her. I'm telling you babe, I'll never love again like that. You're a little runaway, ain't ya? Everybody says it's just a cold. Ere, Cliff, toss us a can will ya?"

They have a twelve-pack in a big bag of ice hanging from a nearby tree, dripping on alarmed passersby.

"Cliff spends all our effing money on ice, and filters for his fish tank," rambles David, stroking my hair with one hand and smoking a roll-up with the other. "We'll effing starve, but at least the effing fish'll be able to breathe."

"One! I only bought one!" retorts the younger, shaggy blond Cliff, slightly embarrassed.

"For fifty-five quid! That's more than I earn in a effing week!"

"Lauren, you look like a lady of refined tastes," says Cliff in his broad Cockney accent. "How'd you like to buy one of these rings, at a specially reduced rate?"

He shows me his wares. Silver snakes with moonstones in their heads, Celtic designs, pentacles.

"Sorry, Cliff, I'm in no position to buy jewelry at the moment."

"Yeah, stupid, ain't you noticed she's been wearing those clothes for at least three weeks?" slurs David, sending gusts of beery breath into my face. "She don't waste money on luxuries, do ya, darlin'?"

"I can't."

I feel desolate. They sense it, and offer me a beer. I loathe the stuff, but accept with gratitude.

We end up in Marble Arch Tube station, they playing *Knocking at Heaven's Door*, and I "bottling": shaking the hat up and down.

"Just smile at the business men, Angel," David tells me, and I do, radiantly. The beer helps. We make £32 in three-quarters of an hour.

"It's 'coz she's a girl," says Bozo, the usual bottler.

"It's 'coz she effing *smiles*!" retorts David, now staggering from foot to foot and slurring all the lyrics.

£20 later, and David is clearly past his best. He wants to dedicate every song, or rather, every round of *Knocking at Heaven's Door*, to his dear departed: his eulogies, though sincere, are beginning to scare children and the elderly.

The Rastafarian ticket inspector is giving us the hairy eyeball, and the suburb-bound, low-level businessmen are starting to exhibit distaste instead of philanthropy. (High-level ones, as everybody who has ever been lost in the metropolis knows, are a no-hope area for the needy. Practised *Big Issue* sellers try to avoid being allotted the city, the most lucrative part of London, for this reason.)

Eventually we support David up the stairs and out of the station, back to our usual benches.

Cliff is so pleased with the day's takings that he gives me one of the rings as well as my cut of the cash.

Some people say the moonstone is unlucky, but I like these guys and refuse to believe it. I read Cliff's Tarot while David lies with his head in my lap. He tells me why he calls me Angel—because he sees light and life in me, apparently.

"I wanna get into your aura, Angie," he says. Well, it certainly makes a change from the usual. "It heals me, it helps me to see her."

As I sit with the David in my aura, I calculate how much money I have accrued, latterly with their help.

With a shock, I realise that I now have enough to put down a deposit on a bedsit.

I opt for a tiny room in North London. It is the first place I see, but the Tarot agree, I should take it. Within one week, I have begun a new incarnation as café assistant, a regular nine to five.

On my first free weekend, I return to an autumnal Holland Park, where I am greeted by Veronica. She tells me, with an intelligent smile, that Jess has asked her (and Jesus) to tell me it's over, because he has a girlfriend already. I smile back, buy her lunch, and read her Tarot yet again. She is still in the same predicament she was when I arrived in the city—thwarted by her mother, the Empress reversed—but I think I can sense a release in the distance.

"It may just be that you decide to leave home," I explain. "Hey, why don't you come to Highgate with me?"

She smiles wistfully at the thought, but I realise, reluctantly, that she cannot extricate herself so easily from her Karma. Veronica has her own abyss to cross.

I leave £20 with her for Jess, and say that I'll be back again soon. However, I never am. Life takes off for me in my new abode, but that's another story.

The Fates mete and dole my elongated future with a generous hand. A year in the café, a year working in a pharmacy, and then I will start at Malynowsky's.

Karma-Burner

Oxford at Easter is a delight indeed. Each college has its own beautifully tended precinct in which any remaining students, fellows, and their friends can sit regenerating their mental and physical bodies courtesy of Apollo's laserfingers, casually tracing time by the chapel bells. The Botanical and University Gardens are full of germinal variety, the magnificent trees that grace the city blooming fresh shade across the lawns, the river misty in the morning and at night, heralding clear skies. In a good year, the narrow stone streets emanate heat as well as history.

On one such Friday, a week before Easter, I was sitting at the till in Malynowsky's, the door propped open to encourage passing sylphs to circulate the breathless shop. We were quite busy, the surprise heatwave having brought the tourists and locals into town to enjoy the cafes, riverside walks, and gardens which characterise the city. Most of the crowd were clad in minimal vestments, with extra freckles and reddened shoulders on display. One, however, was not.

I noticed him initially, through the least warped window, because of his swaying walk, feet pointing inwards. It was the gait of a shy three-year-old, and contrasted completely with his attire, which was formal in the extreme. A slate-grey suit of outmoded cut, a shirt stiff with starch, and yes, as he grew nearer—for the man was staggering into the shop—I detected an actual old school tie. My favourite cousin boarded at Eton, and I would recognise that crest anywhere.

"Good morning, Madam," he began, displaying the pedantic upper-crust English accent typical of the well-bred luminary.

He attempted to bring his body to a halt as he reached the till, but its momentum refused to allow it. He jolted right over the desk, then pulled himself back, giving the impression of a mechanical rag-doll. This physical awkwardness contrasted completely with the certainty of his speech, and with the poker-back, which he now struggled to maintain. His shoulders collapsed naturally into a geriatric hunch. I detected another of Oxford's dysfunctional academics.

"Um, I mean 'afternoon.' Yes, of course, how ridiculous of me. It is afternoon, is it not, Madam? Well, strictly speaking it is, anyway. Though, in the words of Plotinus, of whom I am rather fond—and are you, if I might venture to ask?"

With a start, I realised that he was actually waiting for an answer. As politely as I could manage in my bemusement, I informed the balding patch on his head, which was pointing at me as he gazed down at his shuffling feet, that I had never read any. His swaying was beginning to make me vicariously seasick. I could feel his consciousness tilting with every new move and perception.

He was clutching an envelope in his hands, and I guessed he was here to enquire after the job we had advertised following Eurydice's death. An impecunious academic?

He began to quote the previously announced Plotinus, something about Being and Non-Being, Time and Eternity, but I was unable to follow his fervid monologue, and gazed instead at the elegant hands in which the envelope was becoming ever more crumpled. Then, whilst his meanings claused and subclaused themselves to death, I marvelled at the sartorial oddity of his person—all of the clothes, I could now see, were grubby and ill fitting—and at his face.

This was dominated by a dome-like forehead on which bright auburn hair receded, and had been cut into a wisp of a fringe by, I imagined, his own shaky hand. The forehead was indelibly etched, in contrast to the full cheeks, so that he carried the air of one very old and very young simultaneously. Indeed, his whole person conveyed this paradox, with the cerebral overdevelopment and the physical ineptitude both *in extremis*. The disproportionate dome faded into a gentle full moon face, bisected by an inelegant nose and a thin mouth, naturally downturned in repose.

The overall impression was that of Munch-like elongation of the head, and the squeezing of the body into oblivion. His eyes, of watery blue, were unquestionably sad, but in the cause of Classics, lit by a doctrinaire glow. This was accompanied by the emission, on syllables of immaculate elocution, of vapours of almost pure alcohol.

A characteristic shuffle on the staircase, and Mr. Malynowsky emerged at the back of the shop. I gave him a smile and a nod, causing our Plotinus lover to halt his monologue midsentence and turn nervously toward the object of my attentions.

"Sir!" he cried, rapidly adjusting his body as if just caught smoking in the dorm. "Sir!"

Were they friends, suddenly reunited, I wondered?

Mr. Malynowsky processed down the shop with habitual dignity, his gaze fixed on the man's strange visage. Bad eyesight, or lack of recognition?

"Good afternoon," resonated the mage. The inflexion in his tone suggested that the visitor might give a clue as to the enthusiasm of the greeting.

The man gave a strangled yelp which was presumably a laugh. "Ah, so it *is* afternoon, Madam," he said to me, as if we had been debating the fact for the last half hour. Which, perhaps, he had.

His body was racked with uncertainty. I feared he might keel over with the strain of addressing two people, at opposite cardinal points, at the same time. As with Magwitch, I was tempted to offer him my chair. Instead, Mr. Malynowsky placed himself solidly at my side.

"How may we help you today?" he asked with that wonderfully grounding quality I have so grown to appreciate in this weirdo magnet of a shop.

The man tilted back on his heels, and opened his drooping mouth with an oratorical intake of breath.

"Sir," he began. "I have long enjoyed visiting this fine establishment, and, indeed, buying your wonderful books. I could not help but notice the recent appearance of an advertisement for staff in your window. I feel that the combination of business and scholarship will suit me—please, do take my Curriculum Vitae, though I am quite sure that your present staff are qualified well beyond my own meagre standards—D.Phils are ten-a-penny these days—and that, as one of Oxford's many disenfranchised classicists, antiquarian bookselling is my most desirable prospect. I wish to gain your support and suffrage in this cause."

He looked at me, confusing me even more. I felt deeply sorry for this thin, stressed academic, but embarrassed that he should be appealing to me rather than to the owner of the business. He soon explained his attentions.

"I believe that, in a business such as this, there is always some profitable task to undertake, for however short a duration, and I would certainly take pleasure in whatever it might turn out to be. I feel sure that this good lady has much to teach me about classics and antiquarian books."

I blushed. It was already obvious this man had lived most of his life for the subject, and was aware of possessing a far greater fund of knowledge than my own. Yet his oriental courtesy prevented me from retaliating.

Mr. Malynowsky's face dimmed a little.

"Yes, my staff are excellent, I could not ask for better!" he announced, causing the etiolated man to shudder with a disingenuous smile.

"Indeed," he conjoined. "We were just having a most fascinating conversation about Plotinus, were we not, Madam? The depth of knowledge evident in your staff incessantly impresses me. Perhaps you might take a look at my own qualifications, and mull them over *a votre plaisance?*"

Mr. Malynowsky acquiesced, and both of us were treated to the elaborate departure of what turned out to be Dr. Simon Read. This took the best part of five minutes, and involved much limp hand-shaking and nodding on his part, and much swerving to avoid the alcohol reek on ours. The coarseness of his exhalations provided a sharp contrast to the refinement of his exclamations. I was fascinated.

As soon as he had left, I turned to my favourite touchstone.

"Do you know him?" I asked tentatively.

Mr. Malynowsky gave me a fond smile. "I do not know him, my dear, but I know of him. He visited us regularly when he was an undergraduate, and his knowledge of antiquarian books is unrivalled in Oxford. He used to collect Elzevirs and any fine classics I managed to procure. He was a brilliant scholar. He took all of the University prizes and scholarships in his field, when he was young."

"That must have been a while ago," I murmured, thinking of the thin, pale visage and scant auburn hair. And those clothes.

"On the contrary," replied Mr. Malynowsky, opening the envelope delivered with such ritual. "If I am not mistaken—indeed, I am not—he was born in 1968, just one year before you!"

He flourished the printed date of birth before me. I was suitably astonished. He had seemed middle-aged.

"Hmmm, born in May," he mused. "I see that the Sun, Venus, and Jupiter were all in Gemini. That, you will recall, relates to Hod, and the 17th Path, Zayin, the Sword. It also relates to the 12th Path—Beth, the House, and the Magus."

I looked at him, rather nonplussed. I can concentrate on Qabalah when the references are before me, but I'm useless on the spot. My boss, however, has it all readily available in his cerebral filing-cabinet.

"He seemed rather odd to me," I ventured.

Mr. Malynowsky snorted with glee. "Yes, I rather think he would. What did he make you think of?"

I reflected, enjoying myself. It is times like these that make my job worthwhile.

"Well, he's overdeveloped academically, and underdeveloped psychologically."

Mr. Malynowsky's lips pursed slightly as he gave me a concentrated violet stare from beneath ancient eyebrows. "Well, my dear, Joe Bloggs could have told me that! What do you perceive when you focus on him from a personal stance? Place him in your mind's eye. Take a look at his aura. Think how it interacted with your own. And now cast your mind back a little . . ."

I did as I was told. Tuning in, I perceived first the astral layers of the shop—and with these, the legions of Beths. They, too, seemed unattracted.

"Not as nice as Anna," they whispered. "Something hard and stern about him—false light."

"False light," I muttered. Luckily, there was nobody else in the upstairs part of the shop at this point. Having said that, I'm sure at least some of our regulars come in specifically to enjoy the continual psychodrama of the place. But Mr. Malynowsky is discreet.

"For a Gemini, ruled by Hod, what would that indicate?" he prompted.

"Well, let me think." I was getting onto the right wavelength now. I was recalling my innate knowledge—very difficult when getting on with daily life. I could sense Mr. Malynowsky sending me rays of light to help. Lasers, to aid retrieval. I wished I could do it naturally, as he did. I allowed them to penetrate my personal Akashic Records, feeling trancey. I had become accustomed to these procedures now.

"A major theme for those born with the sun in Gemini is that of duality—the division of time, as by Castor and Pollux, between the celestial and the mundane. Language and communication are also paramount—but—is that it? The tendency to become embroiled with the finer points of language, amusing word plays, etc., rather than the actual communication of thought?"

Mr. Malynowsky nodded encouragingly. "And taken to its extreme, that would mean—?"

"Empty rhetoric. Agility of mind hampered by a love of form."

"Good," he said. "The cure for a Gemini usually lies in the imagination, not the brain. Thus, 'false light,' as you put it, would infer—?"

"Misapplied intelligence. Illumination that seems irrefutable, but is based on fundamental inaccuracies. And the acceptance of doctrine over individual analysis."

"Now, Kala," he said, very seriously. "I would like your personal impressions of Dr. Read. Imagine him standing before you." His tone was lulling, though not hypnotic in the popular sense of the word. With customers such as Aristo working on us, I had learned to discriminate between the facilitation of free thought and its manipulation.

I allowed my mind to explore the essence of Dr. Read as I had just encountered him. I assimilated the obvious, then moved into his third-eye area. His aura began to glow in my mind's eye.

"So brilliant!" I exclaimed, somewhat smitten. I have always been a sucker for strong, disciplined personalities.

"What language does he think in?" asked my mentor suddenly.

It came to my mind instantly. There was no doubt about it.

"Latin," I announced.

"Bravo! And if we had explored the two breast pockets of that disgraceful jacket, we would have discovered a text of selected Latin literature in one, and its twin in Greek in the other."

"Is this some kind of previous incarnation thing?" I asked, though I barely understood what it might imply. I did not know the man, after all.

The owner of the Edwardian Stationery Shop next door, a neat woman characterised by a perpetual two-piece and pearls, trotted in for, she hoped, some change.

"I shall put the kettle on," whispered my boss as I rooted around for two fives and ten ones.

"I see you were visited by that drunkard earlier," she smiled con-spiratorially at me. "He came into our place for an envelope—I've never seen so much mess! Managed to drop most of the envelopes on the floor, digging one out that would fit his CV. He said he was applying for the post of Antiquarian Manager or something."

I laughed. The actual advertisement said "Part-time Book-shop Assistant."

"I think he'd spent most of the day at the Oxford Union Bar, by the looks of him," she hissed with the cruel satisfaction of a non-academic.

I handed the change over with a grin, but my thoughts were far from cheerful. If I analysed it properly, my heart had gone out to this inept man, whomever he might be.

Our neighbour exited, leaving me musing while Mr. Maly-nowsky clattered about with teaspoons and mugs in our atom of a back room.

Why had I felt empathy for him? After all, he was trying to oust me from my job with his backhanded compliments.

Involuntarily, an image arose in my mind. He was standing be-fore me in a white tunic, and he emanated all the power of the realm. Which realm?

The Roman Empire, of course.

Who, then, was I? I looked down at myself.

A neat, clean tunic, but cast in the dour colours of the slave.

Surely not? My imagination was running away with me now. I coughed, to bring myself down to earth.

Outside the window, the crowds were growing thinner, but they were real. This image in my head—which grew stronger even as I refuted it—seemed crazy. In some ways, it was too obvious. I must have been imagining it because, to certain academics in this city, I am indeed a slave. A vendor of books, not even their acquirer. That Plotinus must have gone to my head.

Mr. Malynowsky brought me my drink.

"Nice to be served, is it not?" he asked mischievously. I watched his strong grey back recede into the kitchen to collect his own, which of course must brew for as long as possible, wondering at the knowledge he exhibited so gradually. If it were me, I'd probably blow it in a garble.

"Okay," I said on his return, "I had an image of Dr. Read as some sort of Roman authoritarian, and myself as a slave. But that seems terribly twee*—"

"Hah! Twee was far from what it would have seemed at the time! Clichés exist because they are frequently encountered experiences. We are not dealing with the 'original' here, my dear, except in the sense that the experiences described are rudimentary. We in the occult are dealing with the Archetypal."

"But surely that refers to common patterns of consciousness, not individual experiences?" I asked, sipping the Malynowsky brew with gratitude. I was tired, I realised.

"It means both, Kala. Life is just a pattern of shadows thrown by astral and spiritual solids—true Realities. But we come here, and in the necessary amnesia of birth, we forget. Our classicist has not forgotten—his soul yearns to bask in the glory of its former referents. However, owing to . . . certain acts perpetrated in his time of power, he has been debilitated."

I looked at the magickian, supping on his energy and wisdom as much as on the tea. The more I dwelt on Dr. Read, the more exhausted I found myself. His very existence felt like seeping wheals on my astral body.

"We are going to employ him," announced my boss.

I nearly choked. Truly. I gave him a horrified stare, visions of public humiliation coursing through my mind.

---

* Quaint.

"No!" I cried, for the first time ever, to my beloved boss. *He'll crucify me*, I wanted to say, but I resisted. Mr. Malynowsky detests melodrama, as you know.

Instead, I stared fiercely at the mahogany desk. I could see a line carved by Eurydice when she was in fear for Orpheus. She had dug her little mother-of-pearl penknife right into the beautiful wood. Now, I felt, Mr. Malynowsky was allowing more danger into the shop. I could not qualify my sentiment, but it was there, strong and black. Bitter thoughts rose in my mind about our boss not protecting Eurydice, though I knew all the arguments about spiritual progression. I went into self-defence mode at the mere thought.

"I am not happy with that," I stated.

"I have registered your dissent, Kala," said my boss. "But Simon starts on Monday."

My heart sank. I considered leaving.

"He was drunk," I stated baldly. "You want alcoholic staff?"

Mr. Malynowsky gave me a wry look, and returned the mugs to the kitchen without further comment. I knew he had something up his sleeve, but was piqued despite this. Perhaps it was the idea of replacing Eurydice as much as anything.

I remained sullen until closing time, and bid my goodbye with a pointed omission of eye contact.

Nothing like this has ever happened between me and Mr. Malynowsky before. My weekend was wrecked before it had even begun.

I spent two days with friends in London. Oxford was annoying me; so many people in so small a space, it was impossible not to run into customers at every turn. Normally I enjoy this, but now I was reluctant to think about work. I had a sense of impending

Malynowsky trauma, which I attempted to assail by concentrating on extracurricular company, and by downing large quantities of wine. Still, the face of Dr. Read kept rising in my mind, the mouth belying a continuous, pale frustration, the eyes plaintive but emanating, from a far deeper source, a cruel arrogance.

The white tunic seemed to me now to represent a swathe of lies. Such strong reactions to a man I had barely met! I was reminded of Lauren's description of Ron, and how she had felt a similar excess of emotion on first reencountering him. I hoped and prayed that I was not due for a similar karma-burner.

"It's nice to be served," intoned a voice in my ear as I drifted off, disgracefully late, on Sunday night.

Its resonances played on my consciousness as I drifted up and up the planes. Somewhere in my mental wonderings, it occurred to me that perhaps I could help this man.

I awoke convinced that I could. He was being sent to me for healing. He was my project.

It was a nocturnal revelation of the sort that should have made me suspicious.

When I arrived at work on Monday, a little the worse for wear, it must be admitted, Mr. Malynowsky was nowhere to be seen. I let myself in and retreated to the back of the shop to make a much-needed coffee, where I discovered an envelope labeled "KALA." It informed me that Mr. Malynowsky had been called away to London by a sudden book-buying opportunity, and that I was in charge of the premises until he returned. When this might be was unspecified, but he rarely bothered to leave Oxford for less than a week.

As I rejuvenated the parched pigskin carpet, I wished I had not parted on bad terms with him on Friday. Replacing the watering can, I decided to ring Mr. Malynowsky on his mobile phone (we had insisted he get one after the incident with Aristo and Eurydice) to apologise. I got his answering service. Inwardly desultory, I left a chirpy message telling him not to worry, everything would be fine in his absence.

I think I actually believed it at the time.

Olivia breezed in and did her usual trick of transforming a library atmosphere into one of informative joviality. She excelled in cheerful conversations about classical music, and often inspired lively debate in the customers with her recordings. I always let her loose on the decrepit cassette player, knowing she would bring in something which sounded good, even on our clapped-out machine.

"Schubert today!" she announced with a smile, rummaging in the seemingly bottomless depths of her embroidered velvet bag. "William Primrose on viola, and Gregor Piatigorsky on cello!"

"Oh, wonderful!" came a voice from the back of the shop. A boyish-looking woman who had been lurking in Ancient Greek Magic stood up and smiled over at Olivia. "A rare but exquisite version!"

"Yes, isn't it! Let's put it on . . . there."

The high thin strains of the violin flooded the shop, the cello's rich timbres weaving in and out of their elaborate filigree. The customer's eyelids lowered in appreciation, her face honed into the rapture of a connoisseur of aural pleasure. Olivia inclined her head, nodding slightly. The sonorous, solemn Scherzo that followed reminded me of Eurydice, to the point of bringing tears to my eyes. The combination of this spell-binding music and the sudden uprush of emotion caused me to look for an excuse to extricate myself. I should go to the bank, before Dr. Read arrives.

"We have a new chap starting today," I announced over an anguished melody. "His name is—"

A stagger in the doorway.

"Simon!" cried our only customer.

"Good heavens, Augusta, what on earth are you doing here?"

The lanky academic lolloped into the shop, toes turned inward, knees all but knocking together. He was incredibly thin, I noticed.

"I'm visiting Father."

Ecstatic recognition animated our new employee's face.

"Ah, I had the pleasure of attending one of the professor's lectures at the Philological Society only the other day. Lucretian biographical myths—absolutely top-hole, of course."

I caught the edge of a gin-soaked breath as Dr. Read strained in a frenzy of politeness to shake Augusta's hand at the same time as greeting myself and Olivia. His confident speech was in complete contrast to his overwrought demeanour. I felt nervous just watching him.

"You're early!" was all I could manage.

He looked at me whilst still holding Augusta's hand.

"I have yet to hear of anyone being found lacking on the grounds of excessive enthusiasm for the job, Madam. But hours will in future be observed."

We all stared at him. I noticed a certain look on Augusta's face—something I would dwell on later. She removed her hand from his.

I attempted to alleviate the atmosphere. "Please, call me Kala! 'Madam' makes me sound ancient!"

I was smiling, but only with disbelief at his over-reaction. Olivia was looking from him to me and back again, flushed with surprise. She loathes impoliteness, especially of a University member. There could be no doubt that Dr. Read was of her own educational establishment. The accent and the old school tie spoke volumes.

"Olivia, this is our new assistant, Simon," I said, deliberately dropping the "Dr."

"Simon, Olivia."

Olivia's plump hand gripped Simon's skeletal digits.

"Is that Schubert's *Trio number three in B-Flat* I detect?" asked Simon, rapidly retrieving his forelimb.

"Indeed it is!"

"Marvellous!"

"Isn't it?" interjected Augusta. All three harkened to the Adagio. I wondered at what point it would be politic to remind my staff that they were here to work, not listen to quintets, but I suspected my motives in so doing. Apart from the occasional Requiem Mass, I am more a lover of modern music. Faith and the Muse, Dead Can Dance, Kate Bush, that kind of thing. I was possibly feeling ignorant and ignored.

"As it happens, I was listening to Schumann's *Dichterliebe* as I prepared for the day's industry, and was finding it rather difficult to cast from my mind—" began Simon.

"*In wondershcone Monat Mai!*" interjected Olivia. "Isn't it glorious! And almost in season!"

They all laughed. This was really beginning to annoy me now.

"Simon, if you'd like to follow me, I'll show you where you can put your jacket."

He was sporting a thick tweed today, far less seasonable than his music. Augusta's face fell.

"What, you're working *here*?"

Simon tilted back on his heels. "Indeed, I am. These charming—and intelligent, of course" (looking at me) "people have been good enough to employ me in—a modest role."

He said this in the same way that he had called his qualifications "meagre," giving the impression that his modesty was false. Now Augusta would assume he was Mr. Malynowsky's right-hand man, at the very least.

"How super for you to have such an expert to hand!" she proclaimed to me. In her eyes I saw that look again. What was it? Disbelief? Disdain?

I led our new recruit to the minuscule kitchen-toilet area, pointing out a hook for his jacket. He looked terrified.

"No, no, I shall keep my jacket on, if it's all the same, Madam!"

"Kala," I reminded him. "My name is Kala. And it's boiling out there . . ."

"No, no, Mad—Kala, I do apologise—I rather think it is not 'boiling.' That would indeed be uncomfortable! No, I am quite all right as I am, thank you."

There was no arguing with that tone. It denoted utter finality.

"Right, well, that's the kettle there—and the loo is just through the door," I said. At the mention of the latter facility, he gave a cough, embarrassed. "Anyway, if you're not going to hang your jacket up, no need to stay in here . . ."

The lanky man was leaning over the sink, staring into it. "Ah, I um, I spilled some sort of *substance* on my hands earlier—I'd hate to get it all over your wonderful books—might I just be permitted to wash them now?"

I was taken aback by the sudden switch from arrogance to humility, and smiled.

"Of course you may," I said. "I'm just off to the bank now, but Olivia will give you a tour of the top floor until I get back. I'll grab a bite to eat and see you in about an hour's time, Okay?" I added the final word in an attempt to gain eye contact. The fraught academic seemed hypnotised by the sink.

"Certainly, Madam," he said perfunctorily. I could tell that he was seriously distracted.

I returned a little early, concerned about leaving Olivia with our new recruit. To my surprise, she was sitting alone at the till.

"Where's Simon?" I asked.

Olivia looked awkward. She nodded toward the back room.

"He's in there," she whispered.

"What, again?"

"No—still. He hasn't emerged at all yet." I could tell this admission was difficult for Olivia. She hates anyone being in trouble.

I decided to knock before entering. He might be ill or something.

"On my way!" he replied, with the jollity of a child about to be smacked.

At first, when he emerged to our expectant faces, we could perceive nothing different about him. His hands were in his pockets, causing his tipsy perambulations to seem even more perilous.

"I *do* apologise—it took me rather longer than I had expected to get that wretched stuff off." As he said this, he instinctively pulled his hands out and held them before his eyes to scrutinise.

Olivia and myself both tried not to gasp. His thin white hands had been scrubbed raw. Streaks of blood defined his Fate and Health lines.

"Should I go and do some tidying up?" asked Olivia with alacrity, freeing her chair and ebbing towards the sections designated to her.

"Please."

I was suffering another strange surge of emotion. The sight of those tortured hands filled me with perplexed compassion. Again, I wanted to help this poor trapped soul.

"Is the goodly Mr. Malynowsky to join us today?" asked Simon, with shocking normality, scanning the shop for its proprietor.

"No, he's in London for a week," I informed him, regaining my equilibrium. "He's left me in charge. Do sit down. Then I can show you how the till works."

I felt in control now. I realised anew that, despite the elaborate displays of "top-hole" education, I was dealing with a frightened child. My tone adjusted accordingly. "It's not as difficult as it looks," I assured him. He was shaking.

I placed Simon in situ behind the counter and turned the till key to "Practise" mode.

"Right, let's imagine we're putting through a book at £9.99," I began. Simon stared at me.

"Ought we not to have the object before us, for reference's sake?" he vied.

I stared back. It was tempting to refuse, but it occurred to me that he was going to need all the help he could get. I decided to humour him.

"Sure."

I leapt up and fetched a book at £9.99 from the Greek Language section.

"Right, let's imagine a customer is buying this . . ."

"Ah! Abbott and Mansfield! A text we *all* have to master at some point!" he cried. "A relic of Classical Victoriana which might compliment the extraordinarily wordy American grammar of Mastronarde (you are, of course, familiar with the 'Introduction to Attic Greek,' learned by most of the inhabitants of the Rocky Mountains?)—if only as a quick source of reference!"

"Yes, it's priced at £9.99. So we just press the 9 key . . ."

All ten of Simon's long fingers, now pink, waggled above the keyboard. He was clearly unable to find the key.

"It's just there," I said.

"Of course." He aimed, and tapped it with pained gentility.

"And now we need another two . . ."

"A two? Surely, Madam, if the book is priced at £9.99 . . ."

"No, Simon, I mean we need another two nines."

Was Mr. Malynowsky winding me up here?

Dr. Read was staring intently at the keyboard. He swiveled his gaze to meet mine.

"I am unable to detect the wretched key," he admitted petulantly.

He was still drunk, of course. Amazed that my boss would allow such a buffoon to work here, I pointed it out again. He pressed it once.

"And again," I encouraged. "Just press the same key again, Simon."

He strained to relocate the key. When he tapped it, I almost felt like yelling "Bravo!"

"Right, and the book is then placed in a bag . . ." Simon began to search under the desk.

"No, not yet," I interjected. "So far, all we've done is type the price into the till. Now we need to register it, by pressing that key—" (I pointed to it) "—right there."

Simon pressed it with a victorious flourish. "And now, of course, the bag . . ."

"No!" I almost shouted. "Now, the customer hands over the money or card. Let's imagine it's a ten-pound note, to make it easier . . ."

By six o'clock, I was at the end of my tether, and Simon was still utterly unable to use "that dratted machine." Olivia had long since left, and I was aware of many of our regulars observing Simon and myself with bemusement. Some of them knew him, and evangelical conversations ensued about the Oxyrynchus Papyri, German grammar, and even Piers Plowman. He rose to his feet whenever a female entered the shop, and while talking, kept his hands thrust deep in his pockets as he tilted backward and forward on his heels. He was, I realised, a total freak. Genius and ineptitude defined him entirely. I was beginning to feel strangely protective.

At eleven o'clock the next morning, a bouquet of flowers walked in on a pair of pigeon-toed feet. A card landed on my desk, and a ruffled Simon emerged from behind the abundant blooms. The card was addressed to "The Kindest and Most Patient of Manageresses."

"Do open it," he encouraged.

Thank you for your help in teaching me a new profession, I read. This was followed by three lines in Greek and one in Latin, none of which I could translate.

"Thank you," I said uncertainly.

"I shall put these in water!" he announced, beginning to head for the back room.

"But you're not due in for another two hours!" I protested, recalling the strain he had inflicted on me the day before, but feeling rather mean for it.

"Oh, Mr. Malynowsky will hardly complain of *that!*" he proclaimed, vanishing into the back room and leaving an astringent trail of alcohol vapour behind him. I got up and opened the door. I heard him crashing about in the kitchen, and then the tap being switched on. I correctly deduced that I would not see him for a while.

Right, I thought as I sat at my desk. We have an alcoholic dysfunctional genius who exhibits some sort of obsessive compulsive
disorder. He is likely to be more of a hindrance to the business
than a help, so Mr. Malynowsky must have some other reason for
bringing him here. He was possibly a Roman senator or some
such in a previous life, and I was possibly his slave. He may have
done terrible things to me—that would be the obvious explanation—and he's here to atone.

But this glib explanation did not ring true, somehow. What
was it all about?

I rang Mr. Malynowsky, and got the answer-phone again.

That dratted machine, I found myself thinking.

That week was Herculean. I expended optimum effort at every
challenge, only to be greeted by a new dilemma at its resolve. I was frustrated, elated, and humiliated by turns. Some of
the customers present at our till-side trysts clearly thought I was
patronising a remarkably intelligent man—others looked at me
as if to say "If Mr. Malynowsky only knew who you had employed
in his absence . . ."

Simon's practical inability was staggering. He made coffee
with cold water (claiming to be unable to ascertain the correct
process of delivering electricity into the equipment provided),
and spiked his own with gin. I was forced out of exhausted sub-
mission to sip beverages on which granules floated in tiny pools
of dark brown. He destroyed Olivia's trusty classifications, moving every specimen on which his waggling fingers alighted to "a
more eye-catching position," that meaning into the wrong section, face-out. He used liquid paper to blot out prices he did not
agree with, and inked his own version over the top.

He still could not sell a book.

y desk groaned with flowers. At night, I returned home and pored over books on magick and Qabalah, seeking some explanation. I developed the themes delivered in seed form by Mr. Malynowsky, but was still unconvinced. I knew I had been set a task, but the code was proving difficult to crack.

I found myself obsessed with the protocol that obscured Simon's fundamental suffering. He was adept at concealment. Yet his problems were recognised—witness Augusta's strange look when she heard that he had been employed by us. I saw that combination of respect and disdain in many who engaged Simon in conversation. His drunkenness was one explanation; it is difficult to wholeheartedly admire a person who is swaying visibly, no matter how sound their analysis of the Byzantine translation of Euripides' *Orestes*. But there was more to it than this.

Where did he go at night? My attempts at drawing him into personal conversation had proved futile. He would always change the subject, claiming to lead a "terribly dull existence." And how had a high-flying scholar come to crave a job in a shop? It was obvious from his speech that he was a born teacher. And equally obvious that bookselling was far from his forte.

All of this time, I searched for clues in his demeanour and our interaction that might confirm (or render redundant) this concept of Master and Slave. And what were these "certain acts" Mr. Malynowsky had talked of, that had caused him to be so debilitated in this life? I was so busy concentrating on the mundane running of the shop, however—preventing Simon from keeling over into our glass cabinets, arresting his pen before it defaced another book, and checking for gin and vodka in the kitchen (I had poured two bottles down the sink, and now he kept them, I suspected, in his jacket pocket) that nothing spiritual seemed to be on the cards at all.

There was just one small incident of possible relevance, but I could not explain it. One day, when Simon was dithering about behind the desk, *La Boheme* blasting (he continually turned the most emotional operas up to the point that they lost all quality, and sat rapt and dewy-eyed, quoting French and Italian arias with drunken gusto), a tall thin man entered with a Greek manuscript. Simon fell on it, almost literally, with great interest. I wandered over to its owner, who looked a little alarmed, and introduced myself.

"I have a rather unique specimen here," he told me. "A rare Greek magickal text. Do take a look."

I peered over Simon's hunched shoulders, and my eyes fell on something I recognised instantly, but could not decipher. The emotional impact, however, was immense. Fear flooded into me. Simon began to give a detailed analysis of the contents, but when he looked up at me, his face was not his own. The eyes were full of power and cruelty. I reeled back, my heart thudding. It was the best I could do to stammer that I would contact the owner, Mr. Malynowsky, about it. I took the man's details with a spidery hand.

Simon reverted to his normal inebriated self as soon as the potential customer departed, but I did not. I felt scared of him. I trembled until five, letting Simon loose on the customers by allowing him to stay behind the till, while I tidied shelves in a welter of confused thoughts.

Who was he? Why had I reacted like that to the manuscript? What was he doing here now? Weakness, in the form of incomprehensible emotion, had invaded me. For the first time ever in my beloved bookshop, I felt truly vulnerable.

On Maundy Thursday, driven to distraction by these questions, I decided to follow him. It is not natural to me to stalk my staff, or anybody else for that matter, but it seemed the only way to glean any truth from the situation.

I tried to let him out early, following a six-hour stretch which was supposed to be only three (and three was all we were paying him for), but as usual, he insisted on remaining until "all the work was complete." This was painfully ironic, as I had to invent tasks for him to perform that would not involve him standing up or interfering with the books. I tried him on the filing system, but he protested with complex academic arguments at every turn, and the results were an incoherent mess. He would file things where he felt they ought to be rather than where they belonged, and wrote elaborate notes, many of these in Greek and Latin, on our papers.

I realise this sounds unbelievable. But it really did happen.

Equally difficult to credit, for me, is the fact that I left him in the street, walked away, hid in the entrance of the Turl Bar, and then followed him at a distance. His ludicrous gait was not difficult to discern among the upright citizens of the city that had emblazoned him with golden stars and then, for whatever reason, allowed him to crash.

He went directly to the Union Bar. Our neighbour was right, then.

I cannot go in, not being a member, so I lurked outside with the beggars, drunks, and traditionally dressed South American Indian buskers. I was not too worried about missing Simon—even among this crew, he was distinctive.

He emerged about an hour later, almost unable to walk. He lurched toward the nearest lamppost, and stood clinging to it as if his life depended on it. Tentatively, I approached him.

His watery blue eyes swam into mine, with no recognition, initially. His pupils were tiny. Then, as if he had received a body-blow, he lurched backward, the word "DARLING!" flying from his lips as he recognised me.

"Hello, Simon," I ventured.

"Darling! What on *earth* are you doing out at this ungodly hour?" he asked, slurring slightly despite the obvious adrenaline hit. It was only seven in the evening, and the streets were still light, though the skies had clouded over. A few drops were beginning to fall.

"I'm just on my way home," I lied. "What are you up to?"

"Why, I'm not 'up to' anything, Darling. Oh, Dear Heart, it's so wonderful to see you!"

His eyes filled with tears.

"You look like you could use some help getting home," I ventured. "And it's about to rain, I think. Shall I call you a taxi?"

"I should far rather be called 'Dr. Simon Read,' if it's all the same, Darling!"

"Please stop calling me 'Darling,'" I snapped, despite my charitable intentions. "It's almost as bad as 'Madam,' in a totally different way, of course. Now, Simon, I want you to concentrate. Where are you going?"

I had his home address in our files at the shop, but had never registered it.

"Going? Going? I am, um, I am on my way to my office. It's very close. I plan to do a little work on my analysis of Theocritos."

"And where exactly is home?" I cajoled, as he swiveled on the lamppost with an attempt at nonchalant *joie de vivre*. His legs entangled themselves, and I was forced to dive into the fray of skeletal limbs to prevent him from falling over entirely. He was as light as a girl.

"You're so thin!" I marveled.

"Ah, but not as lithe as you, nor yet so fragile."

Realising that I was not going to win with this one, I hailed a taxi and bundled him into it.

"Where to?" asked the driver brusquely.

Silence.

"Where to, Simon?" I insisted, as heavy cold patches started to land on my shoulders and head. The sky was now that luminous grey that heralds thunderstorms; the shops, cantering passersby, bins, and bus stops stood out in detail-enhancing light against the ponderous, darkening sky. He looked at me, his face a blear of dismay. His body swayed, even as he sat with his arms folded in his lap, as if protecting himself. I thought he was about to be sick, and began to move into the car in order to help him out.

"Sorry, I think he's forgotten where he lives," I admitted to the taxi driver.

"It's Dr. Read, innit?" replied the man. I looked at him, surprised. "I take him 'ome from 'ere all the time, love," he explained. "And more often than not in a worse state than this."

Simon's consciousness swam to the surface again. "Darling!" he cried, as if we had only just met after a protracted and yearning separation. "Oh, do forgive me," he continued, his eyes teary, and his hand grabbing my arm. It was surprisingly strong. He yanked at it, and in I tumbled.

"Alright, love?" checked the taxi driver.

"Please, just sit with me a while," whispered Dr. Read. He was looking very ill indeed.

"I think we should be getting you home," I repeated, looking with alarm at the taxi's meter, which was already at £4.20. I hoped he had some money left after his day's debauchery.

"Might you escort me home?" he asked at last.

Wondering whether this was the cue to the "help" I was sup-posed to be giving him, and deeply curious as to where he abided, I agreed.

"You *do* have the fare though, don't you?" I probed, aware that I only had a fiver on me.

"Good heavens, Darling, what do you think I am?" he asked, brandishing a wad of notes around which a spotted silk scarf was wrapped. "Some sort of penniless cad?"

I smiled, despite the taxi's motion causing his body to veer vi-olently in whatever direction we were turning, and to flop there in alcoholic flaccidity. At a sudden clap of thunder, he jolted himself round to look out of the window.

"About the heavens, I perceive, Zeus Brontaios—he of the thunderbolt, is plying his trade with assiduity! Only relentless rain to be seen, which does however have an advantage—name-ly, that it is beneficial to our gardens." He gave me an intent stare. "Darkness covers the Earth."

I stared back. The tone of the last statement was profoundly strange, yet familiar. It seemed to contain the "om" sound too—it had limitless spiritual connotations.

The taxi pulled up outside Holywell Cemetery.

"You live in *there?*" I said, more for my own amusement than anybody else's. The drunkard surprised me with an answer.

"I do not—no, I live in the rather more comfortable flats adja-cent to these premises—but one very dear to me does, indeed, inhabit these hallowed grounds."

"Eight pound twenny, mate," announced the taxi driver. Simon handed over a ten and struggled with the door.

"Wait, I'll do it," I commanded, leaping out of my side into the downpour. I could not bear to see those raw hands struggling like that.

I swung it open.

Dr. Read keeled over onto the pavement like a toy soldier, head first. I gasped in absolute horror, never having seen a grown man collapse like this before.

"I seem to have suffered some sort of gravitational mishap," he announced from the ground. I looked urgently at the taxi driver. He got out, glanced at Simon, and said, "Don't worry love. 'E's like this every night, just about. Ends up kipping in the graveyard more times than not, I shouldn't wonder."

"You couldn't give me a hand, could you?" I pleaded, unable to countenance the fact that this high-flying academic was lying in the street like a corpse. The rain was soaking him right through, too, and he did not look in good health even when dry and upright.

The cabbie agreed, clearly for my sake rather than Simon's.

"C'mon, let's get him in then."

The man picked Simon up as if he were fashioned of air, and pulled the Classicist along with his legs protruding, rigid and useless, and pigeon-feet scraping along the street. Simon took the opportunity to stick out his tongue to collect a little rain. Pretty dehydrated, I would imagine. I wondered what on earth his flatmates or partner, if he had one, would make of him in this state, though it sounded as if they might be used to it.

"Stop, please!" cried Simon suddenly. "Um, this young lady will have no desire to visit my humble abode! No, let us go instead to *The Magick Graveyard*, where life and death are intertwined . . ."

Thunder.

"Right, mate, you wanna go to the graveyard, you walk there yourself." The cabby, quite understandably I thought, stopped dead. Simon, to our surprise, tilted from the back of his feet, with a push against our driver, to the front, swayed forward perilously, repeated the motion in reverse, and came to rest upright. We could not help but be impressed.

The poor soaked taxi driver beat a hasty retreat, leaving us at the gate to the graveyard. My normally buoyant long hair was stuck to my face and head.

Luckily, I am a big fan of the gothic. Sitting in a cemetery in a thunderstorm with another ancient soul, however bizarre he might be, is pretty much my idea of heaven. We stumbled in the drenched gloaming to the bench just beyond Kenneth Graeham's headstone.

Clouds rolled across the sky like celestial cannonshot. Flashes of lightning illuminated the towers of rain which slid into silver sheets on stone slabs relating to don, curator, and philosopher. Chokmah splashed down on them all, bringing further wisdom to the materially disinherited. A thin wet hand landed on mine, and gripped it.

As I looked up at its owner, I saw the Tarot image of Judgement in my mind's eye.

The pummeling rain was digging into the earth, burrowing into the corpses, floating them to the surface and rejuvenating them. In an instant, I witnessed these long-dead rising up, rising up to Gabriel's trumpet, reborn out of the Darkness. Just like us.

"It has been so terribly long," wailed the man at my side. He was staring into my face with an intense affection, enveloping my aura with his own. It crossed the bounds of light and life, beaming out of his eyes from Kether, it seemed. He emanated pure and vibrant love. The scene bespoke redemption.

I was shaken, and began to withdraw my hand. But with that secret reserve of strength I had encountered earlier, he pulled me back.

"No, no, my darling—we must sit here whilst the rain washes me clean."

He let my hand drop, held his own in prayerful posture, and began to rub them, at first slowly, and then frantically in the cemetery downpour.

No prizes to Mr. Malynowsky's apprentice for guessing that this had something to do with those "certain acts" perpetrated in a former existence. But what were they?

The alcohol had dissolved the barriers of Dr. Read's normal consciousness. I wanted to ask him, directly, about his sins, but he was already so overwrought that it seemed dangerous to push him further.

"*Ask yourself.*"

The voice was transmitted to me on the unmistakable channel of Mr. Malynowsky's brain-radio. I felt him very close, and was instantly lulled and comforted.

Ask myself? Right.

I stared hard at the penitent academic, now rising to his feet and attempting to keep his balance as he held his face, mouth and body open to the storm. Zeus Brontaios continued to ply his trade with assiduity.

"*Who is he?*"

"Master," I found myself saying.

"Yes, my dear?"

Simon had turned to me as naturally as if I had called him by his first name. His look again shone with positive emotion. It was like a spell. He sat down beside me—gracefully. He turned to me with ease, and then, recalling himself, withdrew.

"Is it still there?"

"Is what still where?" I asked, even more taken aback now.

"The miasma, of course," he said miserably.

His body collapsed once again into the desolate form with which I had become familiar.

"I can see no—miasma," I said carefully.

"No, no, Madam, a miasma is not *visible*." Back to the old patronising Dr. Read. What could I do to draw him out?

"Yes, it is still there," I announced. "Urgh, it's disgusting!"

I had started this as a guise. However, as I said it, I really did begin to see a revolting mess of what looked like congealed blood all over his astral body. That old fear flooded into me, along with the image, very strong in my mind (and coming, no doubt, from Mr. Malynowsky) of a silver sword. It had an emerald in its handle and was shining with clean, clear energy. *The Energy of Justice*, I thought.

All about us, spirits were rising from their graves. They gathered around the blood-splattered man like a silent jury. They hemmed him in.

I took the sword with my astral body. The moment I grabbed it, the memories entered my brain with momentum so vivid that I was there again, entirely, serving my master with loving devotion, and receiving his affections in return, but strictly inhibited in their expression. I loved him, and he loved me, too, but his social standing and moral rectitude prevented him from having a relationship, or any "improper" interaction, with me.

He had, I recalled, been a senator in the time of Alexander. My master's house was one of the few in Rome in which servants were treated with consideration and respect. My master, a brilliant philosopher and politician, was groundbreakingly modern in his social outlook, and a mage beyond compare. He shone like a lamp in the darkness and brutality of those times.

I had once been a priestess in ancient Greece, which I remembered, and which my master deduced and told me, courtesy of his own studies. He had served as a priest of Apollo, I his Pythia. Our relationship had not, at this point, been chaste.

Born into slavery, I submitted myself to whatever karmic balancing acts were required of me for my previous life's iniquities.

The proximity of the one I loved, and my inability to touch him, tortured me. He was determined not to put a foot wrong this time. My master resolved to remain chaste throughout his senatorial existence. He submerged himself instead in politics and magick. The two were not so far removed from one another then as they are these days.

However, he took it too far. He became obsessed with finding the key to the nullifying of karma—he sought the essence of impunity in obscure scrolls, alchemical-style ritual, and complex codices. He became so absorbed in this that his soul withdrew from his outer life, gradually creating the impression of one unreachably stiff and formal. He neglected his body, rarely accepting the platters I brought, and drinking wine until he fell into bed at dawn. He burned so much laurel in the villa that even the cooks were becoming oracular. To me, it seemed as if he had canceled his affections, and I was desolate, though just as eager to please as I ever had been.

He became irascible. A couple of times I was reduced to tears by his unjust scoldings. He recognised their nature as soon as the bile had subsided, and overcompensated with apologies and elaborate politeness, sometimes in front of his colleagues and fellow politicians, which made him seem extremely liberal indeed.

"Aren't you lucky to have such a wise, progressive master?" I remembered one senator's wife saying to me. She thought she was being frightfully fashionable, addressing a slave on a personal level. I could see in her eyes a curious mixture of interest and revulsion.

I was envious of her. She was well versed in Greek culture and magick, and was able to discuss them with my master in public. He and I could talk of these things only in strict privacy, with no one, free or bonded, to overhear us.

The thunder continued to shake Holywell, causing more and more of its dead to rise up and surround us. One of these greeted Simon by his present name, and I realised this must be "the one dear to me" whom he had mentioned earlier. It was the wraith of a certain professor of Demotic Greek, who had trained Simon in ancient languages and magickal arts. He had become Simon's mentor, but all the knowledge he had passed on had fallen on barren ground. Simon's faculties as magus had been debilitated. Why?

As I watched mentor and enraptured student communicate across the Veil, Simon's face became young and earnest again. I recalled that expression on my master, and how serious he had become in his studies.

Then I remembered bringing him the flagon.

He was studying hard, scrutinising a rare and valuable text of Greek magick brought from the Library at Alexandria. He had been drinking the wine absently, and was rather the worse for it. As he turned to accept the refill, he bumped me. The flagon jolted, sending a tidal wave of wine into the air. It hung there, in ruby waves and droplets, for an eternity. It changed the course of thousands of years.

The ink swam out as the papyrus tolerated the wine for a moment, than drank it in until soggy.

My horror at that event would have been punishment enough. However, my master needed to vent his own gut-wrenching frustration.

He turned to me, his face transformed by cold and vicious anger. For a moment he simply looked, and then he rang his bell.

Two of the male slaves entered swiftly, on perceiving their particular summons.

"I accuse this woman of the wanton destruction of my property!" he announced. "Take her to the city guards, and have her imprisoned."

His pupils dilated, his eyes seemed to shrink in their sockets. Humanity had deserted him completely.

I knew precisely what this meant. It was common to my class. Imprisonment, and public death in the Coliseum. Two of the primary "outrages against human integrity" which my master and his friends professed to fight.

Had it all been wit and wordplay, after all?

My death was not an enjoyable one. It was public, and agonisingly slow. I was spared the animals at my master's request, and instead was flagellated to death. The audience considered this quite boring at the time, waiting as they were for the lions and wolves to come on in the next scene.

He was there. He witnessed it.

He was repentant, but too proud to go back on his statements.

Besides, with me out of the way, he could concentrate on his studies without distraction, and be free of the temptations which had so often kept him from valuable sleep.

I fast-forwarded myself to the present. Now, it was I who wielded the power. The sword seemed to be deflecting the rain. It was becoming physical. It weighed in my hand, and I liked the feel of it.

"Yes, the miasma is still there," I announced, a scintillating tingle of cruelty rising in my own soul. We all work in these cycles, of course. "I shall have to punish you for it."

He looked absolutely terrified, more Munch-like than one would imagine possible. On the sodden earth, in the company of the multitudinous dead, he got down on his knees, and begged forgiveness.

Without a moment's hesitation, I thrust the sword cleanly through his heart chakra.

On Good Friday, he did not appear at work. I was unsurprised. Mr. Malynowsky rang, to check that everything was okay. I mentioned that Simon had not turned up today, and the mage replied that no, he did not suspect that he had. There were lots of customers in the shop, hence, partly, our muted communication, but despite this, I was grateful for their company. Mr. Malynowsky never talked of occult matters over the telephone anyway, still suspecting the line to be bugged.

I dwelled on Simon obsessively all day.

I sent out lines of light to deduce his state of being. However, as they sought him out like sun-seeking tendrils, they found nothing but vacuous black.

Was he still lying in a heap in Holywell, I wondered? I had tried to pick him up, after I had thrust the sword into him and our audience had retreated satisfied to their tombs, but he was twice his normal weight with water, and I am no Amazon. He had collapsed in a drunken stupor, and lost all consciousness.

Should I have called an ambulance? The police? Should I have banged on the door to his flat and alerted his housemates as to his condition?

Part of me was thrilled to leave him there, I will admit it. It serves the stuck-up bastard right, I thought to myself. At least he's accustomed to it, by all accounts.

The other part of me was worried sick. Had I done the right thing with that astral sword? What if I had caused him further damage?

So I thought, as I tidied the Alchemy shelves and listened to *Carmen*, rather loudly, a hint of cruelty on my lips.

The Pillar of Mercy, the Pillar of Severity. Between them we descend, like a lightning flash, gathering components as we go, spiritual, mental, emotional, physical. Down and down into the heaviness of rebalance, redemption, and the chance to make fresh mistakes.

"You did what?" cried Mr. Malynowsky when he returned on Saturday. "You stabbed him and left him unconscious in the cemetery?"

The shop had been closed and locked prior to this revelation, thankfully. I could just imagine the faces of some of our regulars at that little conversation.

I gulped.

"But I thought you knew! 'Brain-radio' and all that . . ."

His consciousness bored into my third eye, watching the scene replay itself, exactly as it had seemed to me.

He softened a little.

"I see," he said. "Still, a visit to Holywell might be in order, don't you think?"

I almost burst into tears with relief.

We discovered his body behind the shrubs and thickets to the left of the cemetery. It was lying on the grave of his former teacher, Professor Nigel Stanton. It looked perfectly at home there. Especially as it was dead.

"Oh my God!"

I clasped my hands to my head and screamed, not because I find death upsetting in itself—and I knew, logically, that Simon would have welcomed it—but through shock at the role I had played in his physical demise. It would not be so easy to explain to the police, nor to my mundane conscience, why I had left him there.

Mr. Malynowsky leaned over the fresh corpse with a quizzical expression.

"No, there is no life in that vessel, that is for certain."

Had I done something wrong? Had I mishandled this opportunity, embroiling myself in further complex karmic entanglements in the future? I wanted to ask Mr. Malynowsky; I needed the comfort of his reason and guidance. My spirit reeled as if drunk. On blood rather than wine.

He gazed at the crumpled solar-plexus at his feet, and up. And up still further. Soon he was standing with his head entirely bent back. His throat was stretched in front of me, utterly vulnerable, I noticed with my newly murderous persona. I was suffering belated guilt.

His eyes were fixed into the depths of the cerulean. He cleared his throat, a necessary prerequisite to ritual for one so fond of tobacco.

"Jehovah Eloah Va Daath!" he intoned, very slowly. He repeated the phrase. I felt the ground tremble.

Again, that "om" sound, rumbling from the depths of another dimension.

"Mik-ha-el!" A pause. Then, his vocal timbres very low and long—"Mel-e-kim!"

At first, nothing seemed to happen. Mr. Malynowsky looked very small amidst the tombs and thickets, and more like a mad old man than a powerful magickian.

This was the crunch, I reflected. All our occult philosophy was worth nothing if it could not resurrect the man I had more or less killed.

Jehovah Eloah Va Daath—the All-Knowing one. The key to all consciousness, all incarnations. Was Mr. Malynowsky going to attempt to change the distant past, or to readjust the present? I had no desire to return to Rome, and, though on one level it seemed a ludicrous thought, my mind had reached a point at which anything was credible. I did not want my present incarnation to be canceled out. I was nervous, and was thinking of Eurydice and Lauren and what they would have done in the situation. I tried to attune to Lauren, as the last thing I wanted was to become another Malynowsky tragedy.

Yet, I still did not think my actions entirely misplaced. It was the Sword of Justice, and I had used it to balance the equation. I had thrust it through the heart-chakra, just as my own had been pierced and broken by my master. I had inflicted pain, not even in equal measure, for my own act had been swift and symbolic, whilst that of my master had been slow and literal.

I realised, of course, that on the physical plane, the alcohol and stress had killed Dr. Read. A coroner would have nothing to report but cirrhosis of the liver, or a heart attack; natural causes, whatever they might be. However, my Priestess-self knew that the sword had been the deciding factor. With it, I could have held him in fear of his life, then plunged it into the earth instead. Then, the silver chord would not have been cut.

I recalled reasoning at the time, on a very innate level, that a merciful act on my part would have meant more good karma for me, rather than a nullifying of his miasma. There was certainly no blood apparent about him now.

The evocation reminded me, however, of the Balance which cannot be destroyed. In Tiphareth, the equilateral cross defines the harmony of the Universe, and even if I had made a mistake, Mikhael and the Melekim would fix it. Nothing ever ended, it merely altered. I was surprised only by my inability to contact Simon spiritually. Where was he?

Mr. Malynowsky, despite his distaste for overt ritual, held his hands aloft. He had put us behind one of his invisibility screens, I noticed, as the church warden and his wife sauntered through the cemetery and brushed right past me without a moment's glance. The ancient man of magick was staring at the sun.

The sky, still bright but heading towards sunset, vibrated a little. Behind the façade of blue streaked with clouds, I saw light shake itself like golden locks on an angelic head.

The body on the ground began to stir. Suddenly, it was bolt upright, looking about it.

"Oh, not *again*!" moaned Dr. Read. Then, perceiving us, "Good heavens, what are you doing here, Sir, Madam?" He nodded at us both. "I was just, er, paying my respects to the professor. Yes, his grave gets rather overgrown—I fear the parish gardener prefers the view at the bottom of a whisky bottle to that of sober botanical endeavour!"

"This is mere necromancy!" cried Mr. Malynowsky, disgusted. "I have not gone far enough. Forgive me, Kala!"

Simon looked at me, and gradually, as Mr. Malynowsky intoned further words in Hebrew and Greek, the vessel of Dr. Read began to gibber. His eyes fixed on mine, and I realised he was simply replaying an old persona. His spirit was far away. I felt nauseated, my skin sluiced with sweat as if by a bucket of freezing water. I began to stagger back.

"Careful, Kala!" cried Mr. Malynowsky. "Don't cross the boundary!" I had failed to perceive it before, but, as with Simon's miasma, I could see it now that it had been pointed out to me.

The magi, one in god posture, his arms now folded across the chest and his ankles touching, the other flopped lifelessly back on the professor's plot, were placed at the centre of what was, at its base, a sphere. The upper part of the psychic structure seemed to stretch endlessly upward. The boundaries were keeping mundane energies out, as well as prohibiting any pernicious influences.

Inside, the power was so great now that the air was vibrating with it. Each atom seemed to contain its own tiny sun. Everything glowed.

Mr. Malynowsky was repeating his incantations, trying to channel his mind further and further back into Simon's past. They were both bathed in vivid astral light, at first of orange-tinted gold, dissolving into a deep reddish-pink. The colours then merged into yellow, until finally, they were both carved out in the rosy pink of spiritual and physical rejuvenation. I knew that Mr. Malynowsky had transferred them from Assiah to Atziluth with his mind.

"He has walked the Path of the Devil," pronounced Mr. Malynowsky like the priest he now was, "in search of greater insight. His intelligence has been renewed. Now let the Third Ayin be opened, that he might overview his lives and safely progress from Hod to Tiphareth. Raphael, Mikhael, guide this thy charge along the Path!"

The body again became fraught with identity. It rose up, but this time, I did not feel fear. The blue eyes opened, the face flooded with light. The auburn hair blazed like a torch. He was illuminated by his Higher Self.

This time, he did not beg. Instead, he was couched in celestial solicitude.

"My dear Kala," he began. "I have wronged you greatly, as you know. Now, having trodden the Twenty-Sixth Path to its most solar portal, I wish to progress. I require another body to facilitate this, one that is not dominated by neurotic impulses inflicted by a former existence. I request your support and suffrage in this."

This time, however, the statement was sincere, not mechanical. How could I refuse?

"I would like you to progress," I announced, dizzy with all these deaths and resurrections and quite earnest in my permission. In many ways, I realised, I longed to get him out of my spiritual hair. I looked at Mr. Malynowsky.

"Can you cut the chords that bind us?" I asked, selfishly wishing to avoid further encounters in the future with a man I had more than done the rounds with. We may have been in love in ancient Greece and Rome, but now I was ready for a breath of freshly amorous air. I had the bimillennial itch, it seemed.

Mr. Malynowsky produced the sword. Out of pure ether, naturally. Again, it looked real. I shuddered with the memory of its most recent usage.

The lines of love, experience, and hate became visible between myself and the radiant Simon. Some were thin and clear, like the strings of an angelic harp. Others looked like ropes of storm-cloud, plaited together by some resentful servant of Zeus. Others were Geburah-red and jagged, and made my mouth taste of iron just looking at them.

I was subjected to many flashes of recollection as I witnessed them; scenes of daily life, complete with emotion and referents. I saw myself standing in the temple at the height of my bodily beauty, tempted by the priest, expressing my fears of physical interaction, which he refuted as superstitions. I felt again the allure of one so wise desiring me, and remembered preparing myself in rituals of Apolline hygiene for his caresses. It was not the god I worshipped, but his mortal servitor.

In a flash, too, I perceived Anna, the deferential young Pythia who had replaced me just before I died. I recalled teaching her all that I knew. Her name then had been Corina, and she was a far worthier breather of the divine fumes than I. In that life, I had lived to a ripe and solipsistic old age, fat on honeycomb and offerings to the god whose temple we had defiled.

I realised it was time for us both to move upward, toward Kether.

Mr. Malynowsky held the sword aloft, intoned another word of power, and brought the sword down with an almighty scything movement between myself and the sacrificial priest-king.

I reeled back in unbelievable agony. I span into the Abyss in a tortured amnesia, my only thought that I was cast out into space, whomever I might be, drenched in a sensation of being eternally lost to the gods.

When the pain reduced itself to the bearable, I was surprised to find myself standing in a plot of grass filled with strangely carved stones. I was in Oxford, in a cemetery.

An old man in bizarre vestments was looking at me. His eyes were luminous violet.

"Kala, my dear?"

My present persona flooded back at this call.

"Simon?" I asked, feeling as if I had just awoken from a night of Apolline vintage overload. "Is he . . . ?"

Mr. Malynowsky nodded toward the ground.

There, a headstone jutted its blunt fin from the ground. On the plot lay two books of verse, one in Latin, and one in Greek. But this was Professor Stanton's grave, I recalled. I looked at the inscription. It was exactly as it had been before.

"No, where is Simon?" I asked. "Is he alright? Did we succeed?"

"Keep reading," he insisted. "You really must learn the art of patience, Kala!"

At the bottom of the stone, a few new lines had appeared.

"Erected by his loving student, Simon Read."

"What does that mean?" I asked, nonplussed.

"Time for a cup of tea, I think," said the Mage.

Frustration invaded me.

"At least tell me whether he is safe!"

"Do you think I would be suggesting tea if that were not the case?" replied the magickian.

The shop was spectacularly well organised when we returned, I noticed. Had Olivia been in and tidied up, I wondered?

Nothing untoward was in evidence. However, when Olivia turned up, brandishing a particularly fine recording of Purcell's *Sacred Music* the following lunchtime, I mentioned that Simon had failed to arrive at work on Good Friday. She looked at me blankly.

"Is that our new employee?"

Now, I knew Mr. Malynowsky to be powerful, but surely even he was unable to cancel out the past?

I asked him about it.

"It was not I who changed certain events," he replied. "It was Simon and yourself. Once the bonds had been cut, I was able to identify the point in his past at which the neuroses inflicted by your previous lives together had taken a stranglehold. I simply tipped the equilateral cross back a little, and the Planing Angels—the Melekim—did the rest. Without the imbalances caused by your interaction, Dr. Read was free to develop, as any incarnated spirit ought to be. He suffered throughout his D.Phil., it is true, but once he reached Greece, under the aegis rather than the curse of Apollo, healing took place. He met his wife, Helena, on an archaeological dig, and his spirit became stabilised in his body."

"Are you telling me that all the stuff here never happened?" I asked, feeling like an inept actress in a science-fiction movie. My lines were faltering, and casual acceptance of these impossibilities was far from evident on my face.

Frantically, I sought out one of the books I recalled Simon defacing with liquid paper. The original price was written neatly in it.

"This is ridiculous," I kept repeating. Even Lauren's Ron had not gone this far.

"Are you saying that you've changed the past?"

Mr. Malynowsky frowned a little. "No, my dear, I have not. I merely adjusted the probability levels of the present a little." He sighed, a little weary, perhaps, of having to explain cosmic principles to the comparatively young. "Now, what happened here has been removed to the realms of the Parallel Universes. It has merely become one of the many things which could have happened, but never did."

"But it *DID!*" I protested.

I felt even more exhausted than I had on Simon's first day at the till.

A few days later, a box of books arrived on the subject of Greek magick. The top three were authored by Dr. Simon Read. I took one, and read the biographical notes on the back.

"Dr. Simon Read was educated at Magdalen College, Oxford, and received his D.Phil. in Classics under the tutelage of Professor Nigel Stanton. He moved to Greece in 1998, to pursue his studies of Oracular Magic and Apolline Myth and symbolism. He resides in Delphi with his wife and two daughters."

I decided it was time to take a break. I needed a holiday—my life seemed insane.

Mr. Malynowsky took great pains to talk to me, as one would to a child who has experienced an intense trauma, and I have never had to make so few beverages in my life. He proved especially agile at appearing upstairs when anyone who had talked to Simon was in the shop. The conversations that ensued gave every indication that Dr. Simon Read had been conspicuously absent of late.

"I need some time off, Mr. M.," I told him.

He smiled at me kindly, and nodded. "You may wish to go on a vacation of your own choosing, of course. If so, that is no problem." The wily mage eyed me with gentle humour. "However, should you decide that a fortnight in France or Spain would not entirely satisfy you, I have friends all over the world who are interested in the subjects which occupy us," he cajoled. "Not that you would be subjected to anything as strange as recent events. Indeed not. But a combination of business and pleasure is never a bad thing. I would attend to your fares and accommodation, of course. I have certain *specimens* I am too old to convey in person—if, that is, the idea of a visit to Bangkok and New York is not too distasteful to you?—"

I gawped at him. After recent events, or non-events, I longed to leave Oxford and traverse the globe a little. Who knows, I might even encounter that breath of freshly amorous air I so craved.

"Done," I smiled.